TORCHLIGHT

ROBERT LOUIS
STEVENSON III

G. P. Putnam's Sons/New York

TORCHLIGHT

G. P. Putnam's Sons
Publishers Since 1838
a member of Penguin Putnam Inc.
200 Madison Avenue
New York, NY 10016

LIBRARY OF CONGRESS CATALOGING-IN-PUBLICATION DATA

Stevenson, Robert Louis, III.
    Torchlight / Robert Louis Stevenson III.
        p.   cm.
    ISBN 0-399-14315-7
    I. Title.
    PS3569.T4568T67   1997   97-12395 CIP
    813'.54—dc21

Printed in the United States of America

10   9   8   7   6   5   4   3   2   1

This book is printed on acid-free paper. ∞

Book design by Gretchen Achilles

ACKNOWLEDGMENTS

Even with a name like Robert Louis Stevenson III, getting a novel published is far from easy. I began writing fiction when I was eighteen, and sold *Torchlight* at forty-three, having spent two years putting together the first hundred pages while bartending fifty hours a week to support my wife and two children. That it happened at all I owe entirely to the generosity and support of a few very special people.

First of all, I'd like to thank Theresa Park, whose phone call saying that she wasn't interested in the nonfiction book that I was proposing, but wanted to see the opening chapters of *Torchlight*, sent me racing for the garbage where I had tossed the manuscript weeks before, thinking that I had no chance of ever breaking in as a writer of fiction. I gained not only an agent of exceptional ability, intelligence, and charm, but a dear family friend as well.

No less wonderful has been my editor, Stacy Creamer, who had the courage to buy a partial manuscript from an unknown writer, thus providing me with the chance of a lifetime, for which I will be forever grateful. Her enthusiasm and guidance have been extraordinary throughout the writing of this book. What is good in this book is good because of her.

People often joke about their in-laws, but if I were to enumerate the various ways in which Chris and Neil Pultz lent their support over the years, this book would be twice as long.

The same can be said of my parents, Carol and Bob Stevenson, who in addition to their love and considerable forbearance gave me the inestimable privilege of growing up in a house filled with books.

Special thanks to my stepdaughter Devan McClenny for baby-sitting her sister, Caroline, above and beyond the call of duty, and for keeping her mother company and helping out while I was holed up in my office.

Most of all, I would like to thank my darling wife, Sheila, who for years worked two jobs while raising two children, and whose sacrifices in making this book far exceeded mine. I love you, babe.

For my beloved daughter Caroline

TORCHLIGHT

The convoy moved silently across the water, each ship black against a moonlit sky. On the bridge of the U-157, Korvettenkapitän Hans Müller adjusted his binoculars, grateful that the moon was no larger than a crescent. The wind was cool, yet bracing. A perfect night for hunting, Müller thought. He felt with pride the Iron Cross dangling about his neck and above it the Pour le Mérite, Germany's highest military award, presented by the Kaiser himself for the sinking of two British cruisers on a single day. Even the Kaiser had reveled in his victories, the corners of his eyes wrinkling with delight as he bestowed the cherished award declaring Müller the "Wolf of Malta." Overnight Müller had become a hero of the Fatherland. Soon he would become a hero again, but this time world famous. For in three short weeks Müller had achieved the impossible: He had crossed the Atlantic to within a hundred miles of the Rhode Island shore.

A thousand meters out an escort crossed his bow. Müller watched it tensely for several minutes as the vessel sped past, slipping between the two lead ships to the other side of the convoy. Then he shifted his gaze to the armored cruiser that lay in the middle of the pack—his prize.

She was the flagship of the fleet, and as she approached off the starboard bow, her wake glistening in the moonlight, Müller could clearly distinguish the ornate gilt carving on her bow, her four stacks, and the crow's nest high up on her forward mast. Below the mast lay the darkened area of the bridge. Müller examined it for several seconds, wondering if her officers and crew had any inkling of their imminent fate. Then he realized he no longer felt remorse about the men he killed. This was his ninth patrol. He felt a general weariness that the war had lasted this long—a war he did not expect to survive. He wondered if his beloved Germany would survive. For three long years the war had dragged on to no avail. Gone were the heady days of 1914 when the German army had rolled across Belgium and France to within shooting distance of the Paris suburbs. To the east, Ludendorff had smashed the Russian Army at Tannenberg. How he cherished the memory of those halcyon days early in the war when Germany stood poised on the edge of victory. Ah, the Schlieffen Plan—it had nearly worked!

But the Allies had held on. Then came the battle of the Marne and trench warfare along the western front; interminable days of suffering and unimaginable slaughter. Soissons, Ypres, Verdun, the Somme—a litany of death. At Verdun alone the German army had lost more than 350,000 men—Müller's only consolation being that the French had lost more.

Now Germany lay gripped in the stranglehold of the Allied naval blockade. With stinging rage Müller recalled the sight of hollow-eyed German children as their families prepared to endure yet another "turnip winter." To break the blockade the General Staff had ordered the resumption of unrestricted submarine warfare. All to the good, Müller thought. With the sinking of the *Lusitania* in 1915, it had only been a matter of time before the Americans entered the war. Now that they had taken up arms against the Fatherland, they too would suffer the consequences, as had the Russian tsar, whose autocratic regime, unable to withstand a string of military disasters, had fallen victim to a revolution in March. Müller relished the irony. Three hundred years of Romanov rule expunged by the incompetence of Nicholas II and the weakness of his generals. And now the Americans. Yes, they, too, would learn the true price of war.

Lowering his binoculars, he scanned the slender deck of the U-boat now awash as the dark sea churned around them, breaking white against the cowling of the bridge before receding with a hiss faintly audible above the gusting wind. Then he glanced at the four men around him, squeezed inside the U-boat's narrow chariot bridge. They were lookouts—all except Karl Himmels, the First Watch Officer, Müller's second in command, who would carry out the attack.

They were in perfect firing position. With her deck gun partially submerged, the U-157 would be nearly invisible to any lookouts manning the American ships opposite him. As the moon slipped behind the clouds, Müller examined the convoy once more, straining in the darkness for any sign of the escort that had disappeared to the other side of the convoy. Then he looked at the cruiser. She was close. Very close.

"Open bow caps one and two." The voice was Himmels's. "Target bearing one eight zero point five, range twelve hundred meters. Angle on the bow seventeen green."

Müller felt the tension of the men around him. It was their sixth surface attack in two years, and Müller knew that his men preferred the safety and stealth of an underwater approach. But on this mission Müller had decided otherwise. The Americans would not expect them—not in these waters—and besides, he wanted as many men as possible to witness the historic occasion.

He glanced at Himmels, crouched before the long binoculars of the target aiming device. *Make it good, Karl,* he thought in silent invocation. *Make it good because we won't get a second chance.*

"Depth of run three point five meters!"

An agonizing minute passed. Then through the voice tube the confirmation came and Himmels paused a second longer, Himmels the perfectionist.

"Fire one!"

Müller felt a sudden *whoosh* as the U-boat lifted, the water draining from her decks as the saw-toothed band of the net cutter knifed upward through the water like the jaws of a shark. Instinctively, Müller began counting the seconds, and for a brief moment he thought he could hear the faint ticking of Himmels's stopwatch, marking the torpedo's progress.

"Fire two!"

The U-157 lifted again, and looking out past the bow, Müller saw the twin white bubble trails of the torpedoes streaking toward their target.

"Torpedoes running straight and hot, sir."

The voice, deeper and more resonant than Himmels's, came from below. Müller glanced down the open hatch, nodding at Max Konig, who stood in the conning tower wearing earphones and smiling, his ruddy face glistening with sweat. The U-157's interior was bathed in red light. Strains of music emanated from below, tempting him with their gaiety: *Ain't she sweet. Just knocked me off my feet. . . .* Now there would be hell to pay. La Belle Époque.

"Ninety seconds until contact!" Himmels cried. "Sixty seconds . . . thirty seconds . . . twenty seconds . . . !"

"Full astern," Müller shouted. He pressed the binoculars to his eyes, feeling the deep vibration of the diesel engines as the U-157 began to pull away. Then the first of Himmels's torpedoes struck the cruiser amidships, detonating in a geyser of smoke and yellow flame. Instantly the cruiser began to heel, swinging erratically out of line. An illumination flare shot up, bathing the ship in a pool of ghostly light. Men were scrambling on the decks. Then, a moment later, the second of Himmels's torpedoes struck aft, followed by an explosion of such magnitude that the entire ship lifted from the water as the stern disintegrated before Müller's astounded eyes.

"Herr Korvettenkapitän?"

"We must have hit a munitions room, Karl."

Müller peered through his binoculars once more, staring in silence at the catastrophe unfolding before him. The cruiser was settling fast by the stern, faster than any torpedoed ship he had ever seen. On her main deck amidships men silhouetted by flame and fire were abandoning ship, some leaping overboard, others struggling helplessly to lower lifeboats as the flare dropped into the ocean, snuffing itself out. In the darkness the flames, brick orange, took on an aura of haunting intensity. Müller could feel the eyes of his men—seasoned eyes, staring not in reproach but in horror. Even the lookouts were glancing now as the cries of drowning men assailed them from the darkness. Then, as quickly as she had been lifted from the water the cruiser sank, her bow reaching skyward in one final appeal before vanishing beneath the waves.

No one spoke, and it seemed to Müller that the power of language itself had been sucked into the vortex created by the cruiser's sinking. He glanced at Himmels, gently removing the stopwatch from his shaking hand. Only three minutes had elapsed since the firing of the first torpedo. Then he looked out once more at the blackened sea. The moon now hung on the dark horizon.

18 June

The anchor line angled down into the gray darkness. Hovering at a depth of fifty feet, gripping this line so as not to be swept away by the current, Jack Henderson looked up at the yacht's dagger-shaped hull. He was alone. For the first time in forty-eight hours he felt safe, hidden from the danger above and below. It seemed as though time had been suspended. And as he began checking his equipment, he savored this moment of tranquillity, knowing it would not last.

Bars of sunlight slanted down through the clear water. A jellyfish drifted past, its long gossamer tentacles trailing down like rain. Satisfied that his equipment functioned properly and that there were no problems with his air supply, Henderson began sliding down the anchor line like an aerialist on a guy wire.

He would be diving to a depth of 200 feet. And for a dive of that magnitude Jack Henderson carried a lot of equipment: three lights, three knives, and two large tanks of air. Each tank was connected to its own regulator. Throughout the dive and the lengthy decompression to follow, Henderson would switch second stages every fifteen minutes or so to avoid depleting any one tank of air. That way, if one system failed, he would have another as backup. The spare lights were clipped to the wreck harness he wore over his dry suit. Also fastened to the harness was a razor-sharp knife, hanging upside down from its scabbard for easy access. The other two knives he wore on his hips—gunfighter style. Strapping a knife to your ankle, as most divers were taught, was foolish. In deep cold-water wreck diving where entanglement was a constant danger, you wanted your knives where you could reach them. Fast.

The anchor line seemed to stretch on forever. The water was colder and darker now. Then it became dramatically colder, and Henderson knew that he had passed a thermocline. He cocked an arm to read the twin displays of his dive computers. In unison they ticked off depth: 150 . . . 154 . . . 157 . . . And then he could feel it. Nitrogen narcosis—the famed rapture of the deep, the mild delirium that scuba divers experience at extreme depth. It felt like a thousand electric horses were tap-dancing on his brain.

He continued his descent. He could feel the gentle pull of current, and was grateful for the three layers of long underwear beneath his dry suit. Cold water swept past, and as he descended through the ocean depths his loneliness gave way to a more pronounced emotion: a sharp anxiety, a blend of anticipation and fear. He knew that he would have to bear that anxiety throughout the dive. Not until he was heading back up the anchor line, back toward the world of air and light, would those turbulent and conflicting emotions disappear, leaving him awash in an adrenal flow of ecstatic reunion and well-being.

A vague shape loomed in the semidarkness. He jetted air into his vest to slow his descent. Then, as if by magic, the entire ocean opened up, and the bow and superstructure of a large warship appeared.

She was an armored cruiser of World War I vintage. Lying upright on the ocean floor, she seemed to be moving still, a ghost ship emerging from the fog. Her superstructure, broad, dark, and intimidating, was intact except for her mast, which had snapped off its mount. Draped with commercial fishing nets that wavered slightly in the current, the mast angled down from bridge to foredeck like a fallen tree. On the foredeck, amid the tangled wreckage of the crow's nest, squatted the main turret, whose eight-inch, forty-caliber guns tilted slightly to starboard—an ominous sign.

Gliding down over the foredeck, Henderson dropped off the anchor line and hovered twenty feet above the stranded nets and wreckage. He switched on a light and headed for the superstructure towering above him only a short distance away. Long strands of monofilament fluttered below as he swam past several secure hatches. The teak planking of the foredeck appeared only slightly grooved despite its eighty-year immersion in the Atlantic.

He approached the turret. Sweeping his light over the twin eight-inch guns, he imagined the horror and bewilderment of men trying to save themselves and each other as their world erupted in flames. Then he felt a constriction around his ankle, and abruptly came to a halt.

Monofilament.

With trembling hands he reached for a knife, chiding himself for being so careless. He was alone, swimming along the deck of a United States armored cruiser in 200 feet of water. There would be no hope of rescue should something go wrong—not at this depth. Either he would remain vigilant, or he would die.

Rising up over the turret, his pulse returning to normal, Henderson examined the superstructure in detail. Every steel surface was covered with anemones, giving the wreck a speckled appearance in shades of gray. On the foredeck, below and to either side, empty doorways led into the ship's dark interior. Above, the empty windows of the bridge curved around the mast support.

Somewhere below the windows, amid the wreckage of the fallen mast, lay the ship's bell—the key to the wreck's identity.

Henderson swam closer, taking care to avoid the long strands of monofilament that fluttered in the mild current. Reaching the bridge, he began cutting away at the net that draped the fallen mast. Narcosis blunted his motor skills, making the effort laborious and mechanical. He kept at it, and a minute later a large section of netting fell away.

Reaching into the hole, he directed his light down and to either side. Nothing. He swung his light up, concentrating against the narcosis. Then suddenly he saw it: the ship's bell, vaguely discernible under its thick coat of anemones.

The bell, smaller than he had expected, lay six inches beyond his grasp. Cautiously he slipped inside the narrow space between mast and bridge and began inching up, the world darkening around him as he directed the powerful beam of his light down so that he would not be blinded by the backscatter. He heard his tanks clanging against the fallen mast, and for a split second wondered if this was the place where he would die. Then carefully he reached up and began scraping anemones from the bell's surface.

Minutes passed. Inside his dry suit beads of sweat trickled down his backbone, and he could feel the cold fingers of panic touching his heart. He worked on, quelling the urge to check his air. He worked slowly and deliberately, forcing himself to breathe at an easy rhythm. Only when certain that he had removed all the anemones from the bell's exterior did he drop down again and back away, and then only gradually, praying that he would not become entangled in the surrounding wreckage.

He slipped outside the mast and directed his light inside the hole. The water cleared. And a moment later he had his provenance, engraved in silvered bronze and gleaming in the penumbra of his dive light, the inscription: USS NORFOLK. He hovered transfixed.

So the intelligence reports had been correct after all. Gerhardt had discovered the location of the *Norfolk*. Erich Wilhelm Gerhardt, his most recent employer. Friend of presidents and prime ministers.

Gerhardt, arms supplier to the world.

25 June

The ocean was a storm-washed blue. Standing on the stern of the *Avatar,* Henderson gazed with bleary-eyed appreciation at the four-foot rollers sweeping past, lifting the yacht easily before hurtling toward an invisible shore. The rollers seemed to own a seismic intensity. For a long time Henderson stood there in the changing light, taking it all in: the vastness of the ocean, the cool salt breeze, the mesmeric rhythm and power of the swells that seemed to originate from the very center of the earth, the brightening sky. Then the sun rose and the ocean began to shimmer.

He scanned the western sky. Gray light still clung to the horizon, the last vestige of night dissolving into day. The ocean spread out before him, and in the distance he could see a trawler with its booms extended. He concentrated, focusing on the pale light above. Then he saw it: a black speck enlarging on the gray horizon.

The helicopter was coming in fast and low. A fancy piece of flying, Henderson thought. He wondered who the pilot was, what outfit he had flown with before cashing out to cash in. He glanced up over his shoulder and saw the bearded figure of Captain Alberto Alvarez, the yacht's commander, emerge from the glass-enclosed reception area. Two crewmen stood beside him, waiting to assist the new arrivals.

The helicopter zoomed over the yacht, circling it twice, banking sharply, rupturing the stillness of the early-morning air. Then, with the precision that Henderson associated with carrier landings, the pilot eased the Sikorsky down on the platform and cut the engines.

The helicopter's door popped open. A man stepped out. Crew-cut and muscular, wearing faded jeans, sneakers, and a white T-shirt beneath a blue blazer, he stood in front of the door and quickly surveyed the area. Security, Henderson thought. The man's wraparound sunglasses were tinted metallic green, and Henderson felt the cold appraisal of his gaze. It was like the gaze of a gargoyle. Ravening. Henderson returned it with a cold stare of his own. A minute passed. Then the muscular bodyguard stepped aside and, without taking his eyes off the stranger glaring up at him, said something to the people inside.

A balding man with a military-style mustache appeared in the helicopter's doorway. He wore a nylon jacket and carried an aluminum attaché case, the kind used to store photographic equipment. He uttered a few words to the bodyguard, then descended the short staircase, followed by a woman with chestnut hair. She was young—perhaps thirty—and casually elegant, dressed in a cream-colored pantsuit. She wore a strand of pearls about her neck. She crossed the platform to the reception area, where she smiled at Alvarez. The bald man with the grim expression looked on. Then from the helicopter's doorway two more bodyguards emerged, young and muscular like the first. They hopped off the chopper and fanned out to either side with the lead bodyguard out front.

Something was up. They were a hundred miles at sea and

Henderson could not think of a single good reason for the extra security detail. But he could think of plenty of bad reasons, and as he looked up at the three men, calculating his odds, fighting to keep his gaze steady, fragments of fear and hostility began whirling inside him like burning leaves.

Evade, he told himself.

Now.

Head inside. Make them come to you.

But something held him back. Whether it was fear that welded him to the deck, or a gambler's instinct that the last card had yet to be drawn, he would never know. But whatever the motivation, it was this momentary paralysis that saved his life. For as he stood motionless on the fantail, an old man appeared in the helicopter's doorway. Wearing a blue suit and a raffish grin, he spoke to the lead bodyguard, who nodded and relaxed, peeling off to join Captain Alvarez and the others at the forward end of the platform. And suddenly Henderson's sense of doom vanished.

The old man descended the staircase and stood alone for a moment, surveying the yacht with regal authority. Captain Alvarez, as enthralled by the woman's beauty as the bald man seemed indifferent, quickly broke away from the group and strode across the deck to greet his employer. The two men exchanged pleasantries. They crossed the helicopter platform, pausing briefly to allow Gerhardt to convey instructions to an attendant, who promptly disappeared into the reception area. The two parties coalesced, and Henderson heard the sound of conversation mingled with the woman's laughter. Then the group moved off, taking in one last sweeping view of the ocean as travelers will, and Henderson lost sight of his quarry.

Sunlight filled the afterdeck. The trawler had disappeared, and there were no other ships on the horizon. Henderson peered along the starboard rail, then up along the yacht's gleaming white superstructure, whose graceful windswept design seemed fractured by the ugliness of the helicopter crouched upon it.

"Sir?"

It was the sandy-haired youth to whom Gerhardt had spoken on the helicopter platform.

"You are to wait in the main salon, if you don't mind, sir."

The room was airy and spectacular, flooded with emerald light. He was alone, his escort having closed the oak doors behind him before departing. A mahogany banquet table filled the center of the room, and as he approached it, he looked up at the skylight, an enormous stained-glass rendition of the earth laid flat. For several minutes he stood there, transfixed, staring up at the beautiful image of the earth with its ice-encrusted polar caps. Dolphins frolicked in the emerald seas.

Yet the skylight was a mere diversion. For as he moved deeper into the room, his eyes adjusting to the diminished light, he was suddenly drawn to a large alcove to his left. And with a mixture of curiosity and delight that he had not known since childhood, Henderson approached the hidden display, marveling at its size and at the myriad darting colors it contained.

"The largest private aquarium in the world, if I'm not mistaken," the voice said. The accent was British, mingled with guttural German. Henderson wheeled around. The old man stood in the doorway. He crossed the salon with a confident grin and stood next to Henderson in the shimmering light, gazing with pride at the array of tropical fish swimming inside the enormous tank.

"One of the few remaining accoutrements of the yacht's original owner—a British oil baron. Magnificent, isn't it? Almost forty feet across."

The corpulent arms dealer flicked open a miniature door on the paneled wall and pressed a button. Henderson watched in amazement as a four-foot barracuda swam through an opening on the right side of the tank. The large fish hovered a moment, examining the other fish in silent menace before rocketing across the tank in a silvery flash toward a baby eel. Instantly the eel was cleaved in two, its middle section skewered by the barracuda's stiletto teeth.

"My latest acquisition." Gerhardt beamed with pride. "Prefers the holding tank, but in a week he'll be fully acclimated to his new surroundings. See that little button beneath his dorsal fin? An electrode. Keeps him from eating the other fish. A little Pavlovian urging. Makes for a testy critter, I must say, though an obedient one. But I've forgotten my manners. I'm Erich Gerhardt—the man who hired you."

He was in his late sixties—sixty-nine, to be precise, Henderson recalled from his Langley briefings. There were crow's-feet about the eyes, but otherwise Gerhardt's face was as round and burnished as a plum. The eyes, which roamed with playful delight, were a penetrating blue, but the mouth curled down at the corners when smiling, suggesting either cruelty or mischief, Henderson couldn't tell which. Still, the main impression was one of good-natured hardiness. Perhaps a robust demeanor was one of the advantages of wealth. But as Jack Henderson examined his adversary, he thought it a matter of irony, if not some malevolent twist in the Creator's design, that the man who traded in death should be given the face of a cherub.

"It's one of the most impressive sights I've seen," Henderson remarked, looking again at the aquarium that filled the entire wall.

"Common enough for a man in your profession, I should think," Gerhardt said lightly.

It seemed like an offhand remark, and for a moment Henderson wasn't sure if he was expected to reply. Finally, he said: "In cold-water wreck diving, you don't see a lot of fish. They're there, but you tend to concentrate on the wreck. Keeps you from getting lost."

"Lost?" Gerhardt queried, lifting an eyebrow in feigned astonishment. "Does that happen to such a careful man, such a watchful man?"

"It can happen to anyone," Jack Henderson replied, ignoring the implication. "Even when you're careful."

"Ah, then . . ." Gerhardt smiled. "Let us make doubly sure that it doesn't happen to you."

They were walking down another corridor, another deck, the old man a half-step ahead, a bodyguard two steps behind. They were moving forward along the starboard hull. Portholes lined the wall. As Henderson moved along the corridor he caught glimpses of the ocean, radiant and blue. The opposite wall was lined with watercolors. His legs felt stiff and heavy from tension.

It's up to the girl now, he thought—the dark-haired beauty who brought TORCHLIGHT into being. Would she endorse his proposal? Or in a panicked state of self-preservation, would she cast him off, relegating him to the world of inanimate objects? He couldn't tell. The girl was a mystery.

She was Gerhardt's trusted assistant—the daughter, according to Adams, the old man had never had. But beyond that, what else was she? What motive lay behind her betrayal? Revenge? Or was it something deeper—moral transformation, perhaps?

They must be frantic in Washington. Yet they all knew that this could happen—that the plan could change at any moment. The girl was an unknown quantity. So was the wreck. There were too many variables. Adams had made that clear. "There's no disgrace if you decide to opt out. The mission's bound to be dangerous. And you'll have to go it alone. It's our only chance."

But he couldn't go it alone. The *Norfolk* was a death trap.

They entered a chart room through a side door. They were all there, seated along the far side of a large conference table, waiting.

The dark-haired woman looked up and smiled. Henderson felt a surge of relief. She sat to the left of the table's center, her long chestnut hair falling past her shoulders. The bald man sat to the right, glaring up at Henderson with the smoldering look of the inconvenienced. Captain Alvarez, seated to the woman's right, glanced about the room with an air of perceptible boredom. Bob Maki sat beside the bald man, drumming his fingers with impatience. Wearing a Hawaiian shirt, the young dive instructor possessed the wiry build of a surfer. To Maki's left, the lead bodyguard leaned against the wall, arms crossed, gray eyes gleaming. Gerhardt made the introductions.

"Jack, meet Jennifer Lane, my assistant. Gerald Strickland here is my operations manager. The big fellow standing over there is Dennis Rexer, head of security. Captain Alvarez and Bob Maki I believe you already know."

Henderson shook hands with Jennifer and Strickland, nodding to the others as Gerhardt took his seat at the center of the table. The old man glanced down at the black binder on the table before him. Then, leaning forward on his elbows and joining his hands at the fingertips, he peered up at Henderson, blue eyes narrowed in assessment.

"Well, Mr. Henderson. It seems that you have created quite a stir. In your report you recommend that we take on another diver. That wasn't part of the agreement, was it?"

All eyes were on him, like the eyes of a jury—Gerhardt the chief inquisitor.

"We've got a problem," Henderson said, looking at the girl. "Your original survey is inaccurate."

"Like hell it is," Maki protested. "I compiled that survey myself. There isn't a damn thing wrong with it."

"Anyone got a copy?" Henderson fired back.

Gerhardt slid the black binder across the table. Henderson picked it up and turned to the first page.

"Go on, Mr. Henderson," Gerhardt said, leaning back in his chair.

"Third paragraph, second sentence. I quote: 'The *Norfolk* lies upright on the ocean floor. . . .'"

Strickland cast a sardonic glance in Henderson's direction. "So?"

"That assessment is wrong. The *Norfolk* is listing. Sixteen degrees starboard, fourteen degrees aft."

"Big deal," said Maki, looking to Strickland for confirmation.

"Actually," Henderson continued, "it happens to be a very big deal. Think about it. Let's assume that your survey is correct—that the *Norfolk* lies upright. Your objective is to explore the interior, right? Locate the paymaster's issuing room?

"So let's say you enter the wreck through a hole on the port side. Most likely, as you swim inside the wreck, you won't have any problem remaining on the same deck because the water will be clear. Even if the deck has collapsed in places, you'll still be able to see far enough ahead to remain oriented. But it's a different story when you turn around to head out, isn't it? Suddenly all that clear water has become blackened with silt. You have maybe three feet of visibility, at best. So how do you make sure that you remain on the same deck? Simple. If the wreck lies upright, all you have to do is monitor your depth gauge: By swimming at a constant depth, you'll remain on the same deck. That's what you guys have been doing, right?

"But what happens if you've made the mistake of assuming that the wreck lies upright when in fact it's listing sixteen degrees to starboard and fourteen degrees aft? By maintaining a constant depth as you retrace your route, what you're actually doing is moving lower inside the wreck, inadvertently dropping down from one deck to another. Easy to do in silt-blackened water, especially inside the *Norfolk*, where offset decks exist and large areas have rotted away. Suddenly, instead of returning to that big exit hole on the port side, you wind up running straight into a steel wall. And at that point, gentlemen, you might as well kiss your ass good-bye."

In the silence that followed, Henderson could tell that Strickland and Maki had been caught off guard. His logic had been irrefutable, and both men appeared momentarily stunned, mulling over their mistake with an embarrassment that would no doubt ripen to anger.

"Your point is well taken," Gerhardt said, casting an admonitory glance at Maki and Strickland. "Go on."

"The other problem is explosives. The *Norfolk* might be an armored cruiser, but after lying on the ocean floor for eighty years, she's as fragile as a house of cards. Even a minor explosion could cause a whole section of the ship to collapse, and if that

happens, you can forget about finding whatever it is you're looking for. Not to mention the danger of setting off the live munitions aboard. There's a room full of eight-inch shells just two
decks below the room you want to access. So if you want some
good advice, forget about explosives."

Gerhardt nodded. Henderson glanced about the room, hopeful for the first time in days. They were buying it. They had to be.
Even Strickland and Maki, despite their anger. It was time to
close the deal.

"Basically, it comes down to this: Your only hope of salvaging
the paymaster's issuing room is to find a passage that leads to it.
And that's where the *Norfolk*'s deteriorating condition works in
our favor. There are bound to be areas where decks and bulkheads have rusted through or collapsed. But I need someone who
knows what he's doing down there. The *Norfolk* lies in two hundred and seventy feet of water, and in order to find the passage or
series of passages that lead to the room, we'll have to travel a long
way inside the wreck, probably changing deck levels. We'll need
to use lines."

"We can do that," Maki asserted.

"No, you can't. Because it's not simply a matter of using a
line. It's knowing when you can use one and how to navigate in
murky water when you can't. It's knowing how to time your air
supply when you can't read your gauges. It's knowing how to ori-
ent yourself while fighting the effects of nitrogen narcosis. Or
how to stay calm when you think you're lost. It's knowing how to
control your breathing. This isn't some Bahamian reef wreck lying in sixty feet of water. This is a United States warship lying
beyond the range of all but a handful of the world's most accomplished scuba divers. It's going to get hairy down there, and
your guys simply don't have the expertise to handle it. From what

I understand, most of your divers have never seen the inside of a shipwreck before. I need someone with hard-core wreck-diving experience. I need someone I can trust. I need Drake."

Maki turned to Gerhardt, his blue Hawaiian shirt a veritable garden of hibiscus blossoms. "I don't see why we need to bring another diver in on this when we've already got ten divers who, with a little training, can do the job."

Strickland nodded in agreement. "It's bullshit," he averred. "If Henderson needs help, then we've got the talent right here. No need to jeopardize operational security. Unless, of course, Henderson doesn't think he can do the job in the first place."

"You've already lost one diver," Henderson snapped, peering deep into Strickland's eyes. "You lose another and I'll guarantee that Maki's divers will start backing off big time. If they haven't already. You're not paying me enough to commit suicide. Now, Drake's the best there is. If the two of us can't find what you're looking for, then it was never there to be found in the first place. So either hire Drake, or start looking for a new boy."

Gerhardt smiled. "Let us not be rash, Mr. Henderson. You have made your point."

Henderson could see that both Maki and Strickland were furious. He thought of glancing up to see how Rexer was handling it, but reconsidered. Better to ignore the muscular bodyguard, make him think you've minimized his importance.

"But what about operational security?" Strickland demanded.

"The operation is already secure, Gerald," the old man said with weary expostulation. "Jennifer?"

The dark-haired woman gave Strickland and Maki a reassuring look. "I've taken the opportunity to check Mr. Drake's credentials and believe he will fit very nicely into our operation."

"What if he doesn't?" barked Strickland.

"Then Maki's divers get another opportunity to commit suicide," Henderson replied. "But don't worry about Drake. He'll accept."

"What makes you so sure?" Maki demanded.

"We served together in Panama."

Gerhardt grinned.

"There's one more thing," Henderson added. "I need to know what's going on. Drake won't get involved unless he knows what he's in for."

"Tell him he's in for a lot of money," Captain Alberto Alvarez suggested, smiling at the young woman.

"Not good enough."

"Fuck this," Strickland said.

But with an upraised hand, Gerhardt cut him off, his cherubic features turning grim. Then he cast a cold eye on the man who stood opposite him.

"May I emphasize the importance of operational security, Mr. Henderson. As Gerald indicated, we take this matter very seriously indeed. Think of it as the central clause of your contract. Any perceived breach will necessarily void that contract. Restitution is Mr. Rexer's domain. Do I make myself clear?"

"Crystal."

"Good."

Gerhardt turned to his operations manager. "Gerald, we must make arrangements to recruit Mr. Drake as soon as possible. He his currently holed up in Bimini. Runs a diving operation, as I recall."

"Yes," said Jennifer brightly. "Operates a schooner named the *Lady Ann*. Corporate name: Blue Water Adventures. Pays the mortgage by squiring wealthy clients to exotic dive locations. Apparently takes people to places in the Caribbean no one else has ever seen."

Gerhardt looked at Henderson. "A romantic!" He smiled. "How nice." Then he patted Jennifer's hand, gazing at her with pride and affection. "You've done well. I want Henderson to fly out in the next couple of days, with Gerald and Dennis acting as escorts."

"I'll arrange that immediately."

"Does that agree with you, Mr. Henderson?"

"The sooner the better."

"Good." The old man smiled broadly. "Now, Mr. Henderson. What do you know about the provisional government of Alexander Feodorovich Kerensky?"

The name sounded vaguely familiar. It was obviously Russian, and Henderson thought that it might be connected to the Russian revolution in some way.

"I'm not even sure that I recognize the name," Henderson admitted.

"Not many people do, I'm afraid. The government in which he served as prime minister was a flicker of light in the dark abattoir of Russian history. Kerensky was a lawyer and a socialist. I use the term 'socialist' with reluctance, for the obvious distinctions between Kerensky's brand of socialism and the radical Bolshevism of Lenin have fallen prey to the crude assessments of the Cold War. Without taking too much time discussing the distinctions among the Social Revolutionaries, Social Democrats, Mensheviks, and Bolsheviks who vied for power following the March Revolution of 1917, let me say that Kerensky was not dogmatic in his political beliefs. He was a moderate socialist who sought to institute basic civil liberties: freedoms of speech, press, assembly, and religion, as well as universal suffrage and equal rights for women. With respect to instituting these basic liberties and rights, he was successful. For a brief eight months, from the March Revolution of 1917 to the November Revolution in which the Bolsheviks seized power, the provisional government of Alexander Kerensky provided the Russian people with their first taste of democracy. Unfortunately, it didn't last."

Gerhardt looked at Henderson and smiled again. There was a boyish enthusiasm in the way he told his story, as well as a cynic's delight at its odd reversals, and Henderson could feel himself being drawn in.

"Though the tsar was gone, the March Revolution unleashed a groundswell of radical social change that Kerensky and his fellow moderates in the provisional government were unable to contain. Yet it was Kerensky's continued support of the war that ultimately led to the provisional government's downfall in November 1917.

"You see, Mr. Henderson, the Russian army may have suffered a string of defeats, but its continued presence did force the Central Powers to fight a two-front war. It didn't take the Germans very long to figure out that they stood little chance of winning the war until Russia either capitulated or withdrew. Lenin, who was living in Switzerland at the time, seemed their best chance of accomplishing the latter.

"Recognizing the common soldier's disaffection with the war, Lenin had long promoted Russian withdrawal. In April 1917, the Germans conveniently arranged for the young Bolshevik to be smuggled back into Russia, hoping that he would fan the fires of antiwar sentiment. True to form, the fanatical Lenin wasted little time. Supplied with German money with which to build his organization, Lenin quickly began planning a Bolshevik uprising.

"Naturally, the Allies were quite alarmed by the prospect. Hoping to curtail the rise of Bolshevism and the likelihood of Russian withdrawal from the war, the governments of France and Great Britain sought to stabilize the Kerensky regime by providing financial assistance. Unfortunately, the cost of the war had driven both Britain and France to the brink of financial ruin. Any financial assistance would have to come from the United States, which had entered the war on April sixth.

"That assistance was forthcoming. On the foggy night of August eighteenth, under the most stringent security, the USS *Norfolk* set out from the Boston Navy Yard, bound for London. She was to link up to a convoy forming south of Martha's Vineyard. An hour after she set sail naval command received a transmission confirming that she was on course. All seemed well. Then, shortly after midnight, she exploded. She sank within minutes."

"Torpedoed?"

"Precisely, Mr. Henderson. Picked off like a tin duck in a shooting gallery. Think of it: a random event altering the course of history. One of God's malicious jokes. You could even call it the opening salvo of the Cold War. Makes you wonder if that U-boat captain had any inkling. . . ."

"And the money?"

"Oh, it's down there, all right. Resting inside ten steel coffers that were loaded aboard the *Norfolk* on that fateful night in August 1917."

"Coffers?"

"What we're looking for, Mr. Henderson, is a billion dollars' worth of gold."

26 June

From the back of the bulletproof limousine, Charles Francis Adams gazed down on the swirling dark waters of the Potomac. They were driving along the heights of the George Washington Memorial Parkway. It was Adams's favorite route, and he often instructed his driver to take it. A cloudburst the night before had turned the historic river black with runoff. And as Adams gazed across its wooded banks, he could see the white marble of official Washington rising in the distance.

The view was bucolic and reminiscent of an earlier age, a time when his forebears had presided over a young and flourishing nation. However illusory, it was a view that Adams found sustaining. The view from the north was another matter. Enter Washington from that direction and you encountered war-zone ghetto stretching within three blocks of the White House. It reminded Adams of Berlin after the war.

General Walter McKendrick, Chairman, Joint Chiefs of Staff, gazed out the opposite window with a tension that was palpable. The truth was that both men were feeling the pressure of having to account for a turn of events that they did not completely understand. As Director of the CIA, it was Adams's task to brief the President and win his consent; by law the mission could not continue without it. McKendrick would supply the operational details. But in the end a decision would have to be made. And both men knew that Jefferson Marshall would have little choice in the matter. Lives were at stake. And they were running out of time.

A tall, barrel-chested man of fifty-five whose lantern jaw and stalwart appearance often gave subordinates the mistaken impression of stern inflexibility, Walt McKendrick was one of the most highly decorated and revered officers in the United States Army. During the last of his three tours of duty in Vietnam, he had led more than forty reconnaissance missions deep into Indian Country without losing a single man.

Now, as the black limousine sped across the Arlington Memorial Bridge, Adams thought about his own wartime experience as a nineteen-year-old in the OSS and the month he had spent in France prior to D day, blowing up railway lines and dodging the SS, each day a struggle against the uncertainty and fear that could grind you down.

"Tell me about Drake."

"Ever hear of the *Andrea Doria?*"

"I remember the day she sank. Collided with the *Stockholm* about seventy-five miles south of Nantucket Island. . . ."

"That's the one. She went down where two major ocean currents intersect—the Labrador Current and the Gulf Stream. Wreck divers call her the Mount Everest of shipwreck diving. And not just because of the currents. She lies in two hundred fifty-four feet of water—about twice the maximum depth limit set by the certifying agencies for recreational diving. Last summer a group of cave divers decided to explore the wreck. Three went inside; only one came out. The kid died of severe decompression sickness eight hours later. Drake recovered the bodies of the other two. Found them in a mud-filled room three decks deep inside the wreck in about two hundred and forty feet of water. Maybe three men in the world could make a dive like that. Maybe."

"He's that good?"

"The best. Without question. Born and raised in Monterey, California. His father was killed in the Ia Drang in '65. I was there. Damn fine officer. First in his class at West Point. Drake was two at the time. After Phil's death the mother took the family to Birmingham, Michigan, near Detroit, to live with her parents. Drake began diving at fifteen. By the time he graduated from Michigan he had explored almost every major shipwreck in the Great Lakes, many at depths exceeding two hundred feet. Graduated with a degree in American history. Class valedictorian, like his father. Wrote his senior thesis on Vietnam."

"Have you read it?"

"It's brilliant. Says the Cold War drastically reduced the concept of government by an informed citizenry. What followed was the rise of the national security state."

"Yes," Adams reflected. "In his later years, even Harry Truman, who created it, expressed alarm."

"Under the pretext of national security, Johnson and Nixon conducted the war largely through secrecy and deception—Johnson telling people that there was 'light at the end of the tunnel' when CIA estimates painted a far grimmer picture, Nixon pursuing 'peace with honor' while secretly broadening the war, that kind of thing. Except there was no way they could conceal all those body bags."

"Yet Drake enlisted in the Navy."

"I believe it was something he felt he owed his father. He goes on to say that even though the United States lost the war in Vietnam, the courage and sacrifice of the men who fought there stand as an everlasting reminder to all Americans that they have a moral obligation to demand honest government. If Vietnam is our national tragedy, then the rediscovery of that lost ideal will be our anagnorisis—the point of self-knowledge at which we acquire wisdom. He says that if Americans undertake the serious task of becoming involved citizens, then those who died in Vietnam might have won for America its most hallowed victory."

"A requiem for the dead . . ."

"Or an article of faith."

"Will he help us?"

"It's hard to say. We're talking about a man who has a strong sense of duty, yet an equally strong sense of estrangement. Can't blame him, really. The guy lost a father in Vietnam, then several buddies in Panama. Go through something like that and it's hard to feel much affection for the people in charge. If he agrees to help, it will be for Henderson's sake, not ours."

"Paitilla was that bad. . . ."

"Four men killed and nine wounded—bloodiest day in SEAL history."

"What happened?"

General Walter McKendrick glanced out the window with an expression of sadness and disgust. "They were ambushed. Never would have happened had the planners exercised a little common sense. Those kids got sent into a meat grinder."

"And Drake was there."

"Wounded twice. Henderson dragged him to safety. Under intense fire, I might add."

"I need you to talk to him, Walt."

"I've already made arrangements. I'm flying down this afternoon."

They passed the Old Executive Office Building, turning right onto Pennsylvania Avenue and then onto Executive Drive. The White House looked as beautiful as ever. Adams gazed upon the elegant white columns of the North Portico with its single lantern suspended from an iron chain, suddenly stirred by feelings more numinous than nostalgic, arising from the very bones of history—feelings his great-uncle Henry Adams might have regarded with ironic detachment. Looking at the mullioned windows and the lights flickering within, he thought: *My ancestors lived here.*

He turned to McKendrick, thinking about the message the girl had sent the night before. "What's your read on this, Walt?"

McKendrick lifted his eyebrows. "It's got to be the wreck. Hell, the thing's been underwater for more than three-quarters of a century. It's got to be in an advanced state of deterioration, probably a lot worse than we had expected. Henderson's a good diver, but maybe not good enough to dive something like this. My guess is that he needs an expert."

"And Drake fits the bill."

"To a T."

They signed in at the entrance and were immediately escorted to the Cabinet Room, where two more Secret Service agents in blue blazers and solemn expressions nodded in recognition before ushering them inside.

Situated two doors down from the Oval Office and overlooking the Rose Garden, the Cabinet Room was filled with the men who occupied the upper stratum of the Marshall administration. Graying and venerable, they were seated around the wide mahogany conference table that had been donated by President Nixon. Adams could see that he and McKendrick had been the last to arrive.

At the front of the room, flanking a small fireplace and the portrait of the Constitutional Convention that hung above it, stood marble busts of George Washington and Benjamin Franklin. Across the room, a slide projector and screen had been set up, the tray of slides already in place.

Adams nodded hello to the group as he took his seat across from Harold Reeves, the Secretary of State. Standing next to Reeves, an aide was whispering in Martin Vaughan's ear. A plump, tousle-haired man of thirty-five, Vaughan was the National Security Advisor. Leaning back in his chair, an ear cocked to the information he was receiving, Vaughan exuded the haughtiness of a young Napoleon. To the right of the President's empty chair—two inches taller than the rest—sat Attorney General Everett Smith and Secretary of Defense Richard Elliot. Adams had taught both men constitutional law at Harvard. Both were well respected outside the administration and known for their unflinching honesty. The vacant chair to Elliot's left belonged to Thomas Young, the Vice President, who was in New Hampshire for the week, attempting to shore up the President's flagging re-election campaign.

McKendrick sat beside Adams and began removing a thick folder from an accordion-style briefcase that he had placed to the right of his chair. The air was heavy with expectation. Adams glanced at the General as an aide began distributing sealed folders to each man at the table, placing two copies in front of the President's chair. Each folder bore the designation TORCHLIGHT / TOP SECRET. Then the murmuring conversation ended as Chief of Staff David Ellis entered the room. Behind him, dressed in a blue suit and a red tie, strode the President of the United States.

Adams did not know Jefferson Marshall well. They had met twice prior to Adams's nomination for the directorship, then after the election infrequently, the President preferring to deal with Vaughan in matters of national security. Nevertheless, Adams considered Jefferson Marshall to be a remarkable man.

A star quarterback during his four years at the United States Naval Academy, Jefferson Marshall had been runner-up for college football's most prestigious award, the Heisman Trophy. And it would be the last time in Jefferson Marshall's storied career that he would ever be runner-up for anything.

Following his graduation from the Academy and a year manning the Navy's gun line in the South China Sea, Marshall had been reassigned to Naval Intelligence in Washington before returning home to Texas to manage the family oil business. Having directed the company to record-breaking profits within a few short years, Jefferson Marshall began casting about for something else to do. Oil may fuel the engine of foreign policy, but compared to the brokering and power politics of Washington, the oil business was a backwater, and Jefferson Marshall knew it. A year later, he ran for the Senate, vanquishing a backslapping crony of Lyndon Johnson's who had held the seat as a personal fiefdom for as long as anyone could remember. Married to his college sweetheart, a bright and vivacious brunette named Ann whom he had met at the University of Virginia while being examined for a sprained ankle—she had been one of the breathless medical students the doctor had invited in to meet the handsome football star—Jefferson Marshall had become a national hero, a gracious and self-assured exemplar of the American dream.

Now, as President Marshall took his seat, exchanging greetings with the men surrounding him, Adams saw that the great man still possessed the same aura of natural leadership that had brought the world to his feet those many years before when he had ruled the gridiron as a football star.

"This session of the National Security Council will come to order," the President announced with his customary drawl. "Charlie, I believe you've got something to tell us?"

"I do, Mr. President."

Adams rose to his feet as the Cabinet Room darkened and the image of a United States warship appeared on the screen. The men at the table shifted to get a better view, peering up at the screen with pointed interest.

"Mr. President, what you see before you is the United States armored cruiser *Norfolk*. Originally commissioned as the USS *Virginia*, she was the third armored cruiser in a fleet of ten in the Pennsylvania class, built in 1901 by the Union Iron Works in San Francisco.

"Designed to be faster and more maneuverable than a battleship, yet, with her partial armor belt, safer and more impregnable than a cruiser, the *Norfolk* and her sister ships were to herald a new era in naval warfare. Unfortunately, their genesis also coincided with the advent of the dreadnought era. Dreadnoughts, you may recall, were fast, turbine-powered battleships armed with twelve-inch guns. Unable to penetrate a dreadnought's heavy armor with their lighter-caliber guns, armored cruisers were at the same time extremely vulnerable to the faster and more heavily armed ships. As naval tactics changed to capitalize on these advantages, armored cruisers became increasingly obsolete. Nevertheless, during the First World War they often served with distinction.

"Powered by two coal-burning reciprocating steam engines, the *Norfolk* was approximately five hundred feet long and seventy feet wide amidships. Her armament consisted primarily of four eight-inch, forty-caliber guns. These were mounted two per turret, fore and aft. She also carried fourteen six-inch and eighteen three-inch fifty-caliber guns that lined both sides of the gun deck. In addition, she was fitted with two submerged torpedo tubes located on either side of the bow."

"Tonnage?"

"Fifteen thousand tons full-load displacement."

"Nice ship."

"Yes, she was. Unfortunately, she did not survive the war. On the night of August 18, 1917, shortly after linking up with an escort group bound for London, she was torpedoed, sinking within three minutes of the initial explosion. Of the 1,177 men aboard, only fifteen survived—the worst loss of life the Navy sustained during the First World War."

Jefferson Marshall winced.

"The disaster, as one might expect, was widely publicized. What was not publicized, however, was that the *Norfolk* was secretly transporting a large consignment of gold to the British government to help finance the Allied war effort. The gold was ultimately intended for the provisional government of Alexander Kerensky in an effort to keep Russia in the Great War. As it was, Kerensky's government fell to the Bolsheviks during the November Revolution of 1917."

"And the gold?"

"Lost. The Navy searched for weeks, but not a trace of the *Norfolk* was ever found—until now."

"How much money are we talking about, Charles?"

"One billion dollars."

"Jesus Christ," exclaimed Harold Reeves.

General McKendrick leveled his gaze at the graying Secretary of State and said: "Yeah."

President Marshall gazed at Adams in astonishment. "Are you sure?"

"According to Treasury records, the *Norfolk* was carrying American double eagle coins—twenty-dollar gold pieces. Given the price of gold in today's market, the intrinsic value of the consignment is . . . well, substantial. But it is the numismatic value of the coins that we must consider. Once common currency, these coins have become exceedingly rare. We've now confirmed that the *Norfolk* is being salvaged by this man, a German arms dealer by the name of Gerhardt. Erich Wilhelm Gerhardt, to be exact."

"Gerhardt?" exclaimed Secretary of Defense Richard Elliot, glancing at the men around him. "Don't we know this guy?"

"Everybody knows him," Adams replied. "Gerhardt's been a player in the international arms market for years. A German Khasogghi, you might say. Rose to prominence as a member of the Gehlen Organization."

"The Gehlen Organization?" President Marshall inquired.

"The German intelligence unit that we took over in May 1945."

"You mean we hired a bunch of Nazis?"

"Not exactly. General Reinhard Gehlen was the Wehrmacht's Chief of East Front Intelligence, the formidable Fremde Heere Ost. Like most members of Hitler's General Staff, Gehlen was not a Nazi. He was a brilliant intelligence officer, and an opportunist. By 1944, he was also the world's foremost expert on the Soviet military. Recognizing the Soviet threat that would quickly dominate postwar Europe, Gehlen drew together the trusted members of his staff and concocted a plan that would ensure the future of his organization. They would copy every document in their extensive files, then smuggle the entire collection from their headquarters in Bad Reichenhall in East Prussia to various locations within Germany. The idea was to present the Americans or British with an intelligence bonanza in return for asylum."

"And they did this?" the President asked.

"Gerhardt was instrumental in bringing it about. In February 1945, as the Soviet army advanced along the Eastern Front and Hitler ordered his headquarters north to Flensberg, near the Danish border, Gehlen decided to move his family and the valuable cache of documents south to the Bavarian Alps, beyond the reach of Soviet troops. Sure that he was being watched by the SS, he chose to stay behind, selecting his two most trusted aides to carry out the dangerous mission. One of those aides was the son of Hermann Baun, one of Gehlen's best officers. The other was a seventeen-year-old Berliner of Estonian parentage—none other than our Mr. Gerhardt himself.

"The two youths gathered Gehlen's family and two truckloads of documents that had been hidden in an old wine cellar and began their journey south. The roads were clogged with retreating troops, and once during the night they were caught in an air raid. Later that evening they were stopped by an SS unit looking for deserters. Escorted under guard to the SS compound, Gerhardt spotted an open gate across the courtyard and stepped on the gas, Baun racing behind. Caught by surprise, the SS guards fired at the fleeing trucks without serious effect. Under the cover of darkness Gerhardt and the others escaped, eventually reaching a hidden meadow high up in the mountains along the Austrian frontier. There they carefully stored documents beneath the floorboards of an old hiker's cabin and waited out the war."

"Amazing," Ellis said.

"Yes. It was something. Truly one of the great feats to emerge from the final days of the Second World War. Not only did Gehlen and his senior staff produce cases of documents—the most up-to-date information on the Soviet military available—

but they provided the United States with a network of agents still operating behind Soviet lines. It was a controversial and highly sensitive operation at the time. Yet in the early days of the Cold War the Gehlen Organization fulfilled a vital need, providing the United States with valuable information regarding the Soviet order of battle."

"And Gerhardt worked for these people?" the President asked.

"Until 1954. By then he was one of Gehlen's top analysts, well respected within the Organization—and outside it. The Agency loved him. It was at this time that Gerhardt decided to put his sterling reputation to profitable use.

"His initial success as an arms dealer came in Africa in the early sixties, supplying weapons to CIA-backed forces in the Congo. Corruption abounded. Gerhardt made millions. Then came Angola. Later it was the Shah of Iran, Gerhardt again the principal weapons supplier. By the early seventies he had become one of the richest men in the world, maintaining houses in Monte Carlo, Rome, London, Greenwich, and Washington, D.C. In 1975, he purchased the two-hundred-eighty-five-foot yacht *Avatar*. Then he dropped out of sight for a while, as though in retirement. We believe he was advising the drug cartels. His name reappeared briefly during the trial of Edwin Wilson, the rogue CIA agent who sold twenty tons of plastic explosive complete with microdetonators to Mu'ammar Qaddafi. Then came Iran and Iraq."

"The Iran-Contra affair," Secretary of State Harold Reeves observed.

"Half of it," Adams corrected. "The Iran-Contra affairs were actually two separate covert operations carried out by the Reagan administration in the early 1980s. They became forever linked when Oliver North decided to divert profits from the Iranian arms sales to the Nicaraguan resistance—the so-called freedom fighters, or Contras.

"But it was in Iraq during the 1980s and early 1990s that Gerhardt made his biggest score. Saddam Hussein craved not only weapons but the technology to produce them, as well. Conventional, chemical, biological, nuclear—he coveted them all. Gerhardt helped the Iraqis set up the procurement networks. Quite ingenious, some of them. Very difficult to trace."

"Bastard," Attorney General Everett Smith growled.

"Precisely," Adams confirmed. "And it gets worse. Six years ago Walter Hale, Gerhardt's business partner, offered to testify in exchange for immunity. Not only about the Iraqi business. Hale claimed to have extensive knowledge of Gerhardt's dealings with the drug cartels, as well. He was placed in the Federal Witness Protection Program. The next slide you're about to see is the murder scene. Be forewarned—it's graphic."

Adams looked about the room. No one said a word. He steeled himself, then advanced the carousel.

The scene before them was so shocking in its depravity that two aides instantly bolted from their seats and fled the room. Two women bent over, covering their faces. Adams could hear sobbing.

"Oh, my God . . . are those children?" gasped the Secretary of Defense.

"I'm sorry, Richard. I thought everyone should see what we're up against. The photograph was taken at Hale's condominium in Kansas City. They started with the mother. . . . Hale was the last to die."

The men around him were clearly shaken.

Attorney General Everett Smith looked aggrieved. "But I thought you said they were under federal protection?"

"They were. But their address was somehow leaked. Only time it ever happened. Sent shock waves through Justice. The few people who knew about it were sworn to secrecy and the entire program was revamped. If word got out to the press, no potential informant would ever trust the government again. The investigation proved inconclusive."

"And Gerhardt was responsible?"

"I'm not sure. The savagery of the crime suggests the drug cartels. Crimes of this nature are intended to send a message."

"You're not sure?" Heads turned at the note of incredulity in the National Security Advisor's voice. With a sense of foreboding Adams clicked off the slide projector. He wanted no distractions in heading off the confrontation with Vaughan. And he knew there'd be one. Indeed, he had planned for it. Vaughan had made his animosity plain ever since the Mauranian crisis three years before, when a band of communist rebels took over the Dominican Republic. Vaughan had advocated immediate invasion. Adams had counseled prudence, citing public-opinion polls and the fact that the Mauranians were a shaky outfit at best—likely to be overthrown by their own people. The President had ruled in Adams's favor.

But relations between the two men had been strained from the start. Prior to being named National Security Advisor, Martin Vaughan had served as resident scholar at the Meritage Foundation, one of the ubiquitous think tanks that came to the fore during the eighties. During his more charitable moments, Adams considered institutions such as Meritage to be little more than homeless shelters for the ideologically correct. Specializing in what Adams called the inductive approach to policy—the assembling of facts to fit preconceived notions—these institutions generated policy papers that were the inverse of traditional scholarship, worthless at best and often dangerously misguided.

President Marshall appeared ashen. "So you propose that we bring Mr. Gerhardt to justice?"

Adams glanced at Vaughan. It was time to flush this bird from the covey. "That's the idea, sir."

There were sounds of murmuring assent. Adams looked at the men around him, pleased by their support. Then he noticed Vaughan tapping his pencil on the table's polished surface, a sure sign of the National Security Advisor's displeasure. "But you have no proof. You don't have a scintilla of evidence that Gerhardt was in any way connected to these murders," Vaughan proclaimed.

"True," Adams admitted. "But now I have the *Norfolk*."

Vaughan lifted his chin in disdain. "But you forget, sir, that in the realm of foreign affairs, it is sometimes necessary to work with such men."

It worked.

"Yes," Adams conceded. "Sometimes it is necessary in the world of foreign affairs to seek such men as allies. There is the case of Joseph Stalin, for example. A tyrant and a mass murderer. A loathsome human being. And after the Second World War we paid a price for that alliance—or I should say the people of Eastern Europe paid the price."

Secretary of State Harold Reeves looked perplexed. "So why's he after the *Norfolk*, anyway? It can't be money."

"Actually, we believe that it is, at least in part," Adams explained, turning to the heart of the matter now that Vaughan was out in the open.

A flicker of anxiety darkened the President's face.

"We have reason to believe that Gerhardt is brokering a deal between Saddam Hussein and a cell within the Russian military involving the sale of nuclear weapons."

Vaughan seemed to sway under the sudden shock of Adams's revelation.

"Are you certain of this, Charlie?" Jefferson Marshall asked.

"Mr. President, I can't tell you how we know," Adams replied, thinking of their source within Saddam's inner circle, code-named WINDFALL. "But I can say without equivocation that this source has been reliable in the past. I believe the information is accurate, sir. And the fact that Gerhardt is salvaging the *Norfolk* confirms it."

"How so?" Vaughan mumbled.

Adams glanced down at McKendrick, who despite the gravity of the occasion suppressed a grin.

"Gerhardt needs an untraceable source of funds. Evidently the Russians want the cash before delivering the product and Saddam wants the product before delivering the cash. Not an un-usual arrangement in deals of this nature. No honor among thieves, you see. That's where Gerhardt fits in. He's the middle-man. He antes up the cash, minus twenty percent—his commis-sion from the Russians—and takes possession of the nukes. Then he delivers them to Iraq and receives payment, collecting an ad-ditional twenty percent at that end."

"And everyone goes home happy," observed Attorney Gen-eral Everett Smith with disgust.

"That's about the size of it," Adams remarked. "Walt."

McKendrick rose to his feet. "What we're dealing with here, gentlemen, is tactical nuclear weapons—the type designed for battlefield use, not the kind that sit atop intercontinental ballistic missiles. These weapons are small and concealable—you could fit one in the trunk of a car—and because they are intended for use on the battlefield they lack the elaborate built-in safety mechanisms of larger nuclear weapons. We don't know how many these Russians have in their possession, but I think it's fair to assume that they have more than one. My guess, given the price they're asking, is that they have three."

"How much are they asking?" the President inquired.

Adams replied, "Three quarters of a billion dollars."

"So Gerhardt will rake in a quarter of a billion on top of everything else."

"If he's successful in salvaging all the gold—yes."

"My God," said Everett Smith. "The man's already a multimillionaire. Why's he taking a chance like this?"

"I believe his motivation lies elsewhere," Adams replied. "How should I characterize it . . . within the realm of preeminent gamesmanship, I would say. If he pulls this off, it will be the biggest arms deal of the century."

"One that puts nuclear weapons into the hands of a psychopath," Secretary of Defense Richard Elliot added forcefully.

Adams gazed at the men around him. "Yes—I'm afraid Richard has touched upon precisely the reason why we must act now. Decisively. Once Saddam acquires these weapons, he will be able to deploy them in any manner he chooses. Given their compact size, it is conceivable that he could smuggle one into Israel. Or even the United States. After all, bales of marijuana are smuggled into this country every day."

"Would he do that and risk nuclear retaliation?"

"He might. He's never shown much regard for the welfare of

his people. And he's never possessed a weapon that he hasn't used."

"Charlie's right," remarked Richard Elliot. "We simply can't take that chance."

"If the *Norfolk* is the key, why don't we have the Navy simply run Gerhardt off?" Vaughan suggested with a casual smile.

President Marshall raised his eyebrows hopefully. "Charles?"

Adams glanced at Vaughan with veiled contempt. "I wish it were that simple. Unfortunately, we don't know who these 'Russians' are. Neither does Moscow. They may not even be Russians. These weapons were housed in storage sites all over the former Soviet Union. We had a similar problem with Kazakhstan a few years ago, trying to sell nukes to Iran. Even within Russia security has fallen by the wayside."

"So what do you propose?"

"We have to contain Gerhardt. And we have to uncover the location of these weapons and the identities of the people selling them. Gerhardt is the only person who knows who these people are. We've already managed to place one agent aboard the *Avatar*, his base of operations. We're about to send in another."

"Can you do that without making Gerhardt suspicious?"

Adams glanced at McKendrick, wondering just how much he should divulge about the girl. For three years she had provided the Agency with information—a fragment here, a fragment there—all of it accurate, all of it verifiable.

Testing them.

Even now.

Adams decided to keep it short. "They need another diver," he said at last. "The *Norfolk* lies in two hundred and seventy feet of water. There aren't many divers capable of handling themselves at that depth, especially inside a shipwreck. The guy we're sending is one of the best."

President Marshall looked at the men around him. "All right," he said with a sigh. "It's a go. But I expect to be kept fully informed, Charlie. On a daily basis. Is that clear?"

Adams nodded in compliance. "Count on it, sir."

27 June

It was like orbiting the moon. They were drifting along the depths of the Gulf Stream at 130 feet, gazing down through the clear water at the fractured ledges of the continental shelf. Except for a fan of black coral, the ledges were barren, scoured by the strong current. The ocean unreeled before them, and as they were swept along by the Gulf Stream, Philip Drake spotted a French angelfish hovering in the mouth of a cave. Below the cave, the ledges dropped off into a cobalt abyss.

Drake glanced at the young couple hanging below on the drift line, wondering what they thought of these ancient terraces, a primordial staircase descending thousands of feet to the ocean floor. You either loved this dive or you hated it. Divers who came to the Caribbean expecting to see coral reefs and tropical fish were not prepared for the austerity of these limestone ledges. But Drake loved them. Like the enormous salt rings embedded in the desert mountains of Nevada, these ledges were remnants of another age, signatures of geologic time.

He glanced at his dive computer. They had another two minutes before they would have to ascend. It was Drake's policy to keep his clients within the no-decompression limits of recreational diving. No sense in risking the bends, not when they were miles away from the nearest decompression chamber. They would drift at 130 feet for five minutes. Then they would surface.

A long strand of kelp drifted past. He glanced up through the clear water at the small inflatable chase boat shadowing their progress, and then down again at the young couple transfixed by the desolation unfurling before them. Below, a single fan of black coral bent to the current like the windswept Joshua pines that you sometimes saw along the faces of cliffs, their ancient gnarled trunks twisting up through the fissured granite. Drake looked on. Then in the periphery of his vision something caught his eye.

Movement.

He scanned the water to his left, straining to locate whatever it was that had caught his attention, hidden now by the ethereal blue. Then the ghostly images reappeared.

Drake glided below the young couple and pointed left, and suddenly their eyes widened as three large marlin swam into view. Drake had never seen blue marlin this close before, and as he gazed at their long scimitar tails and at the dark blue hash marks running down their sides, he guessed that each fish weighed close to nine hundred pounds. Swimming in formation downcurrent, the mammoth fish regarded the spellbound divers with golden eyes, their bills as delicately attuned as compass needles. Drake hoped that these magnificent fish would not run afoul of the big-game fishing boats that populated these waters. Big-game fishing required brute strength but no skill, and Drake barely tolerated the beer-swilling businessmen who came to these waters in search of trophies.

He had come to these islands years before to start life over again and to work as a professional guide. Over the winter business had been extraordinarily good, and for the first time in ages he didn't have to worry about paying the mortgage on the *Lady*

Ann, the seventy-five-foot custom schooner that he had purchased from a retired bond trader in Key West. Still, his life of exile had failed to live up to its early promise. Lately, during solitary walks, he had begun to notice a mild distancing between himself and the world. It worried him. Somehow in his desire to escape the past he had failed to unlock his heart's affinities, failed to heed the imperatives of the soul. Sex was no answer. He had tried that but had given it up, tasting mortality in the breath of every woman he had known.

To his friends and associates in the Navy the move to Bimini had seemed incomprehensible—at best a shying away from the strictures of impending middle age; at worst another sad spectacle of a man gifted with good looks and intelligence throwing it all away. But though his loyalties were intact, he had little faith in anything these days, least of all his ability to remain in a country whose face he no longer recognized. The sight of his team getting shot to pieces had taken care of that—that and the image of his father, of whom he had no living memory, the proud Army captain whose eyes had shone with love and protectiveness as he lifted his son to his cheek in the photograph taken when Drake was two, the day his father left for Vietnam.

Taking one last look at the marlin, now paling in the distance, Drake signaled to the couple that the dive was over. From their animated gestures, he could tell that they were giddy with excitement. Drake wondered if they knew how lucky they had been. Only once while diving had he seen a marlin, and that had been for only an instant when the spooked fish had suddenly rocketed into the blue depths. Today there had been three, passing within a hundred feet, moving with the muscular grace of jaguars, their golden eyes reflective of the kind of intelligence that is less acquired than instinctual. And as Drake followed the young couple up the drift line, he smiled to himself, happy that these gracious young people had a chance to see something extraordinary.

They broke to the surface after a two-minute safety stop on the drift line and the young man let out a whoop of joy. "Did you see the size of those fish!"

"What kind of fish were they?" the wife asked breathlessly as they formed a circle, waiting for Drake to swing the large inflatable alongside.

"Blue marlin," Drake said, smiling. "Not many divers are lucky enough to see them in the wild. Beautiful, aren't they?"

The man looked at Drake, his eyes wide with excitement. "They were awesome!"

He was jogging along the narrow beach that lined Bimini's western shore. It was early evening, and he was tired, having spent most of the afternoon aboard the *Lady Ann*, cleaning and making small repairs following his clients' departure.

A red sun was melting into the Gulf Stream, flaring as it sank below the horizon, bathing the ocean in crimson and gold. The air began to darken around him, and Drake could feel the mild offshore breeze cool against his skin. Ahead he could see a grove of coconut palms, marking the southern tip of the island that bordered the channel. He pushed himself, thinking that five years before he could have knocked off three miles without breaking a sweat. Now his body glistened with perspiration as his lungs raked in the warm evening air.

Exercise was always a problem when you lived at sea. For the past three weeks he had taken the couple on a Caribbean tour, exploring uncharted reefs, walls, grottoes, and finally the Gulf Stream. In a few days he would be back at sea again, sailing north to dive the great shipwrecks of the northern Atlantic. He had always been drawn to shipwrecks, first because of the artifacts they contained, later because of the mystery they represented. Like Henry Adams at Chartres, he would hover in the stillness of these underwater cathedrals, seeking the eternal in a world shattered by impermanence and death.

Reaching the grove of coconut palms, Drake slowed to a fast walk, his heart pounding. He wandered over to the low seawall and sat down to take in the last ebbing light of day. The air was cooler now, and in the waning light he could see the irregular patterns of coral skirting the shallows. He sat there, catching his breath as darkness fell. Then he gazed out at the Gulf Stream and the fleet of sportfishermen heading toward the islands, their running lights zigzagging across the horizon like shooting stars.

He loved these islands, with their ramshackle grace. Occasionally, while crossing the King's Highway at night, he could hear the splash of feeding fish. Maybe later he would head over to the Compleat Angler for a drink and then sit on the balcony that overlooked the courtyard. Often he would go there just to listen to the murmur of conversation while gazing at the halo of light surrounding the marina across the street and beyond to the sound of boats moving in the channel.

A couple wandered out through the palms twenty feet to his right, holding hands and gazing out upon the Gulf Stream. Drake watched them stroll along the beach in front of him. They nodded hello as they passed, and Drake returned the greeting. The breeze was picking up, and Drake listened to the coconut palms rattling overhead. Then another couple appeared and moved left toward the channel, enjoying a romantic night in the tropics.

A palm frond snapped behind him. Drake turned as a figure emerged from the darkness—barrel-chested yet slightly stooped, though powerful just the same. And as General Walter McKendrick stood before him, Drake knew at once why this end of the island had suddenly become so popular. The couples weren't lovers at all.

They were bodyguards.

McKendrick hopped down from the low seawall, and for a long moment neither man spoke. He was dressed in an old pair of khakis and a faded blue polo shirt, and as Drake stared with astonishment into his eyes McKendrick placed a hand on the younger man's shoulder.

"It's good to see you again, Phil."

Drake nodded, examining the face of the man he hadn't seen in years, not since the day when McKendrick had stopped by his mother's house the year Drake had left for college. The hair was silver now, the weather-beaten face etched with lines, but the old man still retained the heartiness of spirit that gave direction and purpose to everything around him.

McKendrick surveyed the darkened vista. "I always hoped to visit these islands," he said after a bit. "Never got around to it. Discovered in my later years that the urge to travel begins to pale as other imperatives take over. Such as reconciling oneself to history . . ."

"I've tried. It doesn't work."

McKendrick ignored the remark. "Last vacation I had, I spent sifting through the National Archives. Came across a memo written by an OSS officer toward the end of the Second World War. The man had just spent three years in Indochina organizing resistance to the Japanese. Worked right alongside Ho Chi Minh. Washington wanted his assessment. He gave it in a single sentence: THE WHITE MAN IS FINISHED HERE. An essential piece of information. Cabled, read, acknowledged, and filed away. Twenty years later Johnson shoves us into Vietnam, and fifty-eight thousand men get thrown into a meat grinder. Makes you wonder, doesn't it. Did all those people in Washington simply forget, or did they simply think they knew better?"

"I'm not the one to ask—"

"Oh, yes you are." McKendrick paused a moment, gazing at Drake with stern affection. "The Second World War reaffirmed our idealism. We beat the Axis and took it upon ourselves to rebuild Germany and Japan. Clearly, the forces for good prevailed over the forces of evil, both in the outcome of the war and within ourselves as victors presiding over a vanquished world. But somehow toward the end of World War Two the seeds of disillusionment were sown. The Cold War proved exceedingly fertile ground: Iran, Guatemala, Cuba, Vietnam, Laos, Cambodia, Nicaragua, Grenada, Panama, Watergate, Iran-Contra, the covert arming of Iraq, and the Gulf War. Secret government. Black operations. Idealism betrayed. It's Camelot all over again, and I'm not talking about the Kennedy years. I'm talking about the nation we've become since the conclusion of the Second World War—a nation of cynical exiles. Each one of us exiled from what, as citizens, we ought to have become."

"Why are you telling me this?"

"Because you need to hear it. Because you came to these islands to forget and then went out of your way to help the families of the kids who died inside the *Andrea Doria*. Because you're an idealist, Phil. Just like your father."

McKendrick paused, and Drake could hear the sounds of revelry emanating from the expensive sportfishermen cruising the narrow channel. The General's words pulled at him like a riptide.

"Is that why you came here? To tell me that?"

"No. I came to ask a favor."

"What kind of favor?"

General Walter McKendrick looked at the young man as the surf crashed along the sandy beach. "I'm asking you to help a friend."

President Jefferson Marshall stood behind his desk in the Oval Office and with an air of preoccupation gazed out upon the Rose Garden. His hands were clasped behind his back. He was alone. The spectral distortions created by the thick glass gave the colorful rose blossoms a blurred appearance, and he recalled with mute apprehension that rainswept afternoon long ago when he and his teammates had taken the Greyhound north to Philadelphia for the Army–Navy game—a game that would become the capstone of his already legendary football career.

He had been brilliant that day. Completing five touchdown passes and one dazzling forty-yard run into the end zone against an Army team ranked number one in the nation, he had engineered one of the greatest upset victories in the history of college football, commanding his team with a stellar aplomb that during his presidential campaign had seemed a defining moment of the national character.

Now, as he stood alone behind the enormous oak desk, recalling that time, Jefferson Marshall envisioned not the crowd rising in homage as he bowed his head in silent victory, or the swell of ecstatic midshipmen as they rushed wildly onto the field, or those precious few moments when they gathered around, lifting him onto their shoulders when it seemed as if all the world was his, but that lonely journey the day before when he had gazed out the bus window, seeking the face of destiny in the blurred autumn colors of the Virginia countryside.

He heard the click of the door opening behind him but did not turn from the window.

"Excuse me, sir. The National Security Advisor is waiting outside."

"Yes, yes. . . . Send him in."

Ellis held the door for Martin Vaughan, who ignored the Chief of Staff as he strode into the Oval Office, casting a cynical glance at the empty bookcase to the right, which now served as a display case for presidential memorabilia.

"Martin, please have a seat. And David? Please see that we are not disturbed."

"Yes, sir."

The door closed softly behind them.

Jefferson Marshall lingered at the window, and as Vaughan gazed across the massive oak desk to the rounded shoulders that filled the expensive pin-striped suit, he considered the desk symbolic of the unbridgeable chasm that separated the two men and the offices they occupied. The desk, a gift from Queen Victoria to Rutherford B. Hayes, had been hewn from the timbers of the HMS *Resolute*, a British ship rescued from an arctic ice pack by American whalers. Feeling the vague discomfort of having to guess at the nature of Jefferson Marshall's unexpected summons, Vaughan shifted his florid bulk with perceptible unease.

"Mr. President . . . ?"

With the flexing of hands held gracefully behind the back, chin raised as if addressing the sky, Jefferson Marshall spoke. "I've been thinking about TORCHLIGHT." He turned now to face his National Security Advisor. Vaughan was quick to perceive the apprehension clouding the illustrious man's face.

An opening. Where it would lead, he couldn't say. But after years of bureaucratic maneuvering, Martin Vaughan possessed the manipulative instincts and feigned servility of a Florentine courtier. Selecting his words carefully, Vaughan smiled to himself, taking care not to betray the secret joy that lay behind the contrived seriousness of his expression.

"Mr. President, I think it's important to bear in mind that whatever Gerhardt's failings, he has, beyond doubt, proven to be a reliable source of information, as well as a clandestine source of weapons to countries whose, uh . . . public-relations problems make it difficult for us to arm directly. Destroy Gerhardt and you destroy an invaluable policy resource."

"Yes, so you've said. Still, Adams and McKendrick did make a compelling argument."

"To the contrary, sir. Their assertion that this deal threatens the security of the United States is pure conjecture. I agree that we have to take some action against Gerhardt, but we need to act with finesse."

President Marshall nodded in agreement, a gesture in which Vaughan discerned a note of relief and gratitude.

"I've met the man, you know," President Marshall said, taking his chair. "At a dinner party in Houston. Brilliant conversationalist. Had all the ladies charmed. Talked about the politics of oil in terms of the peccadilloes of the major players involved. Made for some titillating conversation, I must say. Amazing, when you think about it."

Jefferson Marshall pressed his fingertips together in a gesture of deep deliberation. Yet his fingers were shaking. Campaign jitters? Though Marshall had won by a landslide four years earlier, Vaughan had seen the latest poll figures and they weren't good, showing the President losing ground to Massachusetts senator Harold Westerfield, a tavern keeper's son who had clawed his way to national prominence as a congressman during the Arab oil embargo of 1973 and who had successfully hammered away at the President's lead, decrying Marshall's failure to deliver on the sweeping tax cut he had promised four years before. At the White House panic had yet to set in, but at the President's behest, Ellis had revamped the President's schedule to double the amount of campaigning originally planned.

"Martin, what would you say to our offering Mr. Gerhardt a deal." President Marshall gazed at his National Security Advisor, sizing him up. "A kind of amnesty," he explained. "My promise to call off Adams and the Justice Department in return for his promise to drop this nuclear business. If Gerhardt asks how we came by this information, say that we were informed by Moscow."

Vaughan felt galvanized, like a falcon riding the thermals, circling.

"A brilliant course of action, Mr. President."

"I can't help thinking about the lives of our agents. . . ."

It was a lie, and Martin Vaughan knew it. *What is this guy trying to hide?* "You're doing the right thing, sir."

"Yes, well, I hope so. And as you say, it's important to keep our options open."

"Critically important."

"I'm glad you see it that way." The President paused, as though embarrassed.

"Would you like me to handle this personally?"

"I would consider it a favor."

"I'll get right on it."

"And Martin?"

"Yes, sir?"

From the moment he had turned away from the window, Jefferson Marshall had been staring straight into Vaughan's eyes. Now he looked away.

"No one is to ever know that this conversation took place. Do you understand? As far as you're concerned, it never happened."

The Grumman Mallard angled left as it began its descent, and from its cramped quarters Jack Henderson gazed down on the slender island of Bimini with the ineluctable sensation of being swept along as if by the force of tide. He had no way of knowing whether Drake had been contacted—if he had volunteered for the mission or had begged off. He gazed at the dark blue waters of the Gulf Stream, then at the bright ribbon of sand running the length of the island's western shore. The eastern shore was lined with hotels and marinas, whose docks patterned the turquoise water like hieroglyphics. Rexer and Strickland sat two rows back.

The old Grumman made a half-circle, swooping down behind the island, landing in the sheltered water near the docks. Sheets of translucent water curved up from the pontoons as the seaplane skidded along the ocean. Then the Grumman glided to a stop, settling into the water and rocking gently before the teenage pilot revved the engines once more, driving the seaplane up the asphalt ramp to the overgrown parking lot that served as Bimini's airport.

In the customs shack two burly black men sporting gold chains and Rolex watches gazed at Rexer with hatred and fear as Strickland tossed the three passports on the table. Evidently

Rexer's reputation had preceded them. Prior to working for the cartels, the big South African had hired himself out as a mercenary in Zimbabwe and the Sudan. A butcher, Adams had said. All it took was a rumor that Rexer had been seen in a district and entire villages would flee.

"Representatives of Arrow Industries," Strickland barked.

One of the men sat down at the battered wood table, giving each of them a nervous glance before stamping the passports, while the other customs officer looked away.

"Always like a kaffir who knows his place," Rexer said, chuckling as they stepped outside. Squinting in the strong sunlight, he slipped on a pair of sunglasses, looking around at the dilapidated buildings and shabby palms surrounding the parking lot. "This place is a real shithole."

From the wrought-iron balcony of the Compleat Angler, the three men stood gazing out over the King's Highway to the Blue Water Marina, where the rustic deckhouse and the twin masts of the *Lady Ann* provided a stately contrast to the fleet of sportfishermen docked alongside her. There seemed to be a party going on, and through the forest of outriggers Henderson could see people dressed in pastel colors milling about the docks.

"He's there," Rexer said, lowering the binoculars and glancing at Strickland.

"Alone?"

"Yeah, I think so."

With a sardonic gleam Strickland turned to Henderson. "Hope you boned up on your sales pitch, pal."

Rexer chuckled. "Yeah. We'd hate to tell the boss that your kaffir-loving friend gave you the boot."

Even as he strolled through the archway of the Blue Water Marina, Henderson could feel the combined enmity of the two men boring through his back like a sniper's round. As he looked out across the channel he could see several sportfishermen cruising up-island toward the Big Game Club, their tuna towers rising above the helms like scaffolding. A crowd had gathered at the docks, sun-bronzed and animated, and as Henderson stepped out into the sun a blonde offered him a gin and tonic. Henderson stared at the woman and shook his head no, suddenly aware of the stunning indifference with which the world greets catastrophe.

He made his way past the crowd. He could see the elegant deckhouse of the *Lady Ann* at the dock's end. Varnished oak. Brass fittings. A mile of teak. Magnificent, Henderson thought. A large Bertram began backing into the slip to his right, gunning its engines, and Henderson looked down. A man in swimming trunks and a white polo shirt lay sprawled on the fighting chair like a patient etherized on a table. On the flying bridge the Captain looked at Henderson with a wry expression and said, "Limited out." Henderson nodded absently. Then, nearing the *Lady Ann*, he spotted Drake, sitting in a canvas deck chair beneath the canopy that sheltered the afterdeck. On the table beside him lay a stack of unopened mail.

"New Zealand, please. One way."

Drake turned and rose from his chair.

Henderson looked into the eyes of the man he hadn't seen in years. The eyes were blue and serious, the angular face handsome and movie-star tan. A pink scar creased the right temple.

"New Zealand might not be a bad place, considering. . . ."

"You look great, Phil."

"Found my calling," Drake said with a hint of irony, a smile breaking through.

"We're being watched."

Drake nodded without looking up. "Not very good, are they?"

They were heading south. From the wheelhouse of the *Lady Ann* Henderson looked out at the dark blue water of the Gulf Stream as Drake navigated the elegant schooner past a succession of small islands. The islands were either barren or covered with scrub pine, and ringed by coral reefs. For a long while Henderson gazed out at the water in quiet exultation, savoring his sudden freedom.

"It was Adams who came, wasn't it?" he said once they rounded the lee of a small island.

"McKendrick. Offered me a chance to save the world. Uncle Sam been good to you?"

"No complaints."

"How's the construction business?"

"Good."

"Sally?"

"Great. She teaches nursery school part-time."

"What did you tell her?"

"The truth: company business, covert, some risk involved."

"How'd she take it?"

"Not well."

"And Andrew?"

"You should see him, Phil. Got his mother's blue eyes. Turns three in September."

"You shouldn't have taken this on."

"I know. But I couldn't let it go, either."

Drake took this in. Then he said, "Tell me about the wreck."

"What did the girl say?"

"Not much. Adams got the package two days ago. Dead-letter drop, Martha's Vineyard. Said you needed help."

"The *Norfolk*'s a fucking nightmare. Offset decks, rotting bulkheads, mud-filled passageways—the whole shootin' match."

"But divable?"

"Yeah. If we're careful."

Drake thought about that for a moment. "What about the girl?"

"Bright, beautiful, British. Gerhardt trusts her completely."

"Can we?"

"She's a trooper, Phil. McKendrick show you her file?"

"Sketched in a few details."

"The Agency started receiving information about Gerhardt about three years ago. Anonymously. Nothing big. But highly selective—stuff that was easily verifiable, but indicating an inside source. Then, about a year and a half ago, the packages got bigger. Nothing obvious—nothing that would arouse Gerhardt's suspicion—but offering a kind of test, as though she needed to see how we would act, what we would do. Remember the towelhead the Mossad blew up with the cellular phone, the guy who blew up the bus in Jerusalem?"

"She gave the guy up?"

"Safe houses, aliases, relatives, you name it. Adams turned the whole thing over to the Israelis. A month later the tango's head goes boom and the asshole's looking for a new head."

"And now she's offering up the big kahuna."

"We knew Gerhardt was up to something—WINDFALL clued us in to the nuke deal. The girl confirmed it."

"Why?"

"Who knows. Christ, Gerhardt's raised her since she was a child. Maybe she discovered that he was involved in those murders in some way. McKendrick show you the pictures?"

Drake nodded. He could see the muscles twitching in Henderson's cheeks, the jaw clenched in anger and despair.

"Any leads on the nukes?"

"Gerhardt's holding those cards pretty close. The girl knows about the deal, but that's about it."

"What about TORCHLIGHT?"

In the distance a sheet of baitfish erupted from the water. Henderson gazed out at the striations of color that led like banners to the cobalt ribbon of the Gulf Stream. Drake glanced at the school of baitfish, then at the man who had once saved his life, the commando with the bent nose and high cheekbones of a Cheyenne, wondering what deal Jack had struck with himself—if there was any bargain to be made with a soul torn between love of family and the cause of justice.

"You in?"

Drake took a deep breath. "Yeah. What the fuck. I'm in."

Henderson grinned. "It's a good operation, Phil. The best."

Martin Vaughan stood alone on the terrace, gazing down through a grove of cathedral elms to the shimmering expanse of Long Island Sound. The view was breathtaking, even more elevated and majestic than the panoramic countryside of northern Virginia with its rolling hills and broad valleys filled with tobacco fields. Offshore, a regatta was under way, and the multitude of gold sails darting back and forth under the setting sun reminded him of another late afternoon when he had stepped out onto a terrace overlooking the Chesapeake and straight into the azure eyes of the most beautiful woman he had ever seen.

She had stood on the edge of the terrace, her champagne glass slightly atilt, smiling at the conversation of two older men who gathered around her, reveling in her presence. She was the trophy wife of a real-estate tycoon away on business. He had recognized her immediately from the pictures he had seen of her in the society pages. An elegant gown of red silk hung from her tanned shoulders; and as she shook her head in laughter, she glanced casually in his direction as if to say, *I know who you are.* And staring back, the young National Security Advisor knew what it was to be gripped by the desperate longings of impetuous desire.

"Can I get you a drink?"

"I have one, thanks."

He had been seated across from her at the table, trying his best not to stare while keeping up a conversation about cigars with an aging corporate chairman. Afterward, as the orchestra launched into a Baise tune, she had taken his hand, leading him up the central staircase and into a bedroom overlooking a terrace sparkling with paper lights. A warm breeze was coming through the open French doors of the balcony, and Vaughan had stood transfixed in starlight as she slipped the silk gown off her shoulders, her hair streaked in a dozen shades of gold. And for the next two hours, to the strains of murmuring conversation and swing, he had buried himself in her, losing himself in sheer wonderment at the fullness of her slender body, as if she were an offering bestowed by the gods of attainment and power.

Now, standing on the empty terrace, the memory of that night long ago mocked him. As National Security Advisor he served at the President's whim, yet Gerhardt's power seemed inviolable. And as he gazed up at the old stone house, his heart was suddenly filled with envy.

It was Gerhardt's summer residence, and one of several mansions that the arms dealer owned throughout the world. Gerhardt had purchased the estate during the mid-eighties, after a sale of six Mirage fighters to the Iraqis during their war with Iran. The mansion had been built in the 1920s by a former president of the New York Stock Exchange, who managed to retain his wealth during the Great Depression. Since the early fifties, when it was sold by his youngest son, a polo-playing alcoholic, the mansion had gone through a succession of owners. Vaughan considered it a minor miracle that it hadn't wound up in the hands of some football player or rock star—the entertainment millionaires who were beginning to invade the exclusive neighborhoods of Greenwich, Connecticut. Vaughan viewed these parvenus of the entertainment world with contempt, their extraordinary wealth and fame, conferred by a credulous public, glaring proof of America's decline.

A butler appeared on the porch. "Mr. Gerhardt will see you now."

Vaughan followed the man inside the splendid mansion to a small elevator of paneled oak. They rode in silence to the second floor. Gerhardt's study lay at the end of a short hallway.

The room was sumptuous, as Vaughan had expected. Sofas and leather chairs of deep maroon filled the room with the rustic smell of antiquity. The walls were walnut, and a prominent Van Gogh hung above a gigantic fireplace. A rich Persian carpet of red-and-gold arabesques swept across the floor to the balcony, whose doors had been flung open to a magnificent view of Long Island Sound, which lay beyond.

"Ah, Mr. Vaughan," Gerhardt said expansively, striding across the room past an enormous mahogany desk, his right hand extended. "I'm honored that President Marshall has chosen such a distinguished emissary. Everyone is well, I trust?"

"The President and the First Lady are fine, sir."

"And daughter Julia? I understand that she will be attending Yale next fall."

"She hopes to become a doctor like her mother."

"Amazing. When I last saw Julia Marshall she was a delightful child of seven. Came bouncing down the stairs in the middle of the reception to say goodnight to all the guests. Charmed us all, I'm afraid. Yale. Her parents must be very proud."

Gerhardt smiled broadly. Vaughan contrived a good-natured smile of his own, his heart filling with disdain. Billionaires. Always boasting of their connections. It was the same old story. Men who started out with a bright idea and worked hard and got rich, only to let the money go to their heads. Still, to make that much money was an accomplishment. By contrast, all you needed to become a millionaire these days was a mediocre batting average. Vaughan drew himself up.

"Two days ago, President Marshall convened an emergency session of the National Security Council. . . ."

Gerhardt fixed the young National Security Advisor with a look of modest solicitation. "Not another world crisis, I hope? It has been my fondest desire, now that the Cold War is over, that the world's inhabitants might finally live in peace."

"Unfortunately, this crisis concerns one of your ventures, Mr. Gerhardt. It has come to our attention that you are attempting to supply Saddam Hussein with tactical nuclear weapons—a deal which you intend to finance by gold salvaged from the USS *Norfolk*."

Gerhardt raised his eyebrows in mock surprise. "Nuclear weapons? The *Norfolk?* Are you sure?"

It was as though some internal mechanism had been jarred. Vaughan had expected resistance or denial, not sarcasm. With growing dismay, he noted the smile of condescension forming on Gerhardt's lips.

"The information comes from Moscow, Mr. Gerhardt. We believe it to be correct. And we are prepared to take whatever steps necessary to ensure that this transaction never takes place."

Gerhardt peered at the young National Security Advisor as though examining a toy.

"Mr. Vaughan, are you threatening me?"

"In the light of your past services, and as a personal favor to you, President Marshall would like to offer you a deal. If you're smart, Gerhardt, you'll take it."

Gerhardt gave a short derisive laugh, his cherubic features wrinkling with contempt. "Do you believe in God, Mr. Vaughan? Of course you do! Order and hierarchy rank high in your pantheon of values. An amusing spectacle, though, isn't it— mankind's primal need to reorder the universe, to make intelligible what lies beyond the realm of understanding. How much wiser were the great men of religion than all the scientists of the modern world whose epochal revision of fact seems to deny the very existence of order, much less truth. The mystics knew better, didn't they? Define the world through metaphor and possess the eternal. But this is all mere storytelling, isn't it? Reality is something else, indeed. Mysterious. Incomprehensible. A swirling multiplicity of fact. So what's left is a construct, a simplification by necessity—a perception of things. How accurate is yours, Mr. Vaughan? How comprehensive? Care to wager your career?"

Vaughan watched in stunned silence as Gerhardt lifted a

small picture from the wall. Framed in gold, it contained a single nine-by-twelve glossy, a family portrait taken on a bright autumn day of a man with dark eyebrows smiling urbanely as he stood beside his attractive wife and two small girls with ribbons in their hair. They were standing in a field of golden maple leaves that had turned crimson around the edges. One of the girls clutched a black German shepherd puppy. The other embraced a teddy bear.

Gerhardt held the picture aloft with both hands, regarding it with a kind of wistful pleasure. "Please inform President Marshall that I cannot accept his kind offer. But perhaps by way of consolation he would accept this lovely photograph."

"Who are these people?"

"My former business partner and his family. They were killed, you see. Murdered. Cut down in the prime of life. I know the President must have been deeply shaken."

"You're telling me he knew these people?"

"Truth, Mr. Vaughan, lies buried in history."

They were skimming the ocean, flying fifty feet above the waves. Peering through the helicopter's front window from his seat one row back, Drake could see the white superstructure of the *Avatar* emerging in the distance. Blue water raced beneath them, and as Drake studied the yacht, seeking refuge in clear assessment, the world of guiding that had consumed his life until the day before seemed relegated to a previous existence.

"Five minutes, boys," Freddie Spector drawled, tilting his head back toward the three passengers in the rear. Strickland sat in the copilot's seat. Drake looked at Henderson, seated beside him, and the two men exchanged glances. Then he peered across the aisle at Rexer, their minder, evidently. The muscular bodyguard leaned against a bulkhead, one leg draped over the seat beside him, leafing through a *Penthouse* magazine.

Rexer glanced up, then lowered the magazine and looked at Drake narrowly. "You got a problem, mate?"

"You ever handle that stuff? For real, I mean?"

From the pilot's seat Freddie Spector laughed. It was high-pitched and wild, like the laughter of a hyena. Jack was laughing, too.

"Blow me," Dennis Rexer said.

They shot past the bow of the yacht, banking sharply, then hovered a moment before Spector made his final approach. Drake looked down at the *Avatar* through a side window, envisioning the assault that would take place when it came time to take Gerhardt down. The yacht was beautiful—as sleek and poised on the blue Atlantic as a sailfish. The *Avatar*'s superstructure gleamed in the early-morning light. It was difficult to believe that a single man could own such an opulent vessel. Several crew members stood in the sheltered bay of the afterdeck, shading their eyes from the sun. Drake looked down along the *Avatar*'s stern, taking in his new surroundings, his sense of radical disjuncture complete. He located the glass-enclosed reception area, examining it carefully for the woman whose face he had memorized from the photograph McKendrick had shown him two days before. Then he saw her, standing beside a bearded man in an officer's uniform. She was wearing a blue summer dress, patterned with cornflowers. Gerhardt was nowhere in sight.

Drake looked at the young pilot. "You handle this bird pretty well."

"This? Aw, this is nothing," Spector drawled, keeping his eyes locked on the instrument panel. "You should have seen me in Desert Storm."

"What did you fly?"

"Apache AH-64s. We were the first to go in—the first unit to cross Iraqi airspace. Task Force Normandy: two teams of four Apaches with two Pave Lows for guidance. It was wild, man. Night flying. Thirty feet above the desert floor. We took out two Iraqi early-warning installations with the air force strike package right behind us, headed for the Scud batteries in western Iraq. Nailed 'em first with Hellfire missiles, then Hydra rockets and

30mm cannon fire. Each team took out a mile square installation in less than four minutes—trailers, antennas, buildings, vehicles—all of it bursting into a ball of flame. One guy saw the ghostly image of an Iraqi soldier reach for the doorway of a van the second it exploded, the Iraqi somersaulting backward through the air. Then we headed home, hugging the desert floor, the F-15E bombers and British Tornadoes streaking into Iraq only a few hundred feet above us. We opened up the corridor, man. We were the lead element."

"Must make this job kind of boring."

Spector glanced back at Drake and winked. "Where else can a pilot make three hundred thou a year."

The Sikorsky eased over the platform. Drake looked out the window once more, his stomach taut with nervous energy. He could see the long cables of the four-point mooring system holding the yacht in place. Then he looked at the girl. She was watching them, looking up with a mixture of curiosity and determination while the uniformed man chatted away. Parents deceased. Raised by Gerhardt since she was ten. A trooper, Henderson had said.

Like me.

"You must be Mr. Drake," she said as they stepped onto the sunny platform. "I'm Jennifer Lane, Mr. Gerhardt's assistant."

"Welcome aboard the *Avatar*," Alvarez announced in a smooth Colombian tenor, extending a hand.

They were standing in a group: Jennifer, Drake, Henderson, Strickland, Rexer, and Alvarez. Drake looked around. "For a moment I thought we were landing on the *Queen Mary*."

"Quite impressive, isn't she," Jennifer quipped with a trace of pride. "Perhaps you'd like a tour?"

"Sure," said Drake.

She smiled. Her eyes were emerald, flecked with gold. Beautiful, Drake thought. It seemed an admission—of what, he couldn't say.

Strickland looked around with impatience. "Where's the boss?"

"Called away on business. Something urgent, I'm afraid," Jennifer explained. "By the way, Dennis, don't unpack. He wants you stateside."

Jennifer turned to Henderson. "I've taken the liberty of informing my father of your success. He is very pleased."

"Let's see what they come up with first," Strickland barked. He peered at the two crewmen unloading the chopper. "Unpack the scuba gear first. I want these two in the water ASAP."

"Time to get crackin', mate," Rexer said, grinning.

Startled, Jennifer glanced at Rexer, then at the others, her eyes hardening again as she regained her self-possession. She turned to Strickland and Rexer, her chestnut hair brushing past her shoulders as she asserted herself with brisk efficiency.

"Dennis, help with the unloading."

"The guy's being a fucking pain in the ass," Rexer protested.

"Now, Dennis. And Gerald? It would be good of you to remember that while my father's away, *I'm* the person in charge."

"Yes, ma'am." The operations manager grimaced.

"Good. Now, Mr. Drake? What are your chances of diving this afternoon?"

"I'll need to study the deck plans first."

"Yes, of course. Anything else?"

Glancing at Strickland and Rexer, Drake began fumbling through his pockets, shaking his head in mock befuddlement. "It seems I've forgotten my wallet. Say, Jennifer. You wouldn't mind tipping the bellhops, would you?"

In the electric moment that followed, Drake noted the smirk crossing Henderson's face. Jennifer gazed at them in shock. Then there was something else in her eyes—a piercing look of confidentiality mixed with fear. Like a secret telecommunication burst, it lasted a nanosecond. "Fuck you, asshole," Strickland said. Then Drake glanced at the muscular bodyguard. Rexer's eyes glared with rage.

A crewman carried the luggage as Henderson led them down two decks and then along a central corridor. In addition to two master suites, the *Avatar* housed four deluxe staterooms. Drake occupied the most forward of these along the port hull.

The room, like everything else aboard the *Avatar*, was spacious and elegant, consisting of a king-size bed, a sofa, a coffee table, two upholstered chairs, and a walnut desk. Oil paintings, depicting the clipper trade, graced the walls. Through the open portholes Drake could hear the slapping of waves against the *Avatar*'s hull.

The crewman deposited the luggage on the floor and left without a word. Drake locked the door behind him, lifted the large duffel onto the bed, unzipped it, and removed the padded liner from the bottom as Henderson watched in silence. Opening the blade from his Swiss Army knife, Drake slit the liner and removed a seamless plastic board. The board was designed to appear solid if X-rayed or closely inspected. Drake tilted the board on its side and carefully examined the nicks along the edge. Then he inserted the locking blade into two of the deeper indentations and tapped hard twice.

The board slid apart.

He reached inside and removed a miniature sensor, placing it on the bedstand and clicking it on. A green light blinked.

He looked at Henderson and smiled. "No bugs."

Henderson grinned.

Then Drake removed two Glock-26 nine-millimeters with six spare magazines. The Glocks were fitted with laser sights. With ten rounds in the mag plus one up the pipe, the Glocks would provide ample firepower in addition to being compact and concealable.

"A gift from McKendrick," Drake said. "Test-fired one the night before you arrived in Bimini. Gunsmiths did a nice job."

"They give you a SATCOM?"

"In here," Drake said, lifting a laptop computer from its case. "We'll use the computer for running decompression schedules. That way, nobody will think twice about our having it. We're going to need a place to hide this other stuff, though."

"Got a few ideas in mind. What time you supposed to meet the girl?"

"Fifteen minutes."

"Lucky you."

"Yeah," Drake replied with feigned nonchalance. "Lucky me."

She was waiting on the afterdeck, looking out at the bright orange buoy that marked the location of the *Norfolk*'s bridge. The wind was picking up, ruffling the ocean beneath a china blue sky. He had hustled up a flight of stairs and had stepped out onto the afterdeck, only to pause in midstride as the wind curled Jennifer's dress around her body.

"Oh, you're here!"

Drake felt his face redden—a voyeur's blush. "I'm sorry," he stammered, fumbling for an excuse. "You looked . . . uh . . . pre-occupied."

"Actually, I was thinking about you." She seemed annoyed. "How's your room?"

"Better than I expected."

"Better than what you would have gotten had Gerald been in charge. Do you think it was wise—baiting them like that?"

"Probably not."

"Try not to let it happen again."

She looked at him a moment longer, her features softening only slightly as she turned and walked along the starboard rail. So much for the warm welcome. Drake walked beside her, thinking that what he really needed was a vacation.

"The *Avatar* is two hundred and eighty-five feet long and sixty feet wide amidships," Jennifer explained with a mirthless smile. "My father bought her from Lord Brooks, who was a Minister of State under Margaret Thatcher. Fleet Street used to call it Brooksie's floating bordello. This is the lounge."

Drake looked around. Wrought-iron tables and chairs painted teal. A well-stocked bar sat opposite a screen-and-glass enclosure that looked out upon the afterdeck.

"Great place to have a party."

"So thought Brooksie's more impressionable guests," she remarked without irony. She walked over to a small glass panel beside the bar, opened it, and pressed a button. With an electrical whir the forward wall began to part, revealing a row of sliding glass doors. They stepped inside.

"We call this area the main salon."

The room was impressive—one of the largest Drake had ever seen aboard a ship. A Persian rug sixty feet long spread across a marble floor. Drake walked over to the mahogany banquet table that filled the center of the room and looked up.

"The skylight is a Chagall original from one of the Rockefeller estates. Along the walls are frescoes by Picasso and Miró. My father had them commissioned years ago. Do you like modern art, Mr. Drake?"

"Sometimes."

"The aquarium is over here."

They entered the darkened alcove and stood before the enormous tank, bright with its array of tropical fish. The barracuda bumped its snout against the thick glass before languidly swimming away. Drake recognized angelfish, grunts, wrasses, trumpetfish, sergeant majors, and garibaldis, as well as a dozen other species. A scrawled filefish gazed down at him with disapprobation.

A Jennifer fish.

"Jack said you employ about fifty people?"

"Fifty-five, actually, including the security staff," Jennifer replied. "They are berthed on the deck below yours. The crew's mess is there also. Jack will show you."

She moved away in the blue light and opened a door, revealing a galley of indeterminate proportions. Beyond the fluorescent lights and stainless steel, Drake could see two professional gas ranges set side by side and four men preparing food. With a muffled click a door opened and an elderly black man in a chef's uniform emerged from a walk-in cooler, carrying a large salmon and humming a reggae tune. He looked up and broke into a wide grin.

"Philip, I'd like you to meet Clarence, our head chef." From the warmth of Jennifer's expression, Drake could tell that she adored this man.

They left the galley and exited the main salon through a side door, walking in silence along the starboard rail, Jennifer's momentary happiness dissolving into an enigmatic expression in which Drake discerned a note of wistfulness and sorrow. Whatever she was thinking about, it wasn't Clarence or him. He scanned the horizon, momentarily at a loss for words. A tanker was edging over the horizon, its white superstructure brilliant against the china blue sky. They entered another hallway, lined with black-and-white photographs of a rocky Mediterranean countryside.

"My father's office," she said, unlocking a plain walnut door.

A long curving rectangular window of smoked glass filled the opposite wall, affording an expansive view of the foredeck and the shimmering Atlantic. Drake followed the lines of teak as they swept to the bow. On either side of the foredeck two cedar deck chairs rested at forty-five-degree angles. A seagull darted across the sky.

Below the window were bookshelves. History and philosophy in French, English, and German. A tall antique Victorian desk stood against the right wall and beside it a Diebold safe. The desk had once belonged to Sir Basil Zaharoff, the legendary Turkish-born arms dealer whose lucrative career began as a gunrunner in northern Africa and ended as Vickers's coveted representative throughout the world. On the opposite wall above the wainscoting were photographs of Gerhardt standing beside the titans of the latter half of the twentieth century. De Gaulle, Nasser, Mao Tse-tung, Stalin, Adenauer, Churchill, the Shah, Sadat, Brezhnev, Reagan, Hitler, Kennedy, Thatcher, Begin—they were all there, and more. Most of the photographs bore personal inscriptions. And for the first time Drake began to sense the vast power and influence of the man whose life he had been sent to destroy.

"Seen enough?"

Drake nodded.

"Let's go upstairs."

From Gerhardt's office they climbed a small private staircase to the observation deck, two decks above, emerging by a small pool. During the entire time Drake had peered into Gerhardt's office Jennifer had remained silent. She did not speak now. She walked over to the port rail and looked out upon the ocean, lifting her face to the sun. A stiff ocean breeze rustled her hair.

Drake scanned the horizon. The tanker had disappeared. No ships. No planes. No birds. They were alone, aboard this beautiful white yacht amid a sea of shimmering gold. They stood there for several minutes, not talking, neither one willing to broach the subject that lingered between them. Then she said, "Come. I'll show you the bridge."

The last of the sailboats were heading back to shore, back to the harbors invisible across Long Island Sound. From the small balcony of his study, Gerhardt looked out upon the stately procession, the boats beating against the whitecapped gray as the weeklong regatta came to an end. Like the stone mansion itself, the view seemed emblematic of his stature in the world, the sails a golden convergence, their receding grace a harbinger of immortality. Then the wind shifted, and as the boats became close-hauled, the sails vanished. Only the delicate pencil lines of the masts remained. High up on the masts the spreaders glinted in the last light of day. Gerhardt stared at them for a while, the crosslike images vaguely familiar. Then he knew why.

Gun sights.

Clearing his mind, he returned to his study, thinking about Vaughan's visit the previous day. *So they know.* Well, that was to be expected. He knew he was being watched. He knew since the day Hassan's cell phone exploded and a decade of carefully nurtured dealings had gone up in smoke along with the Hizbollah chieftain's head. According to his sources within the Egyptian Mukhabarat, the bomb had been Israeli, but Hassan's location and identity had come from the Americans. But the most worrisome fact of all was the persistent rumor circulating in the Middle East that the information had somehow leaked from his organization. Among certain Middle East factions there had been talk of reprisal, as whoever was responsible for disseminating the rumor—the Israelis probably, upset over his Iraqi dealings—had doubtless hoped. But his Palestinian friends had interceded. Nevertheless, the rumor had cost him plenty—in a declining market, millions of dollars of business had suddenly vanished along with much of his credibility.

He had been successful in life because he had the discipline to consider a problem from every angle and to analyze the motives of his adversaries. Gehlen had taught him that. General Reinhard Gehlen, the German intelligence chief who had plucked him from obscurity in the winter of '43, the sole member of the Wehrmacht to recognize the young corporal's genius.

Leaning back in his chair, Gerhardt recalled his mentor with a fondness that he reserved for only his daughter. During the war Gehlen had possessed a round face and an air of quiet efficiency.

In later years the face would lengthen as the jowls began to sag, and Gehlen would carefully guard his privacy, a wealthy man embittered by the betrayal of his trusted associate and counterespionage chief, Heinz Felfe, who was finally unmasked as a longtime Soviet mole in the early sixties. But during the war Gehlen had been a man of enormous aspirations. He had taken young Gerhardt under his wing, often bringing him along to the Wolfschanze when summoned by the Führer. Gerhardt vividly recalled Hitler's tantrums as General Gehlen delivered his somber assessments, the Führer running his fingers through his hair distractedly before sweeping a hand across the map in disgust while proclaiming Gehlen's incompetence.

Then, one day in January 1945, the General had taken him aside. "Your fluency in Russian has served you well, Erich."

"My mother was Estonian," Gerhardt admitted. "We are Auslandsdeutsche. She died when I was six. My father took me to live with relatives in Berlin."

It was a fact that he had previously admitted to no one.

But the General seemed to know.

"And your English?"

"My aunt. Her father had business in England. During the summers she would often join him on his travels."

"May it serve us well also."

"General?"

"The war is lost, Erich. We must look to the future. We must seek out the British and the Americans as allies—"

"But our loyalty to the Reich!"

"Do not confuse loyalty with politics, Erich. Ever. It is a fatal mistake. Politics is for the easily manipulated. Politics is for fools. Your only loyalty is to the realm of objective analysis. You must remember that if you are to survive."

And so he had remembered. And survived, though barely, re-calling the frigid night when he and Baun had driven south, cer-tain as they proceeded under guard to the SS compound with Gehlen's wife and two trucks full of stolen documents that they all would die before morning. But they had escaped, even manag-ing to evade the Soviet hit teams that had scoured the German countryside in the immediate aftermath of the war, searching for Gehlen and his organization.

Yes, he had survived. And, not content with the mere trap-pings of success, he had prospered beyond his wildest dreams. He had used his analytical gifts with stealth and shrewdness and had acquired a fortune, employing Cold War antagonisms to trans-form the world into his private chessboard.

Now, in the aftermath of the Cold War, when so many of his associates had either died or retired, he had raised the game to its consummate level. In a single stroke he would reverse one of the primary objectives of the Gulf War: to prevent Saddam Hussein from acquiring an atomic bomb. What a worldwide coalition had fought to prevent he would undo within a few weeks' time. Kon-alov's seduction had been child's play. Accustomed to the lush life of a high-ranking official in the former Soviet Union, Konalov had bridled under the austerity of the new Russian republic. Gone were the trips to European capitals, the Mercedeses, the expensive whores and champagne, the dacha on the Black Sea—gone at least until Gerhardt the magician appeared. The scent of half a billion dollars under the Russian's nose had proven more al-luring than the perfumed neck of the most beautiful Viennese temptress.

It was all coming together. Moscow was in such disarray that they would never catch on until it was too late. And there would be no interference from the United States. The blackmail scheme would ensure that. With considerable pleasure Gerhardt envisioned the stricken look on the President's face as his initial disbelief slowly succumbed to a claustrophobic sense of encirclement and doom. As a young senator Jefferson Marshall had possessed it all—fame, fortune, power—yet had leapt at Gerhardt's business proposition with all the freebooting ambition of the perennial dealmaker, yearning to be on the inside. In order to save his skin, Marshall would have no choice but to allow the salvage operation to continue, just as he had had no choice but to deal with the Hale affair six years earlier.

Yes, he had ensnared them all. But there was one small detail to clear up, a single nagging inconsistency in the way things had played out. Vaughan had mentioned Moscow as his source of information. Unlikely. Was information leaking from another source? The Iraqis? Discretion had never been Saddam's long suit. But it was unlikely that information had been leaking from that quarter, either. So who was left? He thought of the day he had first spotted Jennifer hitchhiking on the side of the road, her stringy hair wet with rain, her defiance captivating, a reminder of the lonely child that still lingered within his soul. She was beautiful and smart, and he had taken her in and loved her like the daughter he had never had. Could she have been fooled?

Possibly.

Not willing to take the chance, he wrote the names of Drake and Henderson on a piece of stationery and slipped it inside an envelope. There could be no hint of a leak coming from within his organization, not after the Hizbollah incident. He opened a drawer and pressed a button. A moment later Rexer appeared. Gerhardt handed the envelope to the muscular bodyguard.

"Hand delivery to Arthur Shay."

"I was just about to grab some lunch. How did it go?" Henderson asked when Drake returned to his stateroom.

"They've got thermal-imaging cameras. They can spot divers in the water."

"How do you know?"

"Jennifer showed me the security room behind the bridge."

Jack nodded appreciatively. "Looks like you got the royal tour. . . ."

"Those cameras are going to be a problem."

"Not if all goes according to plan."

Drake gave Henderson a skeptical glance.

"What do you think of the girl?" Jack asked.

"Bright, beautiful, British—and bitchy."

Now it was Henderson's turn to cast the inquiring look. "Guess the earth didn't move, huh?"

"Not exactly. What about the Glocks?" Drake asked to change the subject.

Henderson walked over to one of the upholstered chairs and carefully tipped it on its side, exposing the bottom. "Taped to the frame."

Drake examined the unblemished lining.

"Strickland stopped by."

"Great," Drake replied without enthusiasm.

"Dropped off a set of deck plans. He's set up a meeting. Wants you to go over procedures."

"What time?"

"One."

"The bastard's really champing at the bit, isn't he?" Drake replied, suddenly angry, his voice strained.

Henderson gazed at his friend. "This ain't Panama, Phil. You're the guy in charge now."

"Basically, from what I can see, we can access the paymaster's issuing room from two directions. We can either drop down directly to the area through a series of hatches, starting here on the main deck. Or we can enter the boiler room through a rust hole here in the port hull and proceed forward along this passageway."

Drake turned from the presentation board and looked at the group assembled in the equipment room. Jennifer, Strickland, and Maki sat in front with six of Maki's divers standing behind. Like everything else aboard the *Avatar*, the room was well appointed and spacious: black linoleum floor, recessed lighting, and to the left rows of scuba tanks in racks beside the soundproofed compressor room. To the right stood the tall cagelike structure that housed the lift.

"What's the situation with those hatches?" Strickland asked.

"Dogged down on the main deck," Henderson replied. "Who knows what lies beneath. Ordinarily, those hatches should have been open as men poured out of the ship. But the *Norfolk* went down in less than three minutes. Only a handful of men survived."

Jennifer asked, "Can they be easily removed?" There was an earnestness in her tone that seemed more than a matter of simple accommodation.

Drake answered, "If the *Norfolk* were lying in a hundred feet of water, it wouldn't be a problem. But obviously that's not the situation here. We're going to need some additional equipment."

"Now, wait a minute," Strickland barked with annoyance. "We've had divers all over that wreck for the past three weeks.

You mean to tell me that you two can't go down there and pull those hatches?"

"It's not that simple," Drake replied with a trace of condescension, noting the smiles lighting up the faces of the divers standing behind the bald operations manager. "Considering the depth at which we'll be working, we really should be breathing trimix. You guys aren't set up for mixed-gas diving, so we'll be diving air, which means we'll be pushing it. Push it too far and we'll have people dying from oxygen toxicity."

"Could you explain that?" Jennifer asked.

"It's a little complicated, but I'll try," Drake said evenly. "For every thirty-three feet you descend, the water pressure increases by one atmosphere. You're at one atmosphere at the surface, two atmospheres at thirty-three feet, three atmospheres at sixty-six feet, and so on. At two hundred feet you're working at slightly more than seven atmospheres of pressure. Now multiply that number by the partial pressure of the air we breathe, roughly twenty percent oxygen and eighty percent nitrogen, and at two hundred feet you're breathing approximately a hundred forty percent oxygen and five hundred sixty percent nitrogen. Why? Because the ambient water pressure condenses the volume of air. At thirty-three feet—at two atmospheres of depth—you need twice the surface volume of air to fill your lungs. At two hundred feet those air molecules are packed together so tightly that each time you breathe you draw a considerable amount of air from your tank, which is one reason why we carry two or three tanks instead of one—at extreme depth you burn through your air supply.

"Rapid air depletion is just one of the problems we encounter in deep wreck diving. Nitrogen narcosis is another. With the equivalent of five hundred sixty percent of nitrogen absorbed into your tissues, you become mildly drunk. Gauges become harder to read, intricate tasks become laborious and mechanical. You really have to concentrate on what you're doing. The other problem concerns decompression sickness, commonly known as the bends.

"In recreational diving, your depth and time are restricted so that in an emergency you can bail out to the surface. That's one of the reasons divers are taught never to dive deeper than one hundred and thirty feet. Venture beyond that depth for any length of time and you absorb so much nitrogen that you can no longer ascend directly to the surface—you have to stop at various points on the way up, allowing the excess nitrogen to dissipate. On a dive like the *Norfolk*, decompression stops begin at fifty feet and increase in time as the diver ascends in ten-foot intervals. Spend thirty minutes inside the *Norfolk* at two hundred twenty feet and you're looking at about two hours of decompression before you can reach the surface. If you get lost inside the wreck and consume most of your air finding your way out and have no choice but to blow past your decompression stops, you are, as the man says, in a heap of trouble. The effect is similar to shaking a Pepsi can and pulling the tab—millions of microscopic bubbles come rushing out of solution. In most cases, you're dead before you hit the surface.

"The problem with oxygen is that once you approach the two-hundred-percent level oxygen becomes toxic. What happens is that you go into convulsions, black out, the second stage falls out of your mouth, and you drown. A diver overexerting himself at extreme depth is at even greater risk of oxygen toxicity, which is why I say that at this depth we should really be breathing mixed gas. What they do in mixed-gas diving is that they takeout some of the nitrogen and oxygen and replace it with an inert gas like helium—a mixture called trimix. It allows you to work at extreme depth with a clear head and without the risk of oxygen toxicity. The downside is that it makes for elaborate decompression requirements. You need a lot of training to handle the stuff correctly. We don't have time for that. So to make the dive on air I need to minimize the risks. I'll need a half-dozen full-face-mask rigs—that way if someone blacks out, he won't drown. And I'll need a blowtorch to make the job less strenuous."

Drake jotted down the information on a notepad and handed the paper to Strickland. "This is where you can get it. If you send Spector, we could have this stuff by tomorrow afternoon."

Strickland looked down at the paper and nodded, at a loss for words at Drake's organization and businesslike approach. Several divers in Maki's group looked at each other and nodded, brightened by Drake's expertise. Jennifer looked at Henderson and smiled.

"In the meantime," Drake continued, "that leaves us with the rust hole on the port side of the ship. If we can access this passageway here on the berth deck—the one running along these coal bunkers—then we should be able to locate a door here that leads to the area of the paymaster's issuing room. It's a longer and more complicated route, but it just might work."

Jennifer looked uneasily at Maki. "That might not be a good idea. . . ."

"Why?" Drake asked.

Maki filled in the void. "We lost a diver there."

Drake nodded. "I know." He looked at Maki and his group. "Anyone been inside that passageway?"

"I have," one of Maki's divers said. It seemed more of a confession than a statement of fact. The young man stepped forward. Slender build. Brown hair that hadn't been combed in a week.

"How long have you been diving?"

"Year and a half."

Drake glanced at Henderson.

The young diver looked around, unsure of himself.

Strickland interjected, "The guy went in. Never came out. End of story."

Jennifer looked at Strickland with disgust.

"I waited outside the passageway for twenty minutes," the young diver said, glancing at Strickland. "When Mark didn't show up I started to go inside, but I couldn't see. Silt was flying up all over the place."

"Were you guys using lines?" Drake asked.

"I was. Mark said he didn't need one. Said there was no way he was going to get lost inside a passageway."

"How deep is the silt layer?"

"Three to six inches."

Jennifer looked at Drake. "Perhaps you should try removing the hatches first," she said with concern.

"We may have to," Drake replied. "We'll find out this afternoon."

Beneath the gilded cut-glass chandelier in his second-floor office, Jefferson Marshall slumped to his chair and gazed down at the framed photograph with the kind of heartsick desperation that made him oblivious to everything around him, even Vaughan's inquisitive stare.

Outside, in the hallway, the sound of approaching footsteps reverberated along the hardwood floor. Vaughan glanced at his watch with impatience. This was no time for interruptions. They'd be lucky to have five minutes alone together. Egyptian President Zaheed was in town. Already the limousines were lining up along

Pennsylvania Avenue. In fifteen minutes Jefferson Marshall would receive the Egyptian president in the Yellow Oval Room. Then, followed by their wives, they would descend the grand staircase to the East Room, where the other guests attending the reception had gathered in a receiving line.

The President was silent, morose. With an expression of concern that in no way belied his secret fascination, Martin Vaughan gazed at Marshall, marveling at the President's sudden transformation. The slumped shoulders suggested defeat, but the face was a study in contrasts—the cheeks sallow and drawn with resignation and shame, but the eyes feverish and defiant as though the great man still refused to accept his fate as his life crumbled around him.

"Perhaps we should talk, sir."

There was no response. Jefferson Marshall wasn't listening. He was lost in the tawdry spectacle of his own imminent demise, envisioning the righteous audacity with which his opponents would rip him apart. Why had he ever become involved with a man like Gerhardt in the first place? He had known about Gerhardt's history of opportunism, his inclination to play both ends against the middle. Yet during his years in Naval Intelligence he had admired the way businessmen like Gerhardt were courted by the men who ruled nations, the men who occupied the inner sanctums of power. He recalled the first time they had met. How long ago was it? Sixteen, seventeen years? It had been at Gerhardt's Fourth of July party and he had been a newly elected senator, swept into office with the Reagan landslide of 1980. He had received the coveted invitation the week Ann and Julia finally moved to Washington once the school year ended. All of Washington society had been in attendance. Gerhardt had taken them in hand and had introduced them around. The party had been lavish, even by Washington standards; the guests, as he and Ann had quickly recognized, inhabited the more rarefied stratum of foreign affairs. The doyens of Washington society had welcomed him with open arms. Thanks to Gerhardt, he had finally garnered the cachet that he had sought for years.

Now he would become another disgraced politician, a pariah. He would lose the election. He might even go to jail. He would become another Richard Nixon—an outcast even among members of his own party. And his family? They would bear the brunt of his disgrace; they would carry the burden of his shame.

He couldn't allow that to happen. He couldn't allow everything he had built in life to go down the fucking toilet because of a momentary weakness and a lapse of judgment. It was fourth down and fifty to go and it was time to put his head down and charge like a man, like the true champion he was, like the hero the country had worshiped since the day he and his teammates had kicked Army's ass on that glorious windswept afternoon three decades before in Philadelphia. But how? The field was mined with too many obstacles.

Clearly, what Gerhardt wanted was the freedom to salvage the *Norfolk* undisturbed. But how could he cancel TORCHLIGHT now? They had agents aboard Gerhardt's yacht. If he shut down TORCHLIGHT now, he would create a firestorm within his administration. In an election year, it would be suicide. He looked around in desperation. Then suddenly he became aware of the man standing over him.

"I need your help, Martin." He felt like a supplicant. It was unbearable.

Vaughan's imagination was in a feverish state, whirling with possibilities.

There was a knock on the door.

"Yes," Marshall snapped with irritation. David Ellis stuck his head inside. "President Zaheed and his wife have arrived, sir."

"I'll be there in a minute." With a diffident nod Ellis withdrew his head and closed the door. Jefferson Marshall stood, glancing at Vaughan as he moved to the mirror to straighten his bow tie. "I need a legitimate reason for canceling TORCHLIGHT," he said, gathering himself. He gripped the younger man by the arm. "Find me a way of getting out that won't destroy this administration."

It was the first time since they had met that Jefferson Marshall had touched him, even to shake hands, and at first Vaughan considered it a gesture of gratitude, if not friendship. But as the President strode out of the room the lingering sensation seemed altogether different. It was a gesture of complicity, not friendship, and the look that the President had given him confirmed it.

Complicity for which there would be ample rewards.

The hot sun arced deep into the western sky as Drake and Henderson climbed into their gear. They were seated on the swim platform of the *Avatar*'s spacious stern, and as they slipped into their tanks and checked their air supply, they could see Bob Maki at the helm of a large inflatable, slowly circling the orange buoy. Equipped with a center console, Bimini roof, and observation tower, the inflatable would act as a chase boat in case Drake and Henderson slipped from the buoy line during their two-hour decompression and were swept away by the current.

Jennifer and Alvarez leaned against the stern rail of the *Avatar*, watching in silence as the two support divers slipped over the edge of the swim platform to check the oxygen lines. Strickland stood to the left, talking in low tones to Maki via headset.

The ocean was a silvery blue. There was not a single cloud in the sky.

Under the hot sun, Drake was beginning to feel a bit strained. He sat on the platform wearing close to a hundred pounds of equipment. Wreathed in his gear, he felt like a tuba player warming up on a concert stage. Slipping the lanyard of his third dive light up past his right elbow, he felt a nudge and looked over as Jack handed him a bottle of water. Drake gulped the ice water to slake his thirst. Then, handing the bottle off, he closed his eyes against the bright sun, calming himself, not thinking about Jennifer, the dive, or anything else, listening only to the sound of the ocean lapping against his knees. He could feel his pulse ebbing as the tension drained from his body.

Without fanfare they slipped over the side and descended along the inverted scaffolding that hung below the swim platform. The scaffolding contained two horizontal aluminum bars—one at ten feet, the other at twenty—which would serve as decompression platforms. Two oxygen lines were attached to each, their second stages as bright and silvery in the dark clear water as baby pompano. Toward the end of their decompression, they would switch from the compressed air in their tanks to the oxygen lines, allowing them to outgas nitrogen twice as fast. But they had to be careful. Breathing pure oxygen at twenty feet would put them in the same zone as diving to 218 feet on compressed air. At thirty-three feet—two atmospheres of pressure—pure oxygen became toxic.

The current was negligible. Drake hoped it would remain that way. Over the wreck the ocean could be as smooth and transparent as a pool of amber, yet halfway down the anchor line or even on the bottom, it could take on the momentum of a freight train. You never knew what to expect until you got down there.

It was like the weather. You could wake up to fog in the morning, enjoy clear skies by afternoon, and by nightfall be fighting twenty-five-foot seas with no alternative but to cut the anchor line and head for home. Fluctuating currents were a part of the mystique of deep cold-water wreck diving. They came with the territory.

Drake looked out into the dark water, wishing he were somewhere else. He would have preferred diving at noon, when the sun was directly overhead, illuminating the ocean depths, but that, too, had been impossible. By the time they reached the *Norfolk* they would be enveloped by darkness, and that could mean trouble if they encountered a strong bottom current. One slip of the fingers and you could find yourself bumping along an invisible wreck shrouded in commercial fishing nets—a good way to get badly entangled.

Now, as he gazed down into the ocean depths, he could feel the apprehension building in his chest. He thought about Gerhardt, out there someplace, the elusive quarry, arms procurer for men who slaughtered millions, an accessory before, during, and after the fact. Then he thought about Jennifer and the way her emerald eyes seemed to draw him in.

He switched on a light as Jack moved past him on the buoy line. Jack would take point, leading the way along the lines that he had rigged the week before that would take them past the *Norfolk's* bridge and down to the hole that Maki's divers had discovered in the hull. Then Drake would take over, entering the wreck and swimming down the long passageway to see where it ended, while Jack waited at the entry point, shining his light inside as a beacon.

The water was dark and clear. They were sliding down the buoy line, picking up speed as the water pressure increased. Jack's light penetrated the dark water below, and Drake felt as though he were plummeting down a mine shaft, down through the very center of the earth. He could feel his dry suit tighten against his body. He jetted air inside to offset the pressure. His lips were cold. By the time he emerged from the water they would be numb.

Maybe they would get lucky. Maybe they would locate the gold right away. But from Jack's description of the wreck, he doubted it. The *Norfolk* would be a disaster area—decks collapsed on decks, bulkheads rotted away, overheads missing, making the hours they had spent perusing the deck plans something of a joke, except that in deep cold-water wreck diving you never knew what crucial scrap of information would save your life in an emergency.

His brain was tingling. They were surrounded by total darkness now. He checked his depth: 185 feet. Then, twenty feet below on the buoy line, Jack halted.

Drake dropped down beside him as his light began revealing surfaces of metal or teak covered by a thick coat of anemones. In the surrounding darkness he wasn't sure which way he was facing—forward, aft, or abeam. Then he spotted Jack's light sweeping over the connecting line that would lead them over the port rail and down along the side of the ship. He swung his light up, illuminating an empty window, then a door. *So I'm facing the bridge.* To his left, a slender column of netting curved away until it vanished, and he tried to recall the layout of the main deck from the plans he had studied that morning. He swept his light farther to his left, hoping to see the turret. Nothing but wreckage and black water. Then he swept his light once more over the empty window and doorway and the interior darkness beyond, feeling the Siren's call, the lure of danger and unsolvable mystery—a primal curse. Jack flashed the OK sign, and Drake returned it. Then they turned and disappeared along the connecting line that led down over the port rail and along the cruiser's hull.

The barrel of a six-inch gun suddenly appeared in the penumbra of Jack's light. Drake followed the line beneath it, and a moment later Jack's light illuminated the edge of a large jagged hole. Drake drifted down beside it and glanced at his depth gauge: 236 feet. He committed the number to memory.

As with any dangerous enterprise, Drake was stacking the odds in his favor. Should something happen to the line, he would at least know the depth location of this hole and any other that he would pass through—under these conditions a very slender reed upon which to hang his life. Or Jack's. It was the unspoken horror that had haunted them both. Penetration lines were excellent safety devices but were far from foolproof, and by no means a guarantee of a diver's safety. In wreck diving such guarantees didn't exist, as shipwrecks were laden with razor-sharp steel that could sever even a well-placed line in an instant. Drake was amazed by the number of divers who refused to take the point, believing their penetration lines to be a kind of talisman. But lines were no substitute for taking the time to gradually learn the country over a succession of dives—a technique called progressive penetration. If the unthinkable occurred and something happened to your line, at least you had an extensive knowledge of the wreck to rely upon. And as Drake knew, that knowledge often meant the difference between life and death.

Now he would have to forgo that precaution. The success of the mission depended on his salvaging the gold as quickly as possible, not spending a month memorizing the region he intended to explore. The longer the salvage operation took, the greater the chance of their covers being blown or something else going wrong. But as he prepared to enter the protective deck, Drake was not happy about the risk he was taking, having to rely on his line to such an unacceptable degree. The divers whose bodies he recovered from the *Andrea Doria* had been guilty of the same mistake. And they had paid with their lives.

Now, as he shined his light inside, the powerful beam penetrated the darkness. He swept the beam over what appeared to be a cofferdam, then down inside a bunker. Coal and wreckage lay scattered everywhere. He signaled to Jack, wrapped his line around a twisted pipe, and, taking point, swam inside the hole.

They swam fifteen feet inside the *Norfolk*'s interior, Drake unreeling the line as Henderson followed, light in one hand, the line trailing through the other. Then they angled up in an area so vast and empty that it seemed as though they were outside the wreck, swimming at night in the middle of the ocean. The hole behind them was now invisible, cloaked in the darkness that surrounded them. They angled up, and a moment latter spotted a sagging overhead, dull orange with rust. The berth deck? They swam closer to get a better look and noticed an opening to the right. Drake studied his depth: 225 feet. He memorized that number, too. Then they swam up through the opening, pausing a moment while Drake wrapped the line once around a steel bar so that it would not be dragged across the hole's jagged edge when they changed direction. Henderson rechecked the line to make sure that it hadn't slipped as Drake moved away. Perhaps they should have waited until noon the following day, when at least they would have light outside the wreck, Drake thought. The dark was wearing on his nerves.

The bulkhead that housed the passageway lay straight ahead. Drake and Henderson swam forward along it until they found an opening that Drake could fit through. Drake memorized his depth again: 217 feet.

He checked his air. He was doing fine. He hovered a moment longer to switch second stages so that he would be entering the passageway with a fresh tank of air, knowing that once he entered the passageway he would not be able to read his gauges. Then very carefully he swam through the hole, silt whirling around him.

The floor of the passageway was buried under at least six inches of mud. He looked back and saw Jack reach inside the passageway, checking the line, holding it in his hand, protecting it from the hole's jagged edge. Rust flakes, dislodged by his exhaust bubbles, rained down everywhere, bright orange in the penumbra of his dive light. He thought of Pliny the Elder, sailing along the dark coast of the Mediterranean toward Pompeii as Vesuvius erupted, sending rock and ash showering into the fiery night air. Pliny had reached Pompeii but had died the following morning, leaving an adopted son to record a father's death and the surreal spectacle of a world coming to an end. And then he thought about his own father, borne into the valley of death called Ia Drang.

He pulled himself along, passing beneath cage lamps affixed to the curved frames that lined the passageway, praying that his exhaust bubbles would rise through the wreck and not collect in an area of structural weakness, causing an overhead to collapse— another unspoken horror. As the silt swirled around him, his light ebbed to a faint orange glow and he felt as though he were swimming through a mud hole and not through a shipwreck in which 1,177 men had died in a matter of minutes. The catastrophe seemed to yield a kind of perspective. Then he thought that mud hole was the wrong analogy. He was swimming through a graveyard.

He looked around. Not even the *Andrea Doria* was this bad.

There was no way in hell they were going to be able to transport gold the length of this passageway. But Drake kept on, knowing that he had not much farther to go. If he could reach the door, then he might have a shot at locating the paymaster's issuing room. And the gold.

Suddenly he was in open water. Though he couldn't see a thing, he could tell that his surroundings had changed, because he wasn't touching objects anymore. Silt billowed around him, and his heart leapt with anxiety and fear. He reached back and felt the line extending into the darkness.

Instinctively he swam forward, the beam of his light lengthening as the dark water became clearer. He checked his air, then his depth. He had dropped ten feet. He swam ahead a couple of yards and turned around, flashing his light in the direction he had come. Silt poured out of the passageway like gun smoke. So this was what happened to Maki's diver, he thought. He had come charging out of the open-ended passageway hauling a ton of silt and hadn't been able to find his way back. No telling where the body lay. In his desperation to find a way out, the diver had probably traveled some distance before running out of air.

Well, there was nothing he could do about it now. Maybe when the mission was over he would look around. No doubt someone—a relative, a friend—would want the body back. But now Drake had other priorities. Besides, it wasn't as though anyone in the outside world was likely to know about it anyway. Gerhardt and Strickland were not about to risk getting the authorities involved by notifying the boy's family.

Drake hovered a moment to get his bearings. He could see a wall ahead. Intact. He was close. He directed his light up and immediately spotted the opposite end of the passageway, sloping at a forty-five-degree angle like a hay chute inside an old barn.

He entered the compartment and continued forward, trying his best not to think about the structural integrity of the corridor surrounding him. The entrance was almost devoid of silt, but he could see mud ahead. Then, six feet inside the passageway, he spotted the door.

He moved toward it, his heart soaring as he realized that it was partially ajar. He pulled himself gingerly along as the silt layer began to thicken, wishing that he had brought more air. He reached the door, quelling an urge to pry it open, not wanting to lose what little visibility remained. He angled his light through the narrow gap and peered into the room. The shower of rust flakes became heavier as his exhaust bubbles collected along the overhead above.

In the distance to the left he glimpsed several long racks of bottles and wire frames twisted and dangling at the edge of an abyss. What were they? Bed frames? Couldn't be. The petty officer's quarters lay on the starboard side of the ship. What would bed frames be doing over here on the port side? He concentrated, fighting the narcosis, trying to recall the exact layout of the area surrounding the paymaster's issuing room. Then it clicked. Operating tables. He was staring at the dispensary and sick bay.

He gripped the door and tried to force it open, knowing the paymaster's issuing room lay only twenty feet beyond. The door wouldn't budge. *Damn.* He tried again, this time bracing a hand against the door frame in an attempt to pry the fucker open. It moved an inch. *Jesus Christ.* By now the rust and silt had blackened the water to the point his light was useless. It was time to turn around. If he stayed any longer he would be approaching the point of no return. No sense in pushing it. The water was black and his nerves were raw. He was getting low on air.

He reached down to locate the line, now buried in the silt,

moving his hand down along the reel and then forward. Divers had died from becoming entangled in their own lines, and he wanted to make very sure that he knew exactly where the line was when he turned. He felt something long and narrow, and as he ran his fingers along the line it felt as though he were pushing his hand through a brush pile. Then the shock of recognition.

Bones.

Four hours later Henderson slipped the laptop computer out of its nylon case and looked around. He was alone, sitting on a deck chair overlooking the *Avatar*'s stern. To the east clouds were stacking on the horizon and to the west the late-afternoon sky was edged in pink. Drake had headed for the bridge to obtain a weather report.

The dive had gone well. In many ways it seemed a miracle that Drake had accomplished so much in a single dive, but then, Drake was the very best. Even the SEAL instructors at Coronado had watched in amazement as Drake arrived on target each time during the long box swims that they would conduct at night. Drake had performed so well in training that he had been invited back as a diving instructor. But Drake had declined, telling them that he wanted to be where the action was.

Setting the computer on his lap, Henderson flipped up the thick screen, typed in a command, and waited until a red bar flashed in the upper right-hand corner. He looked around again, rubbing his neck with one hand, extending the other as though stretching, then began to work up a decompression schedule that would allow them to make two dives a day to 230 feet for the next two weeks—a purely hypothetical exercise, because there was no way that they were going to push it that hard and risk coming up with the bends.

To his left near the stern the lift began to whir and two crewmen appeared. They dropped down to the swim platform and began hauling in the inflatable and the decompression platform. Henderson watched them for a moment, then resumed typing. When he finished he pressed the Enter key and the red bar flashed again and he looked out at the purple sky. It felt good to be out in the open air. The ocean had been dark and confining, reminding him of the winter afternoons when as a child he had shut himself up in a closet during games of hide-and-seek. He wondered how his son Andrew was doing, and he wondered about Sally, recalling her look of quiet despair as he hugged them both before saying good-bye. He had promised to take the boy fishing in the Berkshires. *God, I miss them.*

The message was sent.

The phone rang. From the upholstered chair in his study Adams looked up from his folder. His back hurt and his leg was stiff. There was a phone on the desk across the room, and he stood, struggling to reach it. In the distance he could hear the housekeeper grunt as she crossed the outer hall. Then a knock on the door and a pretty smile masking perturbation.

"General McKendrick, sir."

"Thank you, Brenda."

She handed him the phone.

"Walt?"

"Redskins hired a new quarterback. Just came over the wire."

"About time we had a winning season."

They were in.

. . .

"Anyone got a weather report?"

The three sailors manning the bridge looked at each other, unsure of themselves. Drake took their lack of initiative as a good sign; clearly these men would not act unless ordered, and probably without much enthusiasm, given the way Strickland hectored them about. He glanced at the sunset through the rectangular windshield: bars of yellow light being shorn by the massing of clouds. A world transformed—the story of his life.

"The Captain's asleep," said one of the men with a tentativeness bordering on the apologetic.

"I don't think we've been introduced. I'm Philip Drake, the lead diver on the *Norfolk* operation. I arrived this morning. . . ."

Jennifer was just stepping into her office when Drake entered the hall, weather chart in hand.

She looked up with surprise. "I thought you'd be resting. May I talk to you a minute?"

Even from the opposite end of the hallway Drake could see the brightness of her eyes, the quick and easy smile that had greeted him on his arrival.

They entered an office startling in its understated elegance. The walls were eggshell, the furnishings oak. A linen sofa, flanked by end tables, stood to the right. To the left an antique desk looked out across the room. Above the desk, framed in gold, hung a large seascape with wild grasses swaying in the foreground against a whitecapped ocean of pale green and a blue sky bursting with clouds.

She closed the door behind them. "Please," she said, indicating the sofa, quietly regarding the man whose presence seemed to fill the room around her.

"Nice painting."

"Yes, it is." She seemed distracted. Then her expression crumpled into a chiaroscuro of uncertainty. "My father arrives day after tomorrow."

"You spoke to him?"

"While you were diving." She paused, glancing above to a bookcase on the right. "I'm afraid I must ask you a favor. . . . You did well today?"

"We came close."

"When the time comes . . . when you are very close, I'll need to know. I'm afraid I'll need some time to prepare. . . ." Her smile was small. Brave.

Drake felt like an executioner, and as he gazed at the beautiful woman seated before him he sensed that it was a feeling that they both shared to opposite degrees—that her burden was as vast as his was momentary. And with this revelation came another: that whatever reasons Jennifer possessed for turning in Gerhardt had nothing to do with the way the arms dealer had treated her—that in his relationship with his adopted daughter Gerhardt had been a warm and loving father.

She glanced up at the wall again, and Drake followed her eyes to a small black-and-white photograph above the bookcase. And suddenly it was as though he were looking upon a vista of a long-forgotten past—his past, not hers. She had been glancing at a framed picture of a medieval fortress perched on a mountaintop. The photograph had been taken from above, and the mountain was so rocky and barren as it fell away on all sides that the fortress seemed to be perched on the edge of a cliff.

"Did you take this?"

"It's nothing really," she said with a tinge of embarrassment as Drake moved closer to get a better view. "Just an archaeological site. My father spent some time there during the war. It's the Cathar stronghold at Montségur. In Languedoc. In the south of France. . . ."

But Drake knew. From the books McKendrick had given him as a child and his subsequent forays into Arthurian legend and the ideals that had shaped his life. And he thought of the fractured ledges of the continental shelf, knowing now why he had been captivated by their austerity.

"Esclarmonde," he whispered.

She looked at him in startled wonder.

The temple fortress had been home to the Grail.

From the backseat of the Lincoln Town Car, Martin Vaughan gazed at the small Tudor house to his right. The street was shaded with white oaks of such majesty and grace that they might have been planted during the time of the Revolution. The houses were elegant and small, packed together like tables at an expense-account restaurant. But despite their proximity to their neighbors, the residents of Chevy Chase tended to keep to themselves. For that reason, shortly after being named National Security Advisor, Vaughan had recommended that the Executive Office purchase the house as a haven for its more clandestine activities.

Terry Fox switched off the ignition and looked around at his boss with an expression of mild inquiry that barely concealed his dismay. A thirty-three-year-old former CIA analyst who had left the Agency out of boredom four years before, Fox had become Vaughan's Deputy National Security Advisor with the tacit promise that Vaughan would transform the NSC from its traditional advisory role into an operational base for covert activities over which Fox would hold a good measure of sway, an initiative steadfastly opposed by Adams.

Though accustomed to the National Security Advisor's fluctuating moods, Fox dreaded having to spend the rest of the day dogging Vaughan's heels. Under pressure Vaughan often became snappish. And today the youthful Deputy National Security Advisor wasn't in the mood for putting up with any horseshit. As he watched his boss gather his briefcase, he thought about the raucous night of Mexican food, dancing, and tequila shooters that had ended five hours before. His stomach rumbled. He gazed at Vaughan with a resolve that was more wishful thinking than fact. Last night's tequila bled through his pores.

"Let's go," Vaughan commanded.

The heat of day had begun to spread, and outside Fox could hear the drone of cicadas. He had no clue as to what was going on, only the groggy recollection of Vaughan's early-morning summons. The National Security Advisor had been unusually terse over the phone. "Get dressed and pick me up at home in an hour. In your wife's car."

"Why? What's going on?"

"Our ship's come in."

Vaughan was halfway across the lawn by the time Fox caught up. Down the street, a boy on a BMX bicycle delivered papers. Fox glanced at his watch. It was seven A.M. *Shit.*

The front door was open. They stepped inside and entered the living room off the foyer. A tall man in khaki shorts and a turquoise polo shirt sat in a wicker chair, staring at them both. Fox had seen this man before. At Langley. Black eyes. Salt-and-pepper mustache. The pallor of a carp.

Paramilitary, people had said. A knuckledragger.

The man eyed Fox with suspicion. "What's he doing here?"

"I thought I'd make him a member of the Charlie Adams fan club. Just like you, Chickie boy."

Fox sat down on a sofa at the other end of the room.

"Cut the shit, asshole," Burnham said.

The levity in Vaughan's expression vanished. Fox looked on in amazement. He had never heard the National Security Advisor called an asshole before, at least not to his face. Burnham regarded them with contempt.

Vaughan pulled up a chair, his face deadly serious. "We need an explosive device placed inside the Jamaican Parliament Building."

"We?" Burnham asked.

"This operation has the authority of the President of the United States."

"Payment?"

"Two million dollars."

"Generous." There was a hint of sarcasm in Burnham's voice.

"You want the job or not?" Vaughan bristled.

"I'm listening. . . ."

"The objective is to create substantial property damage but no casualties. Therefore, the device must be set to detonate at two A.M. to ensure that the building and streets are empty. The explosion is to occur on July fifth. It must also appear to be the work of Mauranian saboteurs."

Burnham smirked. Maurania. Something was up. Burnham could smell it. Probably the election. Not like Marshall could promise the folks another big tax cut. Not when he failed to deliver the first time. "Agency boys know about this?"

"This is an NSC operation. Need-to-know basis only."

"Yeah, I thought so."

"Can you handle it?"

"Not for two million," he replied with a derisive chuckle. "I'll need four. Plus one to cover expenses. Four-fifths payable up front."

"Now, wait a goddamn minute, Burnham!"

"Four million in my account in the Caymans this afternoon. That's the deal. Take it or leave it."

She was alone in her stateroom, gazing up through the wide Plexiglas skylight, thinking about the day Gerhardt had taken her to the Cathar stronghold at Montségur. They had flown by helicopter, courtesy of the French arms manufacturer Dassault, to whom Gerhardt had channeled more than a billion dollars' worth of Iraqi business. She had dreamed of this place since she was a child, since the day she had stumbled across the story of the Holy Grail during one of the weekly outings to the library that had become her sole refuge from a life of loneliness and regimentation. She had hated the orphanage and longed to be elsewhere.

It was the Grail quest that had given her the impetus to run away—the story of the cup that had been used by Christ and his disciples at the Last Supper and carried to England by Joseph of Arimathea, where it became the object of a holy quest by the Knights of the Round Table. The Grail quest had become her quest, a yearning for a love that would remain unbroken despite the vicissitudes of life, the kind of love that she imagined her parents must have possessed for her—the primacy of human attachments being the legacy of an orphanage upbringing.

And so when she was old enough she had run away. Gerhardt had found her, hitchhiking on the side of a road outside of London; he had swerved to the side of the road in his silver Mercedes. He had had a beard then. And suddenly he *was* Arthur. He had swept her away from the orphanage and had taken her home to his castle and had loved her as his own. And she had flourished. When she told him of her secret name for him one night while he was tucking her into bed, he chuckled and told her about the temple fortress at Montségur, home of the Cathars, whose priests were called Perfecti—the pure—and how it had been home to the Grail and how he had visited the site during the war. And she knew right then that he really was a king who had come to save her, and believed that in her soul until the day she discovered what business he was in.

A classmate at Westminster: "Your father sells guns to the Egyptians."

"I'm in the defense industry," he explained that night at dinner. "I work for governments."

Then, a decade later, she overheard him joking about the murders.

They had killed the mother first, then the two little girls who had looked up at Gerhardt's London estate with the same startled wonder as she had when she was a girl.

As a lesson to the father.

They had killed the spirit first, then they had killed the body.

Yet she could not turn him in. If she testified against him he would receive the death penalty. And though she despised him, she could not forget his kindness either. He had taken her in; raised her as his own. So she would turn him in for the nuclear-weapons deal. Thank God that had fallen into her lap. He would spend the rest of his life in jail but avoid execution, though she had no qualms about the terrorist she had turned over to Adams two years before, her quest for love transformed by the necessity to protect the innocent from suffering, like the chatelaine of Montségur who would sometimes guide her in her dreams.

The woman whose name meant world of light.

Esclarmonde.

. . .

He was lying on his belly, deep inside the forward storage area of the *Avatar*'s bottom-most deck. The corridor was dark, over-heated. Like his imagination. He was rehearsing the moves he would make breaching the door, lying on his belly in the dark with a set of tanks strapped to his back. But he was also drifting back in time, back to the Crusades and the Inquisition, which had swept across southern France in the early thirteenth century, an-nihilating the most civilized culture of the Middle Ages—Occi-tania.

He had learned of this civilization via Arthurian legend and the books McKendrick had given him as a child. He had started with T. H. White's *The Once and Future King*, then had moved on to Malory. He had devoured Arthurian legend the way other boys devoured comic books, especially the tales of young Arthur and Merlin and Owl. He thrilled at the story of Excalibur, the magic sword that the boy had pulled from the stone to become king of England, succeeding where stronger men had failed. Would he be ready when his time came? Would he be a knight worthy of the Round Table? Would he possess the wisdom of Arthur or the purity of Galahad? There was a time when these legends were not merely symbolic of his aspirations, they *were* his aspirations. Yet he had forgotten. He had grown up and had gone on to other things.

He thought of the inhabitants of Occitania and how fear must have engulfed their lives as the sea had engulfed the lives of the men aboard the *Norfolk* on that fateful night in 1917. The Cathars were early Protestants whose beliefs had become wide-spread in a region known for its toleration. But the Capetian Kings of northern France had for years coveted this rich and vi-brant land, and Pope Innocent III was eager to wipe out the Cathar heresy. So the Pope and the Capetian king joined forces, and what would later become known as the Albigensian Crusades began. At the walled city of Béziers, the army of Simon de Montfort butchered every man, woman, and child—more than twenty-five thousand people. The papal legate had granted Simon and his army a special dispensation; there wasn't time to separate the guilty from the innocent, because the Cathar heresy was too widespread. Simon and his army had been granted absolution for their sins in advance.

So refugees began pouring into the mountain stronghold at Montségur, the legendary home of the Grail. And the chatelaine of the fortress, a woman of exceptional strength and goodness, had opened the doors and taken them in. She had protected them and given them comfort. Even down to the last moments of her life on that awful day in March 1244 when the fortress fell and she, having refused to renounce her faith, had led the Cathar procession down the mountain path lined by soldiers of the Capetian king to what would become forever known as the Field of Ashes.

It's Camelot all over again, and I'm not talking about the Kennedy years. . . .

Esclarmonde.

Noon. They were seated on the swim platform, adjusting their gear in silence and concentrating on the dive. The sea had begun to flatten, and as Drake looked out over its shimmering expanse, he could see a container ship moving slowly across the horizon. The china blue ocean seemed textured like suede. Sunlight glittered off the backs of the rollers.

To the right two support divers wearing single tanks and wet suits entered the water with a splash and popped to the surface. A crewman handed each diver an extra tank and watched as the divers disappeared beneath the surface, their bubble trails length-ening as they angled down the buoy line. They would hang the tanks at the fifty-foot mark just in case Drake and Henderson needed more air to complete their decompression, a distinct pos-sibility, considering that they would be inside the *Norfolk* for up to forty minutes.

In addition to the two large steel tanks mounted to his back-pack, Jack wore a tank slung under each arm, cave diver style. Given the confines of the passageway, Drake could not opt for a similar configuration. Instead he had mounted a big pony bottle to the back of his tanks in a triangular configuration—not the re-serve he would have liked, considering the complexity of the dive, but better than nothing.

Jack tapped him on the shoulder. "Set?"

Drake could see the beads of perspiration forming around Jack's eyes. He looked up at the crewman standing beside him. "Where's Strickland?" Then, from behind, Jennifer's voice, shrill with impatience: "Gerald. We need you here. Now!"

The operations manager leaned over the rail. He was wearing a black baseball cap with the word INGRAM emblazoned on the front. He gripped the rail, and Drake could see that the knuckles of both hands were scarred. His pink cheeks glistened with sweat. Then Jennifer appeared, standing above him in a white cotton shirt and tortoiseshell sunglasses. The allure of a sophisticated woman. And the avidity that he lately felt in her presence swept over him once more.

"Everything okay?" she asked, her brows knitted with con-cern, her hair catching the wind.

"We're fine, Jen."

He wanted to reassure her, but he could think of nothing to say that would mean anything except the truth about how he seemed to rise out of himself whenever she was around. But this wasn't the time.

He looked up at Strickland. "We should be back on the buoy line in forty minutes. Make sure the support team is in the water. I want a diver hanging out at the fifty-foot mark when we get there."

"Yeah, I hear ya," Strickland said. There was an edge to his voice. Straightening, he looked out at Maki circling in the inflatable and drew a cigar from his breast pocket, striking a match with cupped hands. Then, flicking the match into the ocean, he turned to a crewman and said, "Get me a margarita."

Sunlight penetrated the clear depths, radiant as wildfire. They descended along the buoy line, feeling the gentle pull of running water. The ocean was gorgeous and light-shot. A day of exceptional visibility, Drake thought.

They dropped down to the fifty-foot mark and hovered a moment while Drake made sure that the reserve tanks were tied correctly to the line. If there was anything he hated more than relying on tanks he couldn't carry, it was discovering that they weren't there when he needed them most. Satisfied that the tanks were tied securely, he signaled to Henderson and began checking his equipment, making sure that his lights worked, his knives could be reached—that sort of thing. Then they descended, the sea sparkling around them.

Drake gazed into the ethereal blue. He had seen days like this on the *Andrea Doria*, the water so light-filled and clear that he could look up from the sandy bottom at 254 feet to a panoramic view of the superstructure as the enormous ocean liner rose above him on her starboard side. On such days Drake never switched on a light.

A school of baitfish gleamed in the distance, shifting suddenly only to scatter and re-form as a large pollack appeared. Then the baitfish vanished, as though they had been a shimmering mirage. Drake looked around. The ocean seemed devoid of life.

Drake glanced at his depth gauge: 150 feet. He looked below, and a gray shape began to emerge, galvanizing his attention. Then he saw it, the outline of a large shipwreck, lying upright on the ocean floor. He dropped down another twenty feet, marveling at the clarity of the water as the *Norfolk* came into view.

The superstructure towered above them. Straight ahead Drake spotted the fallen trunk of the mast, draped in commercial fishing nets. To either side lay the open doors and windows of the bridge. The mast angled down past the turret, where the crow's nest lay scattered in a tangle of wreckage. They dropped off the buoy line, Drake glancing down at the teak planking clearly visible on the foredeck, then up again at the dark window frames of the bridge. On the main deck open doorways beckoned.

Every steel surface was covered with anemones. Below and to the right he spotted the line that they had followed the day before. And as they began to trace its path, sections of the wreck that he remembered now came together as a whole.

They dropped over the port rail and angled down in the bright, clear water past the barrel of the six-inch gun. The water was colder now and crisp, like a winter sky.

He could feel himself being propelled by a whisper of current. Then he saw Jack swinging down along the edge of a large rectangular opening. It was nearly twice as large as he had imagined, about the size of a garage door. The contrast between what he was seeing now and what he recalled from the day before was startling, literally the difference between night and day. Drifting down, he looked inside.

It was like staring into a cave.

The initial three feet shelved along a cofferdam, then widened abruptly and dropped down into a coal bunker. Coal and wreckage lay scattered everywhere. He looked up and spotted the rusted overhead, shocked by its fragility.

He glanced at Jack and pointed to the opening that would lead them up into the berth deck, now clearly visible where the day before it had been shielded by darkness. Jack nodded. Farther to the right they could see a larger hole through which an air duct had fallen. Having tied the end of his penetration line to a pipe, Drake signaled Henderson and they swam inside, angling up to the sagging overhead. They checked their depth: 225 feet. They were right on the mark. Then they swam up through the hole, taking care not to sever the line. Immediately, they were enveloped by darkness.

The bulkhead that housed the passageway was straight ahead, as delicate and brown as old paper. Inside the berth deck Drake swept his light from side to side as Jack swam up beside him, cupping the thin line in his left hand. They swam forward along the bulkhead and a moment later found the opening.

Drake looked at Henderson, then swam inside the passageway. He was calmer now, acclimated to the darkness surrounding him. He concentrated against the narcosis, trying not to think of the mystery that lay beyond, keeping his mind focused on the task at hand. Still, his heart swelled with anticipation. Did the paymaster's issuing room exist? Was the gold salvageable? In less than five minutes he would know.

Inside the passageway, he checked the line and began heading forward, silt swirling around him. He played his light over the sides of the passageway as rust flakes, dislodged by his air bubbles, began to scatter all around him, the color of medieval fire. Certain ages always seemed to evoke corresponding colors—the jaundiced yellow of Europe in the 1930s, the kaleidoscopic colors of the Renaissance, the black of the Nazi regime, the white and pastel blue of ancient Greece—but the dominant color of the Middle Ages was the color of flames flickering against castle walls. And as he slowly made his way along the dark passageway, he thought again of the photograph of Montségur that he had seen in Jennifer's office and the shared knowledge that had forged the spiritual bond between them, plunging like the fabled staircase of three thousand steps down to the very core of their being. He moved along the passageway, unreeling line, keeping his light aimed slightly down so that he would not be blinded by the backscatter as the silt whirled around him. A minute later he was in open water.

The beam of his light lengthened as the water cleared. To his left a long section of pipe hung straight down. He hadn't remembered that from the day before. Narcosis. Hmmm. . . . He swung his light up, illuminating the opposite end of the passageway. As far as he could tell, it hadn't shifted. It hung from the thick bulkhead like a covered bridge that had slumped into a river. He could feel the anxiety building in his chest. He swam inside.

The hatch lay dead ahead, six feet away. He angled up as the silt layer began to thicken. Then, within two feet of the door, he stopped.

Reaching over his shoulder, he grabbed the nylon bag that he had strapped to the back of his tanks, pulling it free like an arrow from a quiver. He set the bag down in the mud in front of him, loosened the drawstring, and withdrew the jack without letting go of any of the three pieces, knowing that if they slipped from his fingers he would never find them again. Narcosis blunted his motor skills and the assembly seemed to take forever. He worried about his air. He thought about the skeleton that lay beneath him, the remains of a sailor. Then he thought about something else.

Carefully he wedged the assembled jack into the gap of the door. He cranked the handle twice until it was firmly set. The door creaked. This was going to be easier than he thought. He cranked the handle again, feeling the tension increase. With a snap the door gave way.

Elated, he swung the door open, silting up the water so badly that he was immediately engulfed in darkness. For once it didn't matter. He checked the line and moved past the door, dragging mud and silt along with him. As he moved forward the water cleared. He looked down. A shattered rib cage, ghostly white, fluttered into the abyss. The water ahead was as clear and still as desert night.

The berth deck—or what was left of it—looked as though it had been cored by a knife. He swung his light to the left and spotted what was left of the dispensary and sick bay. Steel bed frames and racks of bottles dangled precariously over the edge. For several seconds he hovered above the jagged abyss, reluctant to move until he had oriented himself to his new surroundings.

To the right the massive trunk of the mast support rose like a sequoia. Then, as he moved forward, the beam of his light stabbing the darkness, something caught his eye. A compartment floating in midair. He concentrated, fending off the narcosis. The paymaster's issuing room? His heart raced with anticipation. He swept his light above, and suddenly felt as though he had been jolted by a cattle prod, the electricity zigzagging up and down his spine. He could see straight up through the gun deck. The overhead was honeycombed.

He pressed his light to his thigh, throwing the room into

darkness. He looked around for traces of ambient light—indications of openings in the hull. Nothing. Not even a porthole. He thought of heading back. But the compartment seemed to draw him in, projecting out into the open area of the berth deck like a sagging balcony on the edge of a cliff. Then he saw that instead of one compartment, there were three. Several bulkheads were missing. And as he swept his light over the framework of rusted steel, Drake realized that by some miracle, he had arrived at his destination. The paymaster's issuing room was intact.

Hovering in the clear water, he felt as though he were floating in space. He moved closer and a cage of rusted steel sparkled in the beam of his light. But it was the area beyond that commanded his attention. Inside the cage, beneath a thick layer of silt, stood eight distinct mounds. And beneath them, Drake knew, lay a billion dollars of gold.

For a long moment Drake hovered at the doorway, memorizing the area. Despite his fear, he was brimming with happiness. Barring any problems with the weather, Operation TORCHLIGHT would be over in a matter of days. He checked his air. Then, as he turned toward the passageway, he heard the groan of collapsing steel. Suddenly a heavy object sailed past his nose like a pterodactyl's wing, striking him in the chest.

He was falling.

Stifling nausea and panic, Drake fought to right himself and regain buoyancy as he tumbled downward, his tanks clanging on wreckage invisible behind him. He jetted air into his vest and reached down to a spare light and switched it on. Then he landed with a jolt.

The line was gone. The reel was still attached to his harness, but the line had been severed. *You're a dead man*, he thought. He swung his light around and discovered that he had landed on a field of naval artillery shells. The big eight-inch shells lay scattered everywhere, blanketed by a thin layer of silt. He had fallen from the berth deck past the protective deck to the upper platform deck and had landed in the eight-inch magazines. He scanned his depth gauge: 249 feet. Beads of sweat ran down his chest. *Take it easy*, he told himself. *Take it one breath at a time.* His head pounded from the narcosis. And he knew that if he didn't find a way out of the *Norfolk* in the next ten minutes, he would run out of air and drown.

Instinctively he pressed his light to his thigh, looking for openings in the hull. Black water. He switched his light on again and looked up, searching for the line. Rust flakes skipped past his face like bullets sparking off a runway.

An open hatch stood to his right. He looked at his compass, knowing that he wouldn't get a precise reading because of the surrounding steel, but all he needed was a rough sense of direction. The door lay to the southeast. He was facing aft. A bulkhead towered above him three feet away. The door led to the ammunition passage along the port hull.

He checked his air. At 249 feet he was burning through his air supply and knew that he would have to choose a course of action and stick to it. He was quickly running out of time. He could either ascend and look for the tail end of the line. Or he could try to find another way out. He headed for the door.

He entered the ammunition passage and switched off his light. Nothing. He swam another ten feet and slammed into a bulkhead. He had reached a dead end. In desperation he swept his light over the rusted steel, thinking about Jack waiting outside the passageway three decks above, his heart filling with remorse. Then, two feet below, he spotted an opening large enough to swim through. He hugged the deck and clawed his way through the narrow passage. He switched off the light and prayed. Then, with resurgent hope, he saw it as he peered into the darkness straight ahead. Fifty feet away, a massive bar of radiant light flooded through a large hole. For a long breathless moment he gazed at it in wonder.

Its color was green, the color of life.

The sky was black, filled with stars. It was midnight, and Drake was standing on the observation deck, a blanket draped around his shoulders. He had quietly slipped out of his stateroom and wandered topside with the idea of stretching out on one of the deck chairs beside the pool. On this night of all nights, he did not want to sleep inside a ship. He wanted to be outside where he could lose himself in the stillness of the night, in the radiance of the stars when there was no moon.

In the aftermath of the dive neither Drake nor Henderson had mentioned the accident. On the afterdeck Captain Alberto Alvarez had been ebullient. Even Strickland had evinced a grudging respect when Drake informed them of what he had seen. Spector, back with the equipment they had ordered, slapped Drake on the back and said, "Shit, man. You guys don't fool around!" Jennifer looked genuinely relieved. She smiled at Drake, then gazed at Strickland with a look of complete vindication. Drake glanced at them all without emotion. He felt numb. It had nothing to do with the fact that he had spent nearly three hours decompressing in cold water.

His air supply nearly gone, Drake had headed straight for the buoy line, where he began his ascent and decompression. Henderson had waited inside the *Norfolk* until he could wait no longer. Before leaving he had clipped a fresh light to the inside edge of the hole and switched it on so that the light shone along the passageway. It was the best he could do. Then, leaving the line in place, he had headed back to the main deck and the buoy line, certain that Drake was dead.

On the observation deck Drake found a padded chair and stretched out, pulling the blanket up to his chin. The ocean breeze felt cool and refreshing as he huddled under the warm blanket. He looked up at the stars, losing himself in their quiet splendor. *I used to do this as a boy—sneak out of the house at night and sleep in the backyard, forever a soldier's son. Don't remember there being as many planes in the sky or as high up. Are they satellites? Impossible to tell. Are they watching over me? Maybe.*

Used to be God.

They would dive again in the morning. Henderson had been against it, but Drake had insisted. This time, however, they would not approach the paymaster's issuing room via the passageway. They would drop down through the main deck hatch instead.

"I'm sorry. Were you sleeping?"

She was standing thirty feet away. Drake could barely see her in the dark. Suddenly he was happy. She moved closer, and Drake saw that she was dressed in the same khaki shorts and cotton sweater that she had worn that afternoon.

She examined the sky for a moment. "The stars are lovely tonight—so clear, so bright. . . . May I join you?"

"Please."

Drake got up and pulled a deck chair alongside his. She sat down, leaning back against the padding, drawing her knees up. Drake sat down on his chair again and spread the blanket over them both. The *Avatar* rocked gently in the swells.

She looked up again. A breeze had picked up, and she took a deep breath of the cool salt air. Then she looked at him. "Thank you."

"Lucky break. I brought a blanket big enough for both of us."

"I mean for taking this on."

Drake said nothing, gazing at her in quiet acknowledgment.

"It's funny—you're not what I expected at all."

"What did you expect?"

"Someone a bit rougher around the edges, I think. Men who've served in elite units usually wear it as a badge. It's usually the first thing they tell you about themselves. You're not like that at all."

"I was in the Navy three years. It's not my life."

She looked at him for a moment. "When I was a little girl in London I would look out of my window at night, thinking that heaven consisted of three stars. That's all. Just three. That's all I could see against the bright London sky. The day my adoption papers came through he took me to his country estate. There were two stone gates at the entrance, and the place was so huge that I thought that he had changed his mind and was dropping me off at another orphanage. But it wasn't an orphanage. It was his home—one of his many homes, as I discovered. And that night when I went to bed in my new room—in my own room—I looked out at the sky waiting for the stars to rise, expecting three. But there were millions. The sky was filled with them, breathtaking and gorgeous against the coal-black sky. As they are tonight. I grabbed my blankets and ran downstairs into the garden, gazing up, enthralled, in all my childhood never dreaming that such radiant beauty lay behind that bright layer of London sky. He was there. Sitting in a wrought-iron chair, smoking one of his Cuban cigars. I think for a moment he thought I was running away.

'What is it?' he asked, startled, and I replied, 'The stars . . . there're so many. . . .' And with a smile he gathered me up. 'Do you know what Mr. Einstein says,' he whispered. I had never heard of Einstein before. I thought he was someone he had made up—a magical figure. 'No,' I whispered with excitement, 'what does Mr. Einstein say?' And as I sat on his lap, his breath fragrant with cigar smoke and port as we looked up together at the night sky, he whispered in my ear: 'Mr. Einstein says that when you look at the stars, you look back in time.'"

Drake looked at her, captivated by the romance of the story, caught by the dilemma that must have rended her soul.

"That's what he's like. When you meet him, you'll see. He is like this sky. Dazzling. But he has a layer, too, and when you peel it back you discover something less attractive. Something that is the absence of all light. Something that should be exiled from this world."

"Think of it as Gerhardt's wake-up call." General Craig Hawking stood beside the display board, grinning.

Seated before him in a small semicircle in McKendrick's spacious Pentagon office were Admiral Jack Tanner, Chief of Naval Operations, Secretary of Defense Richard Elliot, and several other high-ranking officers from the Navy and the Coast Guard. McKendrick sat behind his walnut desk, studying the nautical chart the Chief of Special Operations Command had pinned to the board. Hawking had briefed him by phone earlier that morning, but McKendrick needed the approval of men directly in the chain of command. He didn't think that there would be a problem. Tanner and Elliot were two of the finest men he had known, above the petty politics that so often infected the higher echelons of Washington.

"H-hour is set for 0400 hours," Hawking continued, "the day after we receive confirmation from our people aboard the *Avatar.* Thirty minutes prior to the assault the Coast Guard will enforce a ten-mile exclusion zone. Our base of operations will be the *Nassau*. Once she is in position, we will move in fast: three platoons of Navy SEALs aboard Ch-46 Sea Knights, plus two Blackhawks hovering over the *Avatar* port and starboard, acting as sniper platforms. Our first priority is to take control of the *Avatar*. Second priority is prisoner handling. Gerhardt will be immediately transferred to the *Nassau* following his arrest. Depending on the logistics of prisoner handling, we should have the whole operation wrapped up within an hour. Are there any questions?"

Admiral Tanner looked pleased. "I think you've covered just about everything."

"I believe so. If they resist, we can overpower them in minutes. But my feeling is that once they see the firepower arrayed against them, they'll surrender."

Secretary of Defense Elliot pressed his lips together with concern. "What about our people on board?"

"They know enough to keep their heads down," McKendrick said. "They're combat veterans, former members of SEAL Team 4."

"You're kidding?"

"And they're armed."

Elliot nodded. "Who's commanding the assault?"

"Lieutenant Commander Jack Kelly," Hawking explained. "Good man. Led the assault on the *Galveston*, the tanker the Iranians boarded in the Persian Gulf a few years back. Covered the area of three football fields in less than ten minutes. No casualties—at least on our side."

"I remember."

McKendrick looked about the room. "Well, gentlemen? If you have any objections, now's the time. . . ."

"Looks good to me, Walt," Richard Elliot said.

"Can you get your men up and ready on time?" Admiral Tanner inquired.

Hawking smiled. "Training as we speak."

Tanner looked at McKendrick. "I have no objections."

"Anyone else?"

The men in the room were silent.

"Well, then," McKendrick said, rising from his desk. "Pending the President's approval, it's a go."

They were standing in the shelter of the glass-enclosed reception area, waiting with varying degrees of tension as the Sikorsky approached. Alvarez shielded his eyes against the early-morning sun as he looked up, his face taut with anticipation. Strickland glanced about nervously, his eyes flitting from face to face. Jennifer looked quietly at the platform, as though gazing upon a distant land. By contrast, Henderson seemed almost relaxed. Wearing a pair of aviator sunglasses, he leaned against a wall with his arms crossed, but from the rigid jawline Drake could tell his friend was alert, scouting the terrain, a point man by instinct and training.

The water had been cold and dark that morning. Using the equipment that Spector had delivered the previous afternoon, Drake and Henderson had worked in alternate shifts, each taking a team of divers along to help manage the extra gear. Drake had gone first, slicing through the four clamps that held the hatch in place. Ten minutes later Henderson had severed the hinge, the acetylene flame spewing a torrent of bubbles. A third team had rigged the hatch cover to a two-hundred-pound lift bag, sending it rocketing to the surface, Drake, Henderson, and the other decompressing divers watching with delight as the hatch soared past them thirty feet away.

Now, as they waited like schoolchildren, watching in silence as the Sikorsky touched down on the helicopter platform, the sense of accomplishment that had bolstered their spirits began to fade as Rexer emerged from the helicopter's door followed by an old man whose cherubic features glowed with restless energy. The old man squinted in the strong sunlight as he looked in their direction. Drake gazed at his adversary, taking the measure of the man, setting his sights, and for a second their eyes met. A faint smile drifted across Gerhardt's lips. Drake ransacked his brain, trying to elicit its meaning. He felt as though he were back inside the passageway, swimming blind, the world of recognizable signs obliterated by a universe of darkness and fear. A conqueror's smile? No. It was more subtle than that—a mixture of cruelty and guile, but lacking in pride. Then, with an undercurrent of fear and revulsion, it came to him. It was the smile of a man about to deliver the coup de grâce.

"Welcome aboard, sir,"

"Alberto," Gerhardt chimed with an accented flourish as the group filed out onto the platform. He momentarily gripped Rexer's arm to steady himself. "How I despise old age. The imposition. All is well?"

"Splendid, sir," the Colombian replied.

Gerhardt nodded with satisfaction, gazing out past the *Avatar*'s stern at the wide expanse of ocean. Cumulus clouds scudded across the sky, creating ovals of shadow that moved over the shimmering water as they had over the wheat fields of his Estonian youth.

Jennifer stepped forward and kissed the old man on the cheek. Gerhardt beamed at her with pride and affection, gathering her in. Locked in the old man's embrace, she glanced down, then pulled away. "Father, there's someone I'd like you to meet."

Gerhardt looked at the stranger standing across from him and said, "Mr. Drake. Of course. It is indeed a pleasure. Freddie tells me that you've done quite well."

Spector emerged from the helicopter's doorway, issuing instructions to several crewmen, who nodded in compliance.

"We were lucky," Drake replied.

"You were more than lucky," Gerhardt retorted, placing a congratulatory hand on Drake's shoulder. "You were spectacular! You must fill me in on all the details."

They were seated directly beneath the skylight at the mahogany banquet table whose seven leaves had been removed for the sake of intimacy. Gerhardt sat at the head of the table, with Jennifer to his right. Next to Jennifer sat Gerald Strickland. Drake and Henderson sat to Gerhardt's left.

The table setting was magnificent. Orchids sprang from glass centerpieces, and the white linen tablecloth shimmered in a pale chiaroscuro of multicolored light.

To the right of Gerhardt's place setting stood a small silver bell, and with an air of nonchalance Gerhardt picked it up and rang it. A moment later Clarence appeared, dressed in a white chef's uniform.

"Clarence. How good it is to see you again. And how I've missed your cooking!" Gerhardt's voice was full of benevolence and charm, and the elderly chef smiled, deeply gratified by the compliment.

"We have lobster salad today, sah. Missy Gerhardt's favorite."

Gerhardt cast a look of mock reproval in Jennifer's direction, all playfulness and mirth. "Has he been spoiling you again?"

"Of course," she said with a bemused expression. Clarence's presence had been transforming.

Suddenly Gerhardt's eyes went bright. "That reminds me. I'm having a bash. Actually, my lovely daughter and I are having a bash, aren't we, Schätzelein. On the Fourth. At my estate in Washington. Give you a chance to meet some people. What do you say?"

They were all somewhat taken aback by the unexpectedness of the invitation. Strickland gazed at Gerhardt in disbelief.

Drake glanced at Henderson, then at Jennifer, whose face was a picture of uncertainty. He looked at Gerhardt and said, "Are you serious?"

"Live a little."

Drake looked at Henderson, who shrugged his shoulders in diplomatic nonchalance.

"I forgot to pack my tuxedo. . . ."

Strickland looked ill.

"Nonsense," Gerhardt replied.

Drake glanced at Henderson once more. "Well, I suppose we could use a break."

"Sounds good to me," Jack Henderson said.

"You deserve one." Gerhardt beamed. "And Washington is such a fascinating place. One never knows what to expect. Especially during an election year. Now, tell me all about the *Norfolk.*"

Four men in guayabera shirts and gold chains stood inside the air-conditioned hotel room, looking down at the half-dozen reconnaissance photographs spread across the table.

Four dead men, Chickie Burnham thought.

They were Americans of Cuban extraction, sons of men who had fought in the covert war against Castro during the Kennedy years. But unlike their fathers, their anticommunism had a more pragmatic cast. Born and raised in the United States, they had no lingering memories of Cuba, no haunting memories of property being confiscated or family members being tortured and left to rot in one of Castro's unspeakable jails. Absent were the memories that turned hatred into fanaticism. Unlike their fathers, these men had grown up in the land of the Big PX. In short, what motivated these men was money.

It was late afternoon. Burnham gazed at their shiny faces as he arranged the photographs into groups of three. The room they occupied stood on the twenty-seventh floor of a Miami Beach high-rise. Even so, Burnham had ordered the curtains drawn and the radio turned up to ward off possible surveillance. He had chosen these men because they were smugglers and therefore expendable, but also because as far as the DEA was concerned, they were clean. But Burnham wasn't taking any chances. If the DEA or anyone else got wind of what was going down, Marshall and Vaughan would disavow the operation, riding off into the sunset just as their predecessors had done during Iran-Contra. And once again Chickie Burnham would be left hanging by the balls.

He seethed at the memory. The Pentagon boys had wanted no part of the Contra war, and after the botched mining incident, Congress had made U.S. participation illegal. So Ronnie and the boys had turned to the only people left—the loyalists, the hard-chargers. Take it to the Sandinistas, they had said. Roll the motherfuckers back to Moscow.

With bitterness Burnham recalled the humiliation of his dismissal four years later, William Webster quietly giving him the ax in the Director's seventh-floor suite at Langley. Services no longer required. Hell, Webster wasn't even real CIA. They had to call in some FBI stiff to do the job, some former judge. After twenty-five years of loyal service, after years of living in one hell-hole after another doing Uncle Sam's dirty work, this is how you got treated—some FBI guy sticking it up your ass.

While Ronnie ran for cover, leaving his wounded to die in the field.

And they thought Jimmy Carter was bad.

Casey never would have allowed it. Never would have allowed a man to be honored and betrayed. Burnham recalled the medal the old man had awarded him for distinguished service. Private ceremony. Champagne. Casey had honored him, called him one of the great ones—a true warrior in the struggle for democracy. Said the President had wanted to be there but couldn't get away. Later Burnham found out that Nancy's astrologer had nixed the deal. Casey might have mumbled, but he was a standup guy any way you cut it. Didn't take shit from Congress or anyone else. At thirty-one he had infiltrated agents into Nazi Germany for the OSS while Ronnie lounged by a swimming pool. *In Hollywood!* Hell, you couldn't blame a guy for not wanting to go to 'Nam, the way Johnson and the Pentagon boys were fucking up the war, but World War II?

Then the way the military boys lined up to kiss ass, led by all those Perfumed Princes in the Pentagon who went to Vietnam to get their tickets punched and, as far as combat went, didn't do shit. Birds of a feather. Hell, even the fucking war protesters deserved more respect. At least they had the balls to stand up for what they believed, unlike all those pampered white-shoe boys who carefully avoided the draft or sought refuge in the National Guard.

Chickenhawk scum, that's what they were. Every goddamned one of them. Men who talked a big game but didn't have the balls to fight. Men who betrayed. That was the real story of the eighties.

Now it was their turn to get fucked up the ass. And old Chickie Burnham was locked, cocked, and ready for action. There would be an explosion, all right. But not in Kingston. Not in some empty government facility. This time it was going to be bloody. Just like war. And this time the chickenhawks would be left holding the bag.

Burnham arranged the photographs in groups of three, each showing various views of two distinct coves on the northern coast of Jamaica. One cove was lush and overgrown, little more than a thin strip of sand surrounded by triple canopy jungle. The second cove was larger and crescent-shaped, with a white sandy beach and several luxury high-rise hotels. Across the bottom margins of the resort photographs Burnham had written "Ocho Rios" in red Magic Marker.

Burnham pointed to the largest high-rise hotel lining the cove. "Julio, Miguel. I want you guys to fly into Kingston tomorrow. Wear suits. You're businessmen looking to invest in real estate. That's your cover. Drive north to Ocho Rios and register at Lion's Head. This hotel here. The big one. There are two rooms reserved for you in the name of Martinez."

"Plane tickets? Passports?" one of the men asked.

Burnham tossed a rumpled paper bag onto the table.

"What about the money?" the man named Julio asked.

"Fifty thousand each. Up front. You get the rest at the end of the op—provided you don't fuck it up."

"One million dollars each, man. . . ." The smuggler smiled at his friends.

"Like I said," Burnham reiterated. "You get the money if the job's done right. Eduardo, Enrique, we fly to Puerto Rico at six A.M. *mañana*. From there we charter a boat and head to Jamaica. Should take us no longer than twenty hours. At midnight on the third we rendezvous at this cove here and unload the product. Julio, the suitcases stay with you and Miguel in the suite on the seventeenth floor. The following day at five P.M. you take them down to the room on the second floor. Place them in the middle of the room. Then open the sliding glass doors. Make sure that the sliding doors are open—that's the first signal. Then, at nine-fifteen, I want you guys on the balcony of your suite. Order room service, have yourselves some dinner. Your presence on the balcony is the second signal. Got that? Any fuckups and we'll all be in a world of shit. The people we work for don't tolerate mistakes. Neither do I. *Comprende?* We'll meet the following day and take it from there."

Enrique looked at his friends and grinned. "What we smuggling, man?"

"Plastique—two hundred pounds of C-4."

He was standing in her office, gazing at her things, awaiting her arrival. He had suggested they meet in her office, hoping that the proximity of well-loved objects would help to soften the blow of what he was about to tell her. She loved him, and once she learned that the Americans knew about the nuclear deal she would fear for his safety.

He had considered not mentioning it. But if Drake and Henderson turned out to be agents, he would have to deal with the problem. He would have them complete the salvage operation and then, in deference to his daughter's sensibilities, he would let them go. Strickland and Rexer would take care of the rest. Just as they had with the Hales. Gerhardt would blame the Iraqis.

A cooling breeze entered the room and Gerhardt sniffed the air with a gratifying sense of accomplishment, noticing the photograph of Montségur that hung near her desk. He had told her about this place, though hardly the details of his initial visit or the motivation that had brought him there.

He had been a guest of Nazi high priest Alfred Rosenberg, whose organization, the Einsatzstab Reichsleiter Rosenberg, had been responsible for the removal of art treasures from occupied Europe. Rosenberg was Auslandsdeutsch, too—a fellow Estonian. Gerhardt never cared for the man or his racial theories, but his effort to harness the power of Christian symbolism to Nazi ideology had been pure diabolic genius—a modern precursor of psywar. And it was to this end that he had become obsessed with Rosenberg's interest in the Cathar stronghold at Montségur and the priceless treasure said to reside there. Rosenberg's twisted reasoning had enthralled him.

Just as the Cathar priests, renowned for their purity of spirit, had been guardians of the Grail, now the Knights of Pure Aryan Blood would become their worthy successors. No longer would the German people prostrate themselves before the weakness of Jew-tainted Christian values; they would become a master race, a conquering tribe whose eyes glowed with the freedom and splendor of beasts of prey. Once possessed of the Holy Grail they would storm the world in an orgy of destruction and holy terror, bearing Christianity's most elusive and cherished icon, the very embodiment of the eternal. And the world would cower at their feet.

With nostalgia Gerhardt recalled the thin alpine air of the Languedoc region of southern France, the lingering scent of ozone in a land as well known for the sudden violence of its storms as for the violence of its past. Gehlen had granted him a two-week leave following the fall of France, and with a burgeoning sense of self-discovery he had joined the archaeological team searching the medieval fortress for the chalice that lay deep inside the mountain at the bottom of a fabled staircase of three thousand steps.

But as diligently as they searched the ruins of Montségur, they never found the entrance to the staircase or the chalice that was buried there. It didn't matter. His life had come full circle—from the books he had read as a child by SS Obersturmführer Otto Rahn, describing the treasure of Montségur, to his recent discovery of the *Norfolk*. The Holy Grail was lost, perhaps forever. But the *Norfolk* lay within his grasp. And soon the coins would bear magical properties of their own.

Something was wrong. She settled into the small white sofa with a sense of foreboding so strong that she could hardly breathe. Her father looked at Rexer and nodded. "Wait outside, please." The big South African left the room and closed the door.

Stay calm and look them straight in the eye. You know who they are, you know what they do.

They kill the spirit first, then they kill the body.

Gerhardt leaned back in the linen armchair and scanned the wall. Then with a twinkle in his eye he gazed at Jennifer and said, "They're onto us."

"Who?" she demanded.

"The Americans. Martin Vaughan, the President's National Security Advisor, came to see me two days ago. He offered me a deal."

Jennifer felt as though she were plunging down a well. "But that's impossible," she whispered, trying unsuccessfully to keep her voice from quavering.

"It was inevitable, Schätzelein. They've been watching me for years."

Jennifer looked at her father, her face blank with shock, her world distorted once again by events deliberately hidden. She felt as though she were drowning. She thought of the information she had been slipping Adams, and the enormous relief that had rushed through her body cell by cell as she realized that Gerhardt was not yet aware of her betrayal suddenly vanished. She knew what would happen. In an attempt to pinpoint the leak Gerhardt would run additional background checks, just as he had following the Hizbollah affair. She had been impervious to them before because she had always acted alone. But it was different now. She thought of Drake and Henderson, stricken by an overwhelming sense of guilt as the irony of her fate assailed her.

"If you knew about the Americans all this time, why didn't you tell me earlier?" she asked feebly.

"I was afraid you would worry."

"But I *am* worried, Father. Where are the Americans geting their information? From the Iraqis? What about the other people you're dealing with? My God, I don't even know who they are!"

Gerhardt looked at her with tenderness and compassion. "They're Russians, Schätzelein. The man's name is Konalov. Former member of the Politburo. I've never taken you fully into my confidence before because of the danger such information might present to you. But I believe Konalov can be trusted. The Iraqis, too. And as for the Americans, you needn't worry about them. I've taken care of the problem."

"How?"

"Because I know something about Jefferson Marshall that nobody else knows. Did I tell you that we were once in business together? In Panama?"

. . .

They were drifting down to the foredeck, dropping down past the dark superstructure that loomed above them. It was late afternoon. To the right they could see the outline of the forward turret with its battery of eight-inch guns. What little ambient light remained was fading quickly. They drifted down to the main deck and hovered over the open hatch.

Gerhardt was up to something. But what? The day after tomorrow they would fly to Washington just as the salvage operation was shifting into high gear. It didn't make sense. Why would Gerhardt back off now? Gerhardt's invitation had caught them off guard. They should have declined, but an adamant refusal might have aroused Gerhardt's suspicions, if he wasn't suspicious already. They had no choice but to accept. Still, the trip to D.C. would prolong the mission by three or four days—if not longer. *Damn.*

Henderson knelt beside the hatch as Drake swam to the port rail ten feet away and gave it a good shake. It was solid—at least solid enough for his purposes. He tied the end of his penetration line to a stanchion, then swam back to the open hatch, allowing the line to unreel. Then, with a nod to Henderson, he dropped down through the hatch, disappearing into the darkness below.

The gun deck was vast and empty, devoid of silt and wreckage. Drake swept his light across the deck, noting with a good deal of anxiety that the deterioration was far more extensive than he had imagined. There were holes everywhere, and to the right he could see an area where an entire framework had collapsed.

Rust flakes drifted around him. Drake hovered above a jagged hole, directing his light down into the dark water of the berth deck as Henderson dropped down beside him, examining the gun deck in horror. It looked as though it might collapse at any moment. He signaled to Drake to abort the dive, but Drake flashed the OK sign and dropped down through the hole. Shaking his head, Henderson hovered six inches above the gun deck and unclipped a halogen light to which he had taped two powerful strobes. The strobe combination was attached to six feet of line—just enough for it to dangle well into the berth deck where it would be most visible when Drake retraced his route. He switched on the device and lowered the beacon through the doorway, praying that Drake would be all right. Only once had they ventured into anything as potentially lethal. And for a moment he could see Drake leading his squad toward the hangar that housed Noriega's jet.

The water below was dark and clear, free of rust and silt. Drake could feel the anxiety building in his chest as he traveled beneath the rotted overhead. He looked back and could see the strobes punctuating the darkness. In the clear water the light was blinding, and he envisioned the preserved body of an ancient explorer encased in Scythian ice. He kept on. Then he saw the gray outline of the projecting compartments. He could hear blood coursing through his temples, and he wondered for a moment whether it was the narcosis or his pulse quickening from fear. In his youth he might have paused, dwelling upon an array of catastrophes. He could feel himself being drawn in that direction now, pulled by force of imagination like a leaf on a trout stream curling along the edges of a convex pool—the slumberous and dream-filled waters that led down to the pebbly bottom of his psyche.

But there wasn't time. He could see the compartments clearly now, jutting out into the dark clear water like an abandoned mining shack. The door was ajar, and to the left a section of bulkhead was missing, the rusted edges of what remained forming a diagonal of serrated steel. Below, the bulkhead resembled lacework.

No way he could run a line over that. He gazed at the door again with all the enthusiasm of a man about to walk a gauntlet. Then with a single kick he was at the door's edge. He grasped the edge of the door frame and pulled himself in.

Silt swirled around him as he swept his light back and forth over the wreckage. The room was maybe fourteen by fourteen feet. Directly ahead he saw the cage of steel bars. Inside the cage several distinct shapes lay bunched together against a bulkhead beneath a thin layer of mud, reminiscent of Indian burial mounds. Cautiously, Drake pulled himself forward.

The steel bars were spindly, gnawed by rust. He tapped a bar with his finger, then quickly drew his hand back as an orange pointillism of rusted steel cascaded through the water.

He tapped another bar, and the same thing happened. He kept tapping bars, dissolving them, until he had fashioned a rectangular hole large enough to swim through. Flecks of rusted steel billowed around him. He felt like laughing. The *Norfolk's* deterioration had nearly killed him the day before. Now it had opened up the avenue that would allow them to wrap up the mission over the next twenty-four hours. He would not have to spend a week cutting through the steel bars, as he had anticipated. All he had to do was to swim inside the room and see if he could pry open one of those strongboxes.

He entered the cage, taking care to lay his line so that it would not become entangled in wreckage—a truly horrifying situation when trying to exit in zero-visibility water. When he was absolutely sure that he would have no problem finding his way back through the door, he positioned himself over the nearest mound and swung himself around, turning in the direction of the line so that it would not become wrapped around his body.

By now, even before he dipped his hands in the mud, the silt was so thick that the powerful beam of his light had ebbed to almost nothing. He removed the lanyard from his wrist, clipped the light beside the other two on his harness, and opened a small canvas bag. Then, with a larger sense of optimism than he had felt in days, he plunged his hands into the mud.

Immediately he was engulfed by darkness. He felt the top of a strongbox, and running his hands along its sides, quickly located the padlock, the hinges on the back of the coffer having long since rusted away. He reached over his shoulder and withdrew a slender crowbar from between his tanks. Then, locating the lock again, he inserted the crowbar between the bolt and jerked the crowbar up hard. The lock gave way.

Slipping the crowbar back between his tanks, Drake gathered himself, breathing in and out, feeling an interior quiet settle over him like a solar eclipse. He reached down with both hands and yanked the lid up and swung it to one side as the edges crumbled in his hands. He checked his line, running his fingers along it as far as he could reach. It was okay. Thank God. Then he gently probed the coffer. In the darkness he could feel coins in his hands. They were small and heavy, bearing the unmistakable heft of gold.

With trembling fingers he scooped a handful of double eagles into the artifact bag, then another. Minutes passed. It seemed an hour. He worked with steady deliberation, keeping his breathing at a nice easy rhythm. Then the bag was full.

He cinched the drawstring and clipped the bag to his harness, jetting air into his vest to offset the weight. He started forward, reeling up line. He wasn't going anywhere. He felt the panic billowing inside him like coal dust, ready to explode. He was snagged on wreckage, but on what exactly he couldn't tell. He moved forward again in the darkness, struggling to keep his mind clear as he began to isolate the tension that held him fast. He reached down, carefully sweeping his hand beneath him until he had located one of his spare lights that had become wedged in the mud between two of the coffers. A moment later he was moving forward, reeling up line, the fear draining from his body in an icy rush. The door was invisible ahead. Though he had only a short distance to travel, the trip seemed to take forever as he groped through the blackened water. He wondered how much air he had consumed. The mud was so thick that he could not see an inch in front of his face. Then he bumped into something solid. He reached up and with enormous relief felt the door frame. He squeezed through, free at last.

He had stirred up so much silt that even outside the room the water was black. He continued reeling up the line, turning right toward the flashing strobes that he knew were out there someplace. Then, as he left the region of the paymaster's issuing room, he could see them as the water became clearer, pale white in the distance. He was almost home. His spirits soared. He reached the strobes and switched them off, looking up at Jack and giving his friend the thumbs-up sign. A moment later they were outside the wreck, kneeling on the foredeck as Drake directed the beam of his light down at the artifact bag. Wisps of mud streamed out through the holes like smoke. But the radiance inside was unmistakable. Drake opened the bag and removed a single pristine coin, placing it in the palm of one of Henderson's gloved hands, Liberty side up. The size of a quarter, the coin was beautiful; Lady Liberty with her torch and olive branch on one side and the American Eagle on the other.

Henderson closed his hand over the coin and with his other

hand reached out and gripped Drake's shoulder. Inside the bag lay all the gold Adams would need to wrap up the mission.

They would send the message tonight.

A crowd had gathered on the afterdeck of the *Avatar*. Surfacing in the cold water, Drake and Henderson could see Gerhardt, Jennifer, and the others lining the stern rail. A dozen members of the crew looked down from the helicopter platform. The helicopter was gone. Drake turned toward the sound of an outboard throttling behind him as Maki swung the inflatable around and gave Drake and Henderson a big OK sign. "Way to go, guys," he yelled in triumph.

They had sent the gold to the surface via lift bag. Kneeling on the foredeck beside the hatch, Drake had drained the air from his vest so that when he unclipped the gold he would not go shooting to the surface. Within a minute Henderson had rigged the lift bag to the end of Drake's penetration line so that once the lift bag hit the surface it would not go sailing away in the current. Then from a small wing tank Henderson carefully filled the lift bag with air until it began to hover like a hot-air balloon. Another jet of air and the bag began to rise to the surface, the cylinder of the reel spinning in Drake's hands. When the cylinder stopped, Drake cut the line and tied it off to a piece of wreckage.

Now, as they slipped out of their tanks and climbed aboard the *Avatar*, Drake and Henderson looked at each other with relief and happiness as the group surged around.

"Remarkable. Simply remarkable." Gerhardt beamed, clapping each man on the shoulder.

"What was the haul?" Drake asked.

"Gerald?"

"Four hundred and thirty-four coins—about four hundred thousand dollars' worth," the operations manager said soberly.

"So tell me, gentlemen." Gerhardt laughed. "How does it feel to be rich?"

Gerhardt draped an arm over Jennifer's shoulder and gave her a fatherly hug. A fragile smile appeared on Jennifer's lips as she glanced at Drake and looked away. Then the arms dealer looked Henderson straight in the eye. "You were right. He *is* the very best."

They were gathered in the main salon, sipping champagne and nibbling on the salmon and crab hors d'oeuvres that Clarence had prepared. The champagne was pre–World War I vintage Cristal—the best that Drake had ever tasted, the bead so fine that it resembled mist. "Produced exclusively for the Russian tsar," Gerhardt chimed. "In clear glass bottles so that the bodyguards could check for poison." He stood in front of the aquarium, his cherubic features wreathed in happiness. "Any thought about what you'll do with the money?"

"We haven't earned it yet."

"Oh, but you will, Mr. Drake. You will. Then you'll want to move on to other things, I suppose. It's a shame. I could use a man like you. Jennifer says you're quite well qualified."

Out of the corner of his eye Drake could see Jennifer and Jack wandering out to the bar and Rexer discreetly walking out behind them.

There was a hint of challenge to Gerhardt's voice, and Drake peered at the arms dealer narrowly. "Are you offering me a job?"

"Possibly."

"I already have a business."

"Guiding?" Gerhardt scoffed good-naturedly. "Will you really want to do that when you're fifty-five? I should think that a man of your qualities would want something more intellectually ambitious."

"Like arms dealing?"

Gerhardt smiled benignly, unfazed by the remark. "Not a good time to break in, I'm afraid. Governments are the big players now. Trying to bail out their defense industries. Seems they overexpanded in the last years of the Cold War." Gerhardt shook his head with ironic glee. "Soviet Russia a tottering empire, and defense manufacturers gearing up like no tomorrow—the 'Evil Empire' and all that. Who would have thought?"

"Doesn't seem to have bothered you."

"Hard not to take advantage." Gerhardt shrugged.

"I'm not into taking advantage."

"You underestimate yourself, Mr. Drake. Rimbaud was a gunrunner, you know. Abyssinia. Sold arms to the King of Shoa. The greatest poet of his day, a child prodigy who quit writing poetry for the most part by the age of nineteen. Ran away to the ends of the earth—to the region the Arabs call Barr Adjam, the unknown land, the realm beyond the second cataract of the Nile, to which even the ancient Egyptians refused to venture, the kingdom of evil spirits. Who could blame him? The Greeks invented the gods to transpose life to a higher sphere. To cope with the horrors of existence, they created a transfiguring illusion. Worked for them. Didn't work for us. Original sin running headlong into modern man's desire for universal justice, no doubt. So what's left? Götterdämmerung—the twilight of the gods. The uncharted country of the soul."

"He who rules the world must first renounce love."

Gerhardt lowered his glass with genuine surprise, gazing at Drake with rapt attention. "What did you say?"

"Wagner. *The Ring.*"

Then suddenly there was an enigmatic look about Gerhardt's expression of which the dominant note might have been wistfulness. "Oh, I don't want to rule the world, Mr. Drake. No . . . nothing quite that grand. I merely wish to toy with it."

A steward in white livery announced that dinner was served. Drake sat between Jennifer and Rexer to Gerhardt's left, across from Henderson, Strickland, and Alvarez. Jennifer was wearing a summer dress of teal. Like Jacqueline Kennedy Onassis, she possessed the rare gift of making even the simplest articles of clothing appear elegant.

Three servants bearing platters of food began orbiting the table. Drake helped himself to a generous portion of lamb marinated in balsamic vinegar and spices, grilled medium rare. Again, Clarence had outdone himself. There were garlic mashed potatoes and string beans sautéed in bacon. Drake helped himself to a generous portion of these, as well, his head swimming from the alchemy of residual nitrogen and expensive champagne. Silverware glimmered in the candlelight as the melodic strains of a Cole Porter instrumental filled the room.

Later Drake would recall that Jennifer's performance had been brilliant that night. She had entertained them all, she had sparkled, talking about Venice, Amsterdam, and St. Petersburg— the "water cities," as she called them. Not once during the lengthy dinner had she vouchsafed any hint of the impending catastrophe that had loomed over her spirit like a death sentence. Only when she had excused herself and returned five minutes later did she reveal a slight tightening of features. But the effect had been momentary. Drake had scarcely noticed. Then, as a dessert of fresh strawberries appeared in white porcelain bowls, Drake had felt her hand beneath the table, pressing a note into his. She had been talking to Strickland about the fluctuating lira as though Drake hadn't existed. She had pressed the note into his palm, holding his hand for a minute longer.

An hour later, alone in his stateroom, Drake withdrew the crumpled paper from his pocket.

One a.m., the note said. *Main salon.*

Henderson looked at Drake with concern. "Just before dinner she asked me to step out to the bar. You were talking to Gerhardt."

"I remember," Drake said solemnly. "She say anything?"

"Didn't get a chance. Conan walked out behind us."

They were in Drake's stateroom. It was five minutes to midnight, and the *Avatar* was quiet. Even through the open portholes, they could no longer hear the rhythmic sound of waves lapping against the hull. It was as though the sea itself had hardened into a pool of concrete.

He dressed in the darkest clothing he had—an old pair of navy sweatpants, a pair of black running shoes, and a navy T-shirt with the word MICHIGAN stenciled across the chest in faded gold lettering. Not only would he blend into the night, but if he bumped into Strickland or Rexer he could say that he hadn't been able to sleep and had decided to go for a midnight jog.

Though he had no clue as to what was going on, the note itself was a clear indication of trouble. Unsure of what the night would bring, he had managed a half hour of sleep—an old habit from his SEAL days. Sleep when you can, because you never knew when you were going to get another chance. At five minutes to one, he headed topside.

The salon was dark, save for a single lamp in the corner near the aquarium. As Drake moved across the room he found it hard to imagine that it had been the scene of so much revelry only a few hours before—in the darkness even the furnishings seemed to have retreated into hibernation. Jennifer was standing to the right. She placed a finger to her lips and switched off the lamp. Moonlight reflected off the polished surface of the mahogany banquet table. She approached him, and for a long moment held his face in her hands, gazing up at him as though she might lose him forever. But when he bent to kiss her, she turned away and led him by the hand upstairs to her office. "We'll be safe here," she said, locking the door. Then, sitting on the linen sofa, she told him all she had learned in her office twelve hours before, her voice racked with sorrow and guilt.

Well, we're fucked, Drake thought. *The only way off this boat is by chopper, and Spector's gone. We'll never make it in the inflatable; the* Avatar's *thermal-imaging cameras will pick us up instantly. Maybe McKendrick can arrange an exfil. Maybe not.* Jesus. *Vaughan and the goddamned President of the United States! Who in the hell is running this country, anyway?*

Not you. You dropped out.

And as he stood there, holding Jennifer, the full price of his exile stood revealed.

Don't think about that now. Now is what you have in your arms. Think about her. Think about Jack. Think about how you're going to get them off this goddamned boat.

He stroked her hair, calming himself.

"Listen, Jen? We have a SATCOM. It's in my room."

She looked up, her face streaked with tears.

"How?"

"McKendrick had it built into a laptop. I'm going to request an emergency exfiltration. It may happen or it may not. It all depends on what Adams and McKendrick are up against. But they're good men, and they'll never quit trying. And neither must we. Okay?"

"Okay."

"If the exfil doesn't happen, we leave by chopper. When does Spector get back?"

"I don't know. . . . Tomorrow, I think."

"Find out. We'll grab the chopper tomorrow night. I'll also need a key to your father's room. I'm sorry, Jen. But we'll have to take him along as insurance. Strickland and Rexer won't shoot if they know he's aboard. He's our only chance."

"Okay."

"And I need you to scope out the observation deck while I go get Jack. Can you do that and meet us here in fifteen minutes?"

"Yes."

Then he looked deeply into her eyes. "None of this is your fault, Jen. Whatever happens, I want you to know that. You are very brave."

Drake sat at his desk, composing the Flash message on the laptop computer while Henderson watched the door. He kept it simple.

McKENDRICK EYES ONLY

LIFELINE REPORTS VAUGHAN OFFERED TARGET DEAL TWO DAYS AGO. TARGET BLACKMAILING PRES USA RE

BUSINESS VENTURE PANAMA EARLY EIGHTIES. OBJEC-
TIVE: TO ENSURE NUKE DEAL GOES THROUGH. NUKES
OFFERED BY RUSSIAN KONALOV. FORMER MEMBER OF
POLITBURO. TORCHLIGHT BLOWN. COVERS INTACT, BUT
NOT FOR LONG. REQUEST EMERGENCY EXFIL. IF EXFIL
IMPOSSIBLE WILL ATTEMPT EXFIL VIA HELICOPTER
TOMORROW P.M. OTHERWISE GERHARDT RESIDENCE
WASHINGTON D.C. JULY 4.

"Got it?" Henderson asked.

"Yeah. I think so."

"I can't believe this. . . ."

Jennifer met them on the afterdeck outside the main salon. "Strickland's asleep."

"What about the others?"

"Alvarez turned in an hour ago."

"Rexer?"

"He's in the cafeteria."

They climbed the staircase quickly. The ocean was quiet, motionless. Not even a gust of wind to conceal the sound of their movement. When they reached the bridge deck, Jennifer moved forward to cover the other staircase. Drake watched her disappear in the moonlit darkness.

Leaving Jack to cover the aft staircase, Drake hurried to the observation deck. He tilted the screen toward the sky and almost immediately acquired a signal. Then he hit the Enter key and a red bar flashed in the upper right-hand corner.

He thought about what lay in store for them tomorrow night. They would have to move quickly. They would grab Spector first.

They could keep him on ice in Jennifer's office while they went for Gerhardt. When the coast was clear they would dash for the helicopter.

He closed the laptop and headed for the staircase. There were voices below. A man's voice rising in anger. And then Jennifer's voice arguing back.

Rexer.

"Sir, we just received flash traffic from the *Avatar*." It was the duty officer at the Pentagon. McKendrick rolled over in bed and looked at the alarm clock on the nightstand. It was 2:05 A.M. "I think you'd better get over here right away."

2 July

"I've found a way out of TORCHLIGHT, sir."

They were alone, standing in the Oval Office. Jefferson Marshall walked over to his desk and buzzed his secretary: "No interruptions, please." He looked at Vaughan with pointed interest. "Well?"

"Maurania."

"Excuse me?"

"We invade it."

"Goddamn it, Martin. Are you out of your mind?"

The National Security Advisor smiled. "We need a way to derail TORCHLIGHT, correct? What better way of accomplishing that than by ordering a full-scale invasion of an island nation that has been a thorn in this administration's side since practically the day you took office. A communist nation, I might add."

"Jesus fucking Christ. I hand you an assignment and this is what I get, this . . . this *crap?*"

"It's not crap, sir," Vaughan said, calmly enjoying the President's outburst, knowing that Marshall would have no choice but to go along with the plan.

"Then what the fuck is it, Martin? We've been through this before. Remember? Nobody bought it. And you know *why?* Because politically it won't wash—not with Adams, not with other members of this administration, not with the American public."

"It will this time, sir."

"Shit."

"We will have cause."

"Yeah? Like what."

"Communist subversion, sir. The United States will be forced to intercede on behalf of Caribbean nations that have become the victims of Mauranian terrorism."

The President's eyes narrowed with suspicion. "What in the hell are you talking about?"

"Your political future."

"Fuck you, asshole."

Vaughan continued, unfazed; he was immune to Jefferson Marshall's tirades now. "It's really very simple. What is about to occur is exactly what I predicted would happen three years ago when the Mauranian Liberation Front took over the Dominican Republic. The Mauranian rebels will export their revolution."

"If you're suggesting what I think you're suggesting, I won't allow it," the President said, shaking his head. "Absolutely not. I won't risk the lives of innocent people."

"Like the Hales," Vaughan replied matter-of-factly. "Of course, you could always confess your sins to the public—make a clean breast of things, though with Harold Westerfield rising in the polls and the election only four months away, it's not exactly a propitious time to embark on that particular act of contrition. Especially since it might result in a jail sentence. But you could always give it a try."

The condescension in Vaughan's tone had been unmistakable, and startled by the recognition that their roles had been reversed—that Vaughan now occupied the position of authority—Jefferson Marshall averted his eyes in embarrassment and shame. "Terrorism? Subversion? My God . . ."

Martin Vaughan gazed at the President of the United States with contempt. It was the first time he had seen fear grip a man of Jefferson Marshall's stature, and he relished the sight of the most powerful man in the world flailing against the currents of necessity.

"Look. The plan is foolproof. And you know what the best part about it is? That having been warned about Mauranian intentions three years ago, and having ignored that warning, Adams and McKendrick will be caught with their pants down. You will be well advised to seek their resignations on the grounds of negligence. And with Adams and McKendrick gone and a new CIA Director and Chairman in place whose views, shall we say, are more consonant with our own, Operation TORCHLIGHT is history."

"What about the press?"

"Fuck the press. You'll be justified in firing Adams and Mc-Kendrick, and you'll have the backing of the public in going after the Mauranian terrorists. Your approval ratings will soar. We'll call it Operation Restore Democracy. Hell, when this is over, you'll be a shoo-in for reelection. And because it will be an island invasion, press restrictions will be easy to enforce." Vaughan laughed. "Basically like Grenada, the American public will buy whatever story we put out."

That day Spector did not return. When Jennifer announced at lunch that she hoped to spend a day in Newport shopping, Gerhardt regretfully informed her that Spector had taken the Sikorsky in for servicing and would not return until the following day, when they would all fly to Washington for the weekend.

If Jennifer seemed dismayed, no one except Henderson and Drake noticed. Aboard the *Avatar*, spirits were high. After dinner Gerhardt had made the unaccustomed gesture of passing out cigars, the legendary Davidoff Habañas, and Strickland, Rexer, and Maki had smoked them with pleasure. Even though Gerhardt's Fourth of July party was forty-eight hours away, the celebration had already begun. Drake and Henderson had made two more dives to the *Norfolk*, recovering another million dollars of gold. Inside the *Norfolk* Drake had experienced no close calls, as he had two days before. While the world disintegrated around him, the paymaster's issuing room—for all its fragility—remained intact.

Rain slanted against the windshield, a summer cloudburst that would drive the already unbearable Washington humidity up another notch. Terry Fox hated summers in Washington. At thirty-three he was still young enough to remember the long vacations that were the sole luxury of his college years. Now it seemed as though he never got away. But soon that would change. His prospects were rising. Though the subject had never been openly discussed, Fox knew that once Vaughan assumed Adams's job at CIA, he would be first in line to become the youngest Deputy Director of Operations in the Agency's history. Talk about being on the fast track. With abundant satisfaction he imagined the sensation it would create among his former colleagues. Terrence Fox, DDO. Maybe he would take up golf.

Now, as he turned onto M Street, looking for a place to park, the rain subsided. He cast a hopeful glance at the sky. The groceries could wait. Time for a little drinky-poo before heading home to the missus.

He rounded another corner and quickly spotted an empty space at the end of a narrow side street. He gunned the accelerator, pulled into the space, and got out of the car, failing to notice the two men walking toward him from opposite directions or the silver van that had just rounded the corner, pulling up alongside him.

Suddenly there was a wet glove in his face, shutting off his air. Someone was grabbing him from behind. Then a second man came from the front, jamming a knee into his groin as the van pulled up, its sliding door open, and whatever hope Terry Fox had of wrestling free collapsed along with his sagging body. Without ceremony the two men tossed the Deputy National Security Advisor into the van and slammed the door.

Three men gazed down at him impassively, three men he had never seen before. He lay on the carpeted floor, curled in the fetal position, cupping his wounded testicles and groaning in pain. He was being kidnapped. The man in the passenger seat spoke into a cell phone. "The package is on its way."

Fox's eyes grew wide with terror. "W-w-w-where're you taking me?"

"Cuff him," the man said. One of the men in the back, with arms as thick as telephone poles, flipped Fox onto his stomach. The Deputy National Security Advisor screamed as the man buried a knee into the small of his back.

"Who are you guys?" he whimpered as his hands were cuffed.

The driver glanced down at him without compassion. "Federal Express."

He was hooded and tied to a chair. He was inside a room—in what city, in what state, he couldn't say. He had been in the van for less than fifteen minutes, but such was his state of panic and disorientation that he was sure it was an hour, if not longer. The room was quiet. Deadly quiet. The silence seemed to further unravel his senses nerve by nerve. He thought of the hostages in

Beirut. They had been abducted in the same manner, forced to live in solitary confinement for years at a time. He moaned again. Then he did something he hadn't done since he was five.

He pissed his pants.

And he prayed.

Burnham. Burnham must be doing this. He knew what men like Burnham had done to their Vietcong prisoners. Very few had survived interrogation. He began to shake. *Why?* he asked himself. *Why is this happening to me?*

Then he heard footsteps.

The door opened and several men entered the room. Fox heard the shuffling of tables and chairs. Then he heard a voice.

"Unhood him."

The room was pitch black. Suddenly a light snapped on and he was illuminated, the center object in a pool of light, the others hidden by darkness. He thought about what his life was like the hour before his kidnapping and the pathetic circumstances of his life now. In a matter of minutes he had been transformed from ringmaster to clown.

From the darkness the voice came again, the same voice that had spoken a minute before with such casual indifference. This time, however, the voice was peremptory and laden with portentousness.

"The penalties for treason are severe, Mr. Fox. At the very least you're looking at twenty-five years in a federal penitentiary. Probably at Marion. You'll spend decades in an underground cell with minimal human contact. Maybe an hour to exercise each week, if you're lucky. If the agents you betrayed are killed, you'll spend the rest of your life there. In solitary confinement. And believe me, Mr. Fox, you will be grateful for that protection."

"What do you want?" Terry Fox begged.

The voice continued as though he hadn't spoken. "If you co-operate with us you will avoid prosecution. Your involvement in this affair will remain secret. Following your resignation you may accept any position in government that doesn't require a security clearance. You will have references. Or you may pursue employment in the private sector. You will not be harassed. In short, your life will go on."

"Burnham will kill me."

"Burnham?"

"The guy Vaughan hired to bomb the Jamaican Parliament. He's ex-CIA. Phoenix program. The Contras."

"Where may we find him?"

"Kingston. I'm not sure where he's staying."

"Is he working with anyone else?"

"Just Vaughan and me."

"Has he hired anyone?"

"I don't know."

"Tell me about the bomb."

Fox looked helplessly into the darkness. Whoever these people were, they were government—CIA, FBI, or military. No question about it. And whatever else happened, Vaughan was going down and maybe Jefferson Marshall, too. Fox gazed out into the darkness as the last barrier of resistance began to crumble.

"You mean what you say? About keeping me out of this?"

"It's up to you. You cooperate and keep us abreast of what's going on—and I mean completely abreast—then you've got a deal. But if you screw up in any way—if you warn Vaughan off or mislead us and those agents get killed, it will be your ass in the slammer."

Fox began to sob. He couldn't help himself. He cried harder than he had since he was a child. Then, when the tears had subsided, he told them everything he knew, his voice a whisper, his eyes downcast—the quiet enactment of contrition and shame.

"It wasn't my idea. It was Vaughan's," he sniffed. "The President needed a diversion — something that would allow him to curtail TORCHLIGHT without causing suspicion."

"Why?"

"Because of something that happened a long time ago. With Gerhardt. And somebody named Wexler."

"Who's Wexler?"

"I dunno."

"You're an analyst, Fox. Guess."

The Deputy National Security Advisor choked back a sob. "I'M TELLING YOU THE TRUTH!"

"Tell me about the bomb."

"Vaughan figured if we set off a bomb in the Jamaican Parliament and tied it to the Mauranians, we would have a pretext to invade. The President could fire Adams and McKendrick and cancel TORCHLIGHT. It's set to go off in three days, around two in the morning . . . when the building's empty."

"What kind of explosive?"

"I don't know."

"And the payoff? How is that being arranged?"

"The President transferred four million dollars into an account in the Caymans. Through Marshall Oil. It was withdrawn yesterday."

Not since his wife died three years before had Charles Francis Adams felt so old. He was sitting in McKendrick's Pentagon office and Hawking had just played the tape of Fox's confession. He had arrived five minutes before. When he had been shown into

McKendrick's office the Chairman hadn't said a word but his face had spoken volumes. It was bad news, Adams could tell. Taking the message McKendrick had handed him, he had fumbled for his glasses.

Now, as he struggled to comprehend the enormity of Vaughan's betrayal, he thought of the nights he had parachuted into France during the Second World War. They would fly in on Lancasters. It would be quiet over the Channel, then rough as they hit the coast of France, flak bursting all around them, then quiet again as they passed over the countryside. The pilot would throttle back and the jumpmaster would open the center hatch. Sometimes they could see the ground, sometimes not, depending on the moon. Then they would tumble into the darkness, the receding drone of the engines as poignant as a mother's heartbeat, never knowing whether they would be greeted by the Maquis or by the SS.

"We picked him up in Georgetown four hours ago," Hawking explained once the tape had ended.

"My order," McKendrick said. "After we heard from Drake I took the liberty of phoning Reggie Williams. Reggie's the action officer at NSC. Good man—trustworthy. I asked him if he had noticed anything unusual regarding Vaughan's schedule lately. He said that Fox was supposed to review some data on Iraq that just came through the NRO. Evidently that's Fox's domain on the staff. Wouldn't pass it up. Fox canceled the appointment. Then, the next day at lunch, he overheard one of Vaughan's secretaries complain that Vaughan was going through one of his testy moods—that something was obviously going down, and Fox was involved, but no one knew what." McKendrick leaned back in his chair, the gravity of his expression unchanged.

Adams picked up the phone and pressed a button. "Roger, I

need a file. The name is Burnham. First name Chick. Yes. Immediately. Thanks."

"How do you want to handle this, Charles?" Hawking asked.

"We have two priorities of equal urgency—first, to head Burnham off, and second, to get Drake, Henderson, and Jennifer off that ship."

"What about Konalov?"

"We can hand that off to the KGB. But not right away. We have to wait until our people are clear. Konalov disappears prematurely and Gerhardt's nuke deal won't be the only thing that winds up dead. Now, what do we do about the bomb?"

"I've got a DELTA team on standby," Hawking said. "We can be in Kingston within an hour."

"Good."

"We can't notify the Jamaicans," McKendrick warned. "They'll want to contact the White House." He looked at Hawking. "Can you get your people in without anyone knowing?"

"I can try," Hawking said.

"Do it."

"That solves one problem," Adams remarked. "Now, what about Drake and the others? Gerhardt will surely have them killed."

"We get them off that ship," Hawking urged.

"Unfortunately, that's not an option," McKendrick said. "I'd need presidential authorization to mount an operation of that size."

"Or compelling evidence as to why such authorization would not be forthcoming," Adams observed. "A reason to go over the President's head."

"Can you obtain that, Charles?" Hawking asked.

"Yes. I think so. But I'll need a day or two."

"You may not have that long."

"Gerhardt's party," McKendrick said. "We pull them out then."

"Honey, what happened?"

"Bad day at the office." Terry Fox glanced at his wife. Following the interrogation he had been supplied with a clean pair of pants, hooded once more, and taken back to his car. "Have a drink and go home," the voice from the darkness had instructed him. "And remember. Stay in touch."

Now his wife looked at him with sympathy. She was a surgical nurse at Richmond General, and hadn't seen her husband this haggard since the day after his stag party the week they were married.

"Here. Sit down."

But Fox preferred to stand. He had driven home with his pants undone to ease the pressure on his swollen testicles.

"Honey. I've been thinking. Maybe it's time I look for another job. In Arizona. What do you think about moving to Arizona?"

They flew in silence, the black Lear skirting the eastern seaboard of the United States. Jennifer sat up front beside her father; Drake, Henderson, Strickland, and Rexer sat behind, the processed air of the Lear's circulation system inducing a cocoon-like somnolence that for Drake always seemed the primary characteristic of air travel.

They had lifted off in a typical clammy Rhode Island fog, but fifteen minutes later the sky had cleared. Stepping off the Lear at

Dulles, they were struck by the opacity of the air on this hot and humid summer day—the hottest on record, a baggage handler informed them. Even the short walk to the limousine was drenching. At Rexer's signal two bodyguards jumped out of a waiting car to help Gerhardt, who seemed to be foundering a bit, the oppressive heat and humidity apparently depriving the man of his vigor. They piled into the limousine, feeling the scintillating rush of cold air.

Arrowood, Gerhardt's villa on the Potomac, occupied the center of a walled compound that rambled along five wooded acres. The villa was classic Italian—white stucco, red-tiled roof with terraced gardens falling to either side. As they pulled up the long drive, Drake could see at least a half-dozen paneled trucks parked near the service entrance. Security guards roamed the grounds. In the main entrance hall, a blonde with cropped hair directed a team of florists who were setting out lavish bouquets along the tables that lined the dining area and the ballroom.

A servant showed them to their rooms on the second floor. Drake unpacked with a sense of well-being that he had not known in days. All they had to do now was to sit back and enjoy their surroundings. McKendrick's reply had come through that morning, before they left the *Avatar.*

Midnight. From the foredeck of the motor cruiser *Skipjack*, Chickie Burnham scanned the Jamaican coastline. They were anchored outside the reef, a hundred yards from the sandy cove that lay hidden in the jungle four miles east of Ocho Rios. Lowering the binoculars, Burnham glanced up at the moon in disgust. They would have to hurry.

"You guys ready?" he snapped.

One of the Cubans climbed out of the inflatable, and Burnham could see three large suitcases, each sealed inside a waterproof bag. The Cubans were dressed in black. Burnham wore tiger-striped fatigues. He pressed the walkie-talkie to his lips. "Rover, Deep six."

"Go ahead, six."

"The check's in the mail."

Leaving Eduardo aboard the *Skipjack*, Burnham climbed into the inflatable beside Enrique and shoved off.

They rode in silence, the phosphorescent trail created by the prop wash racing toward them like a lighted fuse.

The white sandy beach shimmered in the moonlight, and Burnham could see the surf breaking in a white line against the outside edge of the reef. Enrique steered as Burnham lifted the binoculars to his eyes once more, guiding the Cuban to the ten-foot gap in the reef where the ocean surged without cresting. They passed through the channel, the surf crashing to either side. Then, as they approached the coastline, Burnham could smell land. Just like the good old days, he thought. The musty odor of triple canopy jungle.

A red light flashed from the cove, followed by two more flashes, and Enrique cut the engine. Kneeling on the floorboards, they silently paddled in, the offshore breeze ruffling the ocean around them. Then, thirty feet from the cove, they heard the sound of the engine scraping sand and they hopped out and pulled the inflatable to shore.

A Cuban dressed in black coveralls emerged from the jungle. "Any problems?" Burnham asked.

"*Nada*. Everything is set to go, man."

They each grabbed a suitcase and headed up a steep jungle path until they reached the top of the embankment, overlooking a two-lane road embowered by Spanish moss and trees. The road was empty, nearly invisible in the darkness. Crouching in the bushes, they waited.

"Come on, *cabrón*," Burnham heard one of the Cubans say. Then they heard the sound of an approaching car. Sweat trickled down the back of his neck as the trees began to glow with yellow light. Burnham reached down and felt the reassuring grip of the forty-five tucked in his waistband. The car pulled off the road.

The driver hopped out and opened the trunk as the old Chevy idled on the roadside. They leapt from the bushes and tossed the suitcases in. The Cuban who had met them on the beach stepped out of his coveralls. Like the driver of the car, he was wearing a blue suit. "See you guys in Miami," he said, then laughed and jumped into the passenger seat. The car sped off.

"Let's go," Burnham said. They scrambled down the path to the beach. He could see the *Skipjack* in the distance, moonlight reflecting off her white hull. The wind had picked up, and high overhead Burnham could hear the palms rattling in the breeze. The Cuban grinned and said, "That was easy, no?"

"Piece of cake, Enrique." Smiling, Burnham placed a congratulatory hand on the Cuban's shoulder and quickly kneed him in the balls. Enrique screamed and fell to the ground, writhing in pain. But before he could scream again, Burnham had him by the throat and was dragging him into the water, holding him face-down beneath the surface, the Cuban too stunned to offer much resistance. Burnham held the man underwater until he was motionless, and then for another three minutes to make sure he was dead.

One down, Chickie Burnham thought.

The dead Cuban bobbed on the waves. Burnham dragged the man ashore and laid him out on the beach faceup. A couple of days rotting in the hot Jamaican sun and the guy would resemble a toadstool. The coroner was about to become a very busy man. Unbuttoning the flap of his shirt pocket, Burnham removed a few wadded bills of Cuban and Mauranian currency. He squatted down beside the Cuban and slipped off one of the dead man's shoes, stuffing the currency into the toe. Then he slipped the sneaker back on the man's foot and tied the laces.

Fifteen men on the dead man's chest—
Yo, ho, ho and a bottle of rummmmmmmmmmmmmm.

"Hey, man? Where's Enrique?" the Cuban aboard the *Skipjack* asked when Burnham pulled alongside in the inflatable.

"With the others. Give me a hand."

"You sure?" the Cuban asked nervously once Burnham was aboard. "I thought I heard a scream."

"You spooked, Eduardo? Whatsa matter? You afraid of some voodoo moon? Now, haul the anchor before we get our asses waxed."

Dutifully the Cuban headed for the bow and began pulling up the anchor chain. Burnham slipped the forty-five from his waistband and withdrew a silencer from his pocket, screwing it in place. Then, bracing his hand against the mast, he carefully took aim at the Cuban's head and squeezed the trigger. Skull fragments scattered across the water like the sound of heavy rain as the Cuban toppled into the sea. Burnham walked forward, snapped on a flashlight, and checked for blood. Nothing like a good clean shot. Then he looked down at the faceless body. Garbage, he thought. The sharks would take care of that.

4 July

Early that morning, as the hot sun lit the Blue Mountains outside of Kingston, the DELTA team under the command of Captain Bobby Haines quietly moved into position around Gordon House, the Jamaican Parliament. The team consisted of eleven men and four women, some dressed as tourists, speaking English, Spanish, or German and taking pictures as they strolled the grounds throughout the day, others posing as Jamaicans, cruising along in cars or on foot or riding bicycles or mopeds. One athletic blonde in shorts and a Hampshire College T-shirt set up an easel in front of the building and began painting an elaborate water-color, which took the better part of the day, becoming the focal point of the curious and admiring.

Prior to arriving on the island via a commercial airline, each operative had memorized the photograph of Burnham that Adams had culled from the Agency's files. According to Fox, the bomb was set to explode at two in the morning, which meant that Burnham would have to make an appearance at some point during the day, not wanting to risk the bomb's premature discovery by leaving an unattended briefcase or package inside the building for any longer than necessary.

So they waited and watched, concentrating their effort during the hour prior to the building's closing. Then, with fading hope, they waited and watched some more until shortly after sunset, when the entire town of Kingston suddenly echoed with the wailing of sirens as almost every ambulance and law-enforcement unit sped north to Ocho Rios.

With his feet propped on a table, Chickie Burnham leaned back in his director's chair and from the *Skipjack*'s stern scanned the seventeen-story luxury hotel as though he were staring at a slab of granite. He had cruised into Ocho Rios the hour before, past two giant cruise ships and an argosy of smaller vessels, whose passengers now filled the hotel's nightclubs and casinos. He could see the calypso band on the terrace and people swaying to the beat of steel drums as children took turns diving into the three connected swimming pools. Others lingered on balconies, gazing at the merriment below or up at the moon or out upon the white beach of the nearly perfect crescent-shaped bay. A steady breeze cooled the tropical air. Burnham glassed the second floor, zeroing in on the fifth room from the left. Draperies fluttered in the breeze. He lowered the binoculars and sipped his martini.

The sliding glass doors were open.

Burnham lifted the binoculars to his eyes again and scanned the seventeenth floor, counting the rooms from the left. He had placed them in the penthouse to give them a false sense of security. He could see light-filled windows but no sign of Julio or Miguel. He glanced at his watch impatiently. They were five minutes late. He needed to see them both on the balcony to make sure that they had not wandered off to a place where they might survive the explosion. Then, a moment later, they appeared, and

Burnham saw immediately that they were not alone. Two women in bathrobes stepped out onto the balcony with them.

Fucking spics. All balls and no brains.

Burnham reached down to his lap and palmed the transmitter, sliding his thumb gently over the face until he found the rocker panel. He switched it on. This ought to be good. Should have brought a videocam. The Cuban named Miguel sat down on one of the deck chairs, pulling a woman onto his lap. She ruffled his hair and laughed, then kissed the top of his head. Julio leaned back against the balcony, guzzling a magnum of champagne while the other woman stared out into the darkness. Then he turned and, leaning into her, offered her a drink. She shook her head, and Julio waggled the bottle enticingly in front of her face. Burnham located the second rocker panel with his thumb, keeping an eye on the Cubans. Then he detonated the bomb.

It was as though someone at his feet had struck a match: A flash of yellow light filled the lenses of his binoculars as the Cubans froze, staring out into the darkness in horror, fear, and supplication. Then came a deep rumble, and a shock wave of hot filthy air slammed into him as the earth trembled. Burnham quickly pulled the binoculars away just as the entire seventeen-story structure crumbled in an avalanche of steel, concrete, flesh, dust, and bone.

Where once there had been a hotel of radiant luxury, there was now only a gray cloud of settling dust and darkness beyond— no music, no laughter, only the empty silence of people too terrified to scream. It was as though the very stars had been sucked from the sky. The hotel and everything inside it had been reduced to a fifty-foot mound of rubble that spread across the swimming pools and down to the beach itself. Burnham looked at the neighboring high-rise, noticing that all its windows had been shattered, and it was from that direction that he heard the first sharp cry of pain. Several boats anchored close to shore were missing windshields. Then twenty yards astern the first engine coughed into life, then another, and fifteen seconds later the entire cove looked like the start of a powerboat race as people got the hell out before death dropped from the sky and zeroed in on them.

Burnham glowed with a satisfaction he had not known in years. They had fucked him over and now he had paid them back. In spades. He freed the *Skipjack* from its mooring and climbed up to the flying bridge. He thought he heard a siren in the distance. *All right, Vaughan, you chickenhawk motherfucker. Dance.* Then he started the *Skipjack*'s engines and headed out to the open sea.

The umber walls of the state dining room shimmered with candlelight and festive conversation as a presidential aide quickly approached the center table and whispered into Jefferson Marshall's ear. In reverential tones Marshall had been entertaining the pretty wife of one of his largest contributors, the founder of a drugstore chain. The woman had asked about the inscription carved into the mantel above the fireplace, and Marshall had nearly choked on his fillet when suddenly he caught sight of the aide entering the gilded room.

Now the President glanced up with alarm. He rose and excused himself, four Secret Service agents also rising from their respective tables nearby to escort the great man from the room as the eyes of every dinner guest fell upon them, captivated by the spectacle of power.

Ann was in the Oval Office when he arrived, surrounded by

various advisors and Cabinet members, including Chief of Staff David Ellis and Secretary of State Harold Reeves. The television was on. Ann was crying.

The news commentator broke in: "Yes, Sara, we now have confirmed reports of over nine hundred people dead. Ladies and gentlemen, if you've just tuned in we are bringing you live coverage of the hotel bombing at Ocho Rios, a well-known resort on the north coast of Jamaica. At approximately nine-fifteen this evening an explosive device detonated inside the Lion's Head Hotel, a seventeen-story luxury high-rise, causing it to collapse. The hotel was frequented by many American tourists, and we believe the number of American dead may exceed seven hundred. We have unconfirmed reports that a Mauranian terrorist organization is claiming responsibility for the bombing. According to Jamaican authorities . . ."

"Those murdering bastards," Reeves was heard to say.

"Where's Martin?" the President barked.

"We're paging him now," Ellis said.

"Sir, the Jamaican ambassador is on the line—"

But Jefferson Marshall wasn't listening. He was striding out of the Oval Office and up the stairs, his teeth clenched in grim determination. "The door," he croaked. The Secret Service agent flicked open the bathroom door and the President of the United States plunged in, slamming the door behind him as a burning stream of vomit poured from his throat.

For as long as he lived Adams would remember the next forty-eight hours as the most concentrated in his life. Upon agreeing to a course of action the day before, Adams, McKendrick, and

Hawking had gone their separate ways, Adams returning to Langley to put his affairs in order, McKendrick and Hawking tending to Gerhardt's party and the extraction.

Now, at nine forty-five that night, he was driving south, driving alone, having forgone the obligatory car and driver, having abandoned the trappings of office as unwanted obstacles to the conversation he hoped would take place. He was driving through the Virginia wilds, through Civil War country, following his intuition once more. Through the windshield he could see the distant plume of fireworks. On the radio the Boston Symphony Orchestra was concluding Gershwin's *Rhapsody in Blue*.

The Gershwin piece ended and Adams leaned forward to switch the station. Then the news came on. His finger never touched the radio.

The mailbox read "Ogilvy" in neat handpainted red letters. It was rumored that George had taken up landscapes, a codicil to a life whose work had been formative in creating the landscapes of foreign policy—landscapes marred by the trench lines of the Cold War.

A long gravel driveway disappeared through the woods, headlights revealing puddles of brown water and banks of red clay. In his rented Pontiac, Adams bumped along them and down over a crest to a gravel cul-de-sac. A hundred feet away a house stood at the end of a path. White clapboard and small, but well kept. A deck extended along the back, either new or freshly painted.

Adams tapped the door knocker, a brass lion. A light came on in the kitchen. Then, a moment later, a woman with gray hair answered the door.

"Hello, Mary."

"Charles." She wasn't glad to see him. She stood at the door without inviting him in.

"I need to speak to George, Mary. It's urgent, I'm afraid. . . ."

"He's not receiving visitors these days. Not from Washington, at any rate. That part of our lives is over."

A throaty voice from inside the house: "Who is it?"

"It's Charlie," Adams shouted through the screen door. "Charlie Adams."

George Ogilvy appeared beside his wife at the door. A tall, crew-cut man of fifty-five. The eyes were deep-set and blue, the face haggard. Adams had not seen the former Deputy Director of Operations since his resignation from the Agency ten years before in the aftermath of the Iran-Contra affair. His resignation had been forced, the inevitable result of the furor that the arms-for-hostages deals and the Contra resupply mission had created throughout the United States. Like so many senior officers who had worked for Bill Casey, Ogilvy had been caught in the pipeline, jettisoned through the slippery conduits of political necessity. The truth of Ogilvy's disgrace had been infinitely more complex and compelling. For the man standing before him was, without question, one of the great unsung heroes of the Cold War.

As a young CIA officer assigned to Cairo station in 1970, Ogilvy, against all odds, and the brutal methods of Egypt's Nazi-trained intelligence service, the Mukhabarat, had somehow managed to recruit Ashraf Marwan, one of Anwar Sadat's closest advisors. Following Nasser's death, Sadat had done little to alter his predecessor's pro-Soviet policies. Thanks to Ogilvy, that situation would soon change.

In May of 1971, Ogilvy received a flash cable from CIA headquarters at Langley. The KGB was planning to assassinate Sadat. Involved in the conspiracy were members of Sadat's inner circle, including his sadistic intelligence chief, Sami Sharaf, and his vice president, Ali Sabray, whom the Russians had picked to take Sadat's place following the assassination. Armed with transcripts of the plotters' telephone conversations, Ogilvy spent three harrowing hours shaking his KGB tail and delivered the evidence to Marwan. Within days the KGB plot had been broken. A grateful Sadat quickly transformed Egypt into an American ally. And the story of Ogilvy's persistence and courage soon became one of the enduring legends within the Agency, a stirring example of the unqualified good the CIA could accomplish in world affairs.

But if the early seventies had been a time of personal triumph, the eighties would become for Ogilvy and other senior officers at the CIA a time of anxiety as they tried to keep the Agency and themselves from becoming embroiled in two Reagan initiatives that would finally erupt in scandal: the arms-for-hostages deals and the secret effort to supply arms to the Contras. Ogilvy had been opposed to both.

The arms-for-hostages deals had been lunacy right from the very start. The Khomeini regime had a rap sheet that made Castro look like a jaywalker. And it wasn't simply the embassy takeover in Teheran in which fifty-two Americans were held hostage for 444 days. The Iranians had been tied to the bombing of the U.S. embassy and embassy annex at Beirut that killed sixty-three people, including two of the Agency's top experts on the Middle East. They also had ordered and financed the bombing of the Marine compound at Beirut International Airport. Two hundred forty-one Marines had died that day—the bloodiest day the Corps had sustained since Iwo Jima. Those bombings were followed by still more bombings of the U.S. and French embassies in Kuwait. And yet Reagan, Casey, and North had negotiated with these people.

Negotiate? With terrorists? *Never.* In Ogilvy's opinion, the

United States should have embarked upon a little bombing campaign of its own.

And what did the United States get for the eighteen HAWK and 2,004 TOW missiles that it sold to Iran?

Three hostages. During the course of which the Iranians kidnapped three more.

Now, as he gazed up at Ogilvy and his wife, realizing that he was not going to be invited in, Adams found himself saying, "Have you heard the news, George? If you haven't, please turn it on. CNN."

They were sitting on the deck, a citronella candle flickering on the glass table between them.

"Care for a drink, Charlie? About all there is left these days. If what you say is true . . ."

"Panama, George. The Contra resupply."

"You couldn't talk to those people. It was all mission and madness. You know how they are. Thought they had Armageddon in Nicaragua. You remember, Charlie."

"But you protected them."

"What the hell else was I supposed to do? The Contra business came from on high and the buck was being passed down."

"Was Gerhardt involved?"

"Ran his own show. Shied away from Ollie. Too many people involved in North's operation. Fund-raisers sharking up the bluehairs, that sort of thing. Might as well rent a billboard. Then there was the money siphoned off from the Iranian missile sales. Two separate operations combined into one. Not smart. Poor tradecraft."

"But Gerhardt was there."

"A player. Gerhardt and others."

"Anyone I can talk to?"

Ogilvy rose from his chair and disappeared inside the house. When he returned a few minutes later he handed Adams a card. On it was the name and address of a man of whom Adams had never heard.

"Tell him I sent you."

"A gunrunner?"

Ogilvy looked at Adams with a distant expression.

"DEA."

How many years had it been since he had worn a tux? Drake couldn't remember. Navy days, probably. Good thing it came with a clip-on tie. He regarded himself in the bathroom mirror, examining his mouth and eyes for signs of tension. Then he locked the bathroom door and removed the Glock, silencer, and spare magazines. The bathroom was luxurious: floor and walls of dark green Italian marble, Jacuzzi, sinks with heavy gold fixtures, mirrors that automatically defogged, and an eight-foot shower with five showerheads and benches built into the walls. Drake screwed the silencer to the Glock and slipped the spare magazines into his pants pocket. Then he tested the laser sight. A red wire-thin beam stung the wall.

He tucked the silenced Glock into the small of his back, slipped on his jacket, and examined himself once more, running a comb through his sandy-brown hair, noting the flecks of gray about the temples.

The name is Bond. James Bond.

Yeah, right.

He left his room and headed down the hall to find Jack.

Looking down from the balcony, he could see that the guests were already arriving. Jennifer was standing at the entrance, greeting people as they walked in. She was wearing an evening gown of white satin and a pink top. She looked beautiful, elegant. Jack emerged from his room at the end of the hallway, dressed in black tie. "You look sharp," he said.

"You, too."

Then, gazing down at the procession, he glanced at Drake with a wry expression and said, "I'm going to miss this life."

"Ah, Mr. Drake, Mr. Henderson," Gerhardt boomed expansively from the ballroom, standing beside a tall man with ruddy features and slicked-back hair and an attractive redhead in her mid-forties. "I'd like you to meet Senator and Mrs. Jason Rutledge of Greenwich, Connecticut. Mr. Drake and Mr. Henderson are both former Navy SEALs. Mr. Drake recovered the bodies of the two young men who became lost inside the *Andrea Doria* last summer."

The couple nodded, gazing at Drake and Henderson approvingly. "I recall reading about that in the *Times*," Senator Rutledge said. "A terrible tragedy. Just terrible."

With raised chin and a matronly look, Mrs. Rutledge proclaimed, "I don't know why young men take so many chances when there is so much death in the world. And those poor people in that hotel in Jamaica . . ."

Drake hadn't listened to the news that day. "Pardon me?"

The Senator flushed with anger. "Bastards blew up a seventeen-story high-rise at Ocho Rios. Half hour ago. Leveled the whole building. Over nine hundred estimated dead. Men, women, and children. Mostly Americans. Mauranian terrorists have claimed responsibility. I'm calling for an invasion of Maurania tomorrow. And we're going to hear from Director Adams, too. How could the Agency miss this one?"

Drake felt rocked by the news. He glanced at Henderson just as the orchestra started up. From the narrowed glowering of his eyes, Drake could see that Jack, too, was bristling with anger.

People were moving into the ballroom. Along the outer wall a dozen two-story windows opened out to the dark expanse of lawn and the Potomac, whose languid waters suddenly blossomed with color from the array of fireworks bursting in the sky. People mingled together in groups, chatting with cocktails in hand while servants in white livery circulated with silver trays of shrimp, miniature crab cakes, and sliced filet and toast rounds. Jack had moved off to a table to the right where a group from the Russian embassy hovered around a silver tureen brimming with golden sterlet caviar. Behind the table a bartender was serving chilled vodka in fluted glasses. Drake listened to the breezy sound of the orchestra launching into a bossa nova tune. He scanned the crowd for Jennifer. No time to lose track of her now. Then she entered the ballroom and began talking to a group of men fifteen feet from Jack, who caught Drake's eye and nodded. Drake relaxed. He spotted Gerhardt on the dance floor, twirling a rather heavy blonde with a grace that Drake would not have thought possible.

"Care to dance?"

Drake turned. It was Hawking.

The General was dressed in black tie, and Drake realized that Hawking must have wangled an invitation from one of his Pentagon friends.

Hawking smiled, gazing fondly at the man he hadn't seen since the day a squad of Drake's SEALs had conducted a joint training exercise with Hawking's Special Forces. "I didn't know that you were such a Boy Scout," Hawking said finally. "Why don't we wander outside?"

"How bad is it?" Drake asked when they finally reached the lawn. They had buried themselves in the crowd that had formed outside to watch the fireworks, as the orchestra drifted into a rhythmic version of "Stella by Starlight."

"Unimaginable," Hawking said. "The bombing at Ocho Rios? Vaughan's involved. That means Marshall, too. This thing is going to get a lot worse before it gets better. And until it gets better, your lives are in danger. McKendrick sends his regards, by the way."

"Tell him thanks. Adams, too."

Hawking smiled at a young woman strolling by. "A power failure will occur at precisely twenty-two hundred hours. It is now twenty-one thirty."

"Check."

"There's an orchard to the right. When the lights go out, cross it until you reach the north wall. On the other side of the wall is a black Mercedes, Connecticut plates. The keys are above the visor, driver's side, and ten thousand dollars in cash is locked in the glove compartment. You'll find a change of clothing in the trunk. You need to disappear for a while."

"How long is a while?"

"A week, two weeks, maybe longer. I'm your contact. Reach me at this number. Use the name Edwards. Good luck."

With a frown, Hawking shook the ice cubes in his empty glass and broke away, disappearing into the crowd.

Jennifer was talking to Mrs. Rutledge when Drake walked up. "Philip. We were just talking about the Jamaica bombing. Have you heard?"

"Where's Jack?"

"In the bathroom. He said he'd be right back. Oh, there he is."

Drake looked left and saw Henderson walking toward them. "Excuse me a minute. He walked over to Jack and filled him in. Nothing like the anonymity of a crowd. Then they walked over to Jennifer and Drake slipped his arm around her waist, nuzzling her hair with his nose. "Let's dance," he whispered.

"Now?"

Mrs. Rutledge regarded them with a rosy countenance. "Oh, go ahead. Have some fun," she encouraged. "You won't be young forever!"

"Where's the boss?" Strickland growled.

Rexer pointed across the room. Strickland scanned the crowd with impatience, then spotted Gerhardt seated beside another old man on an oversized leather sofa near the bar. He walked over to where his employer was sitting.

"Excuse me, sir."

Gerhardt looked up.

"A package just arrived by courier. Marked urgent," Strickland explained.

"Yes. Thank you, Gerald," Gerhardt said absently. *Urgent?* He turned to the silver-haired gentleman with whom he'd been speaking, a well-heeled lobbyist for the defense industry. "I'm sorry. Where were we? Oh, yes . . . the Saudis. Not a good market these days. Tell Lockheed to try the Egyptians."

He excused himself and left the bar and took a small elevator to his office. The package was on his desk. It was the background check of Henderson and Drake that he had commissioned from Arthur Shay six days before. Why would Shay mark it urgent? He opened the package as the murmuring sounds of jazz drifted up through the hardwood floor. Worried, he settled back into his chair and began to read with intense interest.

The first part of the report dealt with Drake, and Gerhardt noted with satisfaction that Drake was everything he claimed to be—an ex–Navy SEAL who owned and operated a charter business out of the Bahamas called Blue Water Adventures. But Henderson's background was a mare's nest of inconsistencies. It was true that Henderson was employed by his father-in-law's construction business, but Shay had documented at least seven occasions in which Henderson had taken prolonged leaves of absence. Officially, Henderson had been hired out as a consultant to foreign construction firms, but when Shay checked with these firms no one could remember very much about a Mr. Henderson save that he had visited for a few days and then disappeared. Moreover, these visits coincided with certain brushfires that had gotten out of hand—Kuwait, Somalia, Bosnia, Haiti, and Bosnia again. Taking these discrepancies into consideration with Henderson's background in Naval Special Warfare, Shay had determined that only two conclusions were possible: Either Henderson was a mercenary, which he thought unlikely. Or he was CIA.

But how could this be? Gerhardt wondered with growing alarm. He had hired Henderson upon Jennifer's recommendation; he had placed her in charge of vetting. How could she overlook such obvious discrepancies? Hadn't he taught her what to look for, what agencies to use when trying to verify someone's past, to use Shay if necessary if she had any lingering doubts at all? Hadn't he emphasized over and over again that security in his business was an absolute requirement—a matter of life and death? How could she have failed to notice these glaring inconsistencies in Henderson's background?

Perhaps he had given her more than she could handle. It couldn't be negligence. She had never let him down. Ever. She loved him, he loved her; she was the one person in this world he could trust. It must be that she had been overwhelmed by her responsibilities, too embarrassed to admit that she couldn't cope. Yes, he saw it clearly now—it wasn't that she had failed him; rather, it was that *he* had failed *her.* Thank goodness he had made that discovery before word got out. He would talk to Jennifer, but not right away, allowing Henderson and Drake to complete the salvage operation. Then he would have Strickland and Rexer take care of business. He had to hand it to Vaughan: nine hundred people dead and Congress calling for an invasion. He had misjudged the little fucker. Obviously, Vaughan didn't fool around.

He rose from his desk and stepped out onto his balcony, needing after such turbulent thoughts to catch a breath of air. In the distance he could see fireworks bursting in the sky, long tendrils of shimmering color melting into their reflection on the Potomac. Dozens of people had drifted out on the lawn to watch the display, and Gerhardt watched them with a self-satisfaction that was hard to contain. They were senators and congressmen, lawyers and lobbyists, journalists and television personalities, military men, foreign dignitaries, and administration officials. They were the power elite, and they had come to his home in obeisance, to pay tribute to his stature in the world.

A Lionel Hampton tune floated up through the air and he began to tap his foot, momentarily nostalgic for the nightclubs of the fifties and early sixties and the beautiful women he had bedded in New York, Paris, and Rome. He had been part of the jet set—a rival of Agnelli and the Aga Khan. But he had never been fool enough to marry. He didn't need to; he had the daughter of his dreams, a beauty who would cherish his memory long after he was gone—the woman whose love fulfilled his final dream of immortality.

And then she was there, forty feet below, stepping out onto the terrace. Drake was leading her by the hand, and he watched them as they made their way through the crowd. *Hmmm.* He could see her smiling to people as she passed, but there seemed to be an urgency about the way she moved. Probably rushing to catch the last of the fireworks, he thought. Then he caught sight of Henderson standing on the lawn. As they strolled in Jack's direction, Gerhardt could see that they were talking—or rather, Drake was talking. They paused, and Jennifer leaned down and removed her shoes. She handed them to Drake, who snapped off the heels and gave them back. She held on to Drake as she slipped her shoes back on. Then, with Henderson standing behind them, facing the Potomac, they looked up, not at the fireworks display like everyone else but in the opposite direction—at the lighted windows of the villa. Then her eyes fell upon him. She was staring at him as though he were stone. He opened his mouth as if to call to her, but he couldn't speak. And a moment later his world collapsed in darkness.

"I thought you wanted to dance," Jennifer said as Drake led her out to the terrace. There were people milling about. She smiled at them, sometimes nodding in recognition as Drake guided her through the crowd to the lawn. A skyrocket burst in the heavens and people looked up, spellbound. Henderson was standing at the edge of the lawn near the orchard.

"Phil?"

"In three minutes the lights go out. We're out of here, babe. Are you wearing heels?"

"Of course."

"Take them off."

Placing a hand on Drake's shoulder, she leaned down and removed her shoes. Drake snapped off the heels. She slipped her shoes back on and straightened. Jack was standing three feet away, his back turned, watching the expanse of lawn that led down to the Potomac. Drake was gazing up at the house.

"The bombing in Jamaica . . . Was my father involved?"

"Indirectly."

She looked at the lighted villa. Then she saw him—the man who had murdered two innocent children and countless others—standing in the shadows of his office balcony on the second floor. He was looking down at her, his mouth a rictus of pain. And she stared at him without compassion, pity, or sorrow. She stared at him until she thought she had closed her eyes as the lights went out.

Silence. A skyrocket burst high over the Potomac, followed by the muffled report, the partygoers frozen in a Goyaesque tableau of people acted upon rather than acting. Then someone on the terrace shouted, "Hey!" From inside the ballroom came the sound of a single glass breaking against the hardwood floor.

They were running.

The cherry orchard was four hundred feet wide, the tall grass silver in the moonlight. They ran through the grass, picking their way among the dark trees. Ahead and to the right Drake could see the distant glow of a flashlight. Then he heard barking. *Jesus Christ. Dogs.*

They reached the wall, the flashlight closing in. Drake looked at Jennifer and said, "You okay?"

"Yes." Jennifer nodded, out of breath.

Jack gazed at Drake with a worried expression and said, "We gotta move, buddy."

Drake interlaced his fingers, then crouched to give Jack a leg up on the wall. Henderson swung himself up and around and reached down for Jennifer as Drake lifted her up. He swung Jennifer up beside him, and as he turned for Drake he saw the villa's lights go on in the distance.

A beam of light skittered across the wall. Then there was the sound of a dog whining as it strained against the leash.

Jennifer looked at Henderson in panic as he drew the Glock and scanned the bushes near the wall. "Jack, what do we do?"

"Lie flat and don't move."

She pressed her body to the top of the wall and looked out into the darkness.

"Phil," she whispered.

But Drake was gone.

Gerhardt stumbled back in the darkness. *The phone. I need the fucking phone.* He slammed into his desk and heard the lamp crashing to the floor as he flayed about helplessly. Then he found his desk again and swept an arm across it, gathering in the phone, an ashtray, and a sheaf of papers. In rage and desperation he lifted the receiver. A dial tone. *It worked!*

The buttons felt like Braille beneath his trembling fingers.

Middle key, bottom row. Fuck. Dial it again. The operator came on the line. He gave her the number of Vaughan's private line.

The phone rang twice. Someone picked up, and Gerhardt could hear shouting in the background. Then a voice, brittle with tension: "Vaughan."

"Ocho Rios."

"Who is this?" the National Security Advisor demanded.

Gerhardt did not mince words. "Drake, Henderson, and my daughter are gone. Someone arranged for a blackout to occur at my estate. I want them back, do you understand? In two weeks. And I don't give a fuck what you have to do to find them." He slammed the receiver down, having expended the remaining vestige of his self-control. Then he slumped to the floor, burying his face in his hands as the grief boiled up inside him. The lights snapped on a minute later. The arms dealer lay in a heap on the floor, oblivious to everything except the searing wall of pain that had been erected around him.

"You killed nine hundred people today, nine hundred people, you stupid cocksucker! You hear me, dumbfuck?"

Vaughan's heart shriveled as the President bore down on him. They were standing in Vaughan's second-floor office. Summoned to the White House, Vaughan had ignored Ellis's insistence that he meet with the President in the Oval Office and had headed upstairs. He needed time to think. But no sooner had he seated himself at his desk than the door flew open and Jefferson Marshall stormed into the room. David Ellis stood in the hallway, cowering behind him.

Vaughan had been attending a small dinner party at the French embassy when word of the bombing had come through.

With no visible sign of emotion, he had made his apologies to the French ambassador and left, bidding his driver to take his time in getting to the White House. The request had been unnecessary—Fourth of July traffic had clogged the streets and boulevards of downtown Washington as people descended upon the Mall to watch the fireworks display. But the delay had done little to assuage the panic that gripped his soul as he was delivered from the embassy.

Burnham. You son of a bitch!

Now, as the President slammed the door in his Chief of Staff's face, Vaughan sensed that his nuts would soon be dangling before the Department of Justice if he didn't think of something quick.

The phone rang. Vaughan glanced at it indecisively, then picked up the receiver. "Vaughan . . . Who is this?"

Then he knew who it was.

His survival instinct kicked into overdrive.

The German shepherd pranced around the discarded cummerbund as though it were steak. "Easy, girl," the guard said in a quailing voice, anxiously searching the moonlit grass around him. The dog's whining grew frantic as it homed in on Drake's scent. The guard stared into the tall grass where Drake was hiding in the shadow of a cherry tree and drew his revolver.

Christ, he doesn't even look old enough to drive.

Drake took aim and hit the laser switch. The thin red beam skewered the darkness, striking the boy in the chest.

"Move and you're dead. Your choice, kid."

The boy froze. "Please, mister. Don't shoot. I'll do anything you say."

Out of the corner of his eye, Drake could see another flash-light in the distance moving toward them.

"Drop the revolver."

The Colt Python slid from the boy's hand.

"Now, listen. There's a tree to your right. Tie the dog to it. If the dog gets loose, you die, do you understand?"

The boy dragged the dog to the tree, then looked up help-lessly. "The leash isn't long enough."

"Wrap the end of the leash around the trunk and snap a hand-cuff to the loop and the other handcuff to the long end so that the leash will tighten against the trunk of the tree. That's right. Now back away from the dog."

Trembling, the boy did as he was told, the dog bounding up on its hind legs, barking furiously as Drake stood in the tall grass. "Let's go."

They moved quickly through the grass, Drake holding the boy at arm's length, a hand on the boy's collar. The kid stumbled through the grass, breathing heavily, twenty pounds overweight. When they were ten feet from the wall, Drake signaled Hender-son. "Guard moving in on your two."

"Got 'em."

The boy glanced up at the wall as Henderson took aim. Then Drake ordered the boy to lie facedown on the ground.

The boy hesitated, tears streaming down his cheeks. "Are you going to kill me?"

"Not unless I have to," Drake snapped. Then in a softer voice he said, "Come on, kid. We're running out of time."

The kid hugged the ground.

Drake dashed for the wall. Henderson reached down and pulled him up and swung him over to the other side. Drake could see the black Mercedes parked beneath a chestnut tree fifty feet away. He reached up for Jennifer as Henderson lowered her to the ground. She threw her arms around him as Henderson dropped down to their left, her voice choked with happiness and relief.

"For a minute I thought you might kill the boy."

"Not my style, Jen. Now let's get out of here."

Jennifer drove. It made sense—she knew the area and it left Drake and Henderson free to return fire in case Gerhardt's people blocked the road leading from the estate. But they encountered no obstacles as Jennifer negotiated the back roads and country lanes of suburban Washington. The blackout had been perfectly timed. The festivities taking place around the nation's capital had provided ample cover. They turned north, blending in easily with the holiday traffic.

Drake opened the glove compartment and passed the bundle of cash back to Henderson. Then he withdrew a small black travel folder containing maps and three driver's licenses, plus registration and insurance certificates for the Mercedes.

They drove through the night, stopping only for gas, filling the tank from only the outermost islands marked "Self-Service." They were exhausted but couldn't sleep—at least not right away. They were free of the cloistered atmosphere of the yacht, they were free of Gerhardt, they were free of the mission. No matter how uncertain the future, at last they could be themselves.

The dream came to him in bits and pieces, falling around him like the intricate workings of a shattered watch. Jefferson Marshall shifted in his sleep but did not awaken. He saw himself casually holding out a hand, the tiny springs and levers filling his palm as he stared at them in glorious wonder. They were gold. They filled his hand with light. He held his hand to the sky like a torch-bearer, heedless of the blizzard of golden mechanisms rising around him with each mesmeric second. Then he was blanketed by their soft accretion, the transforming darkness spinning him down into the hold of a ship.

He was in the center of a lighted gallery the size of a football stadium. There were lights all around and the broken mechanisms were drifting down like snow, filling the seats—only this time they had eyes. They watched him in silence. He implored them, reciting his inaugural address. Then one by one they began falling away as though he had taken his hand and had cleaved a row of icicles.

In the distance he could see a square of light. Then the front of the ship fell away and he saw that he was being borne by a powerful current. The bright blue ocean was tumbling off the face of the earth. Afraid, he drew back, but the hold vanished beneath his feet and suddenly he was standing at the edge of the earth looking down.

It was night. He was gazing down to a cove. Palm trees rattled in the wind and the golden sand of a crescent-shaped beach grew luminous in the moonlight. The golden levers and springs drifted down, falling into the sea, and suddenly the lights of a thousand small boats twinkled in the darkness. Then he heard splashing and the excited voices of children. He looked down past his toes and saw three interconnected swimming pools at the base of a hotel, undulating with jeweled light. The hotel was radiant, white. The children were diving into the water while their parents danced to the strains of calypso music on a terrace nearby. Then he could see his daughter Julia walking toward the pool with two other children. She was a little girl again and was talking with the Hale children. They seemed to be sharing a secret of some kind. And as they came nearer, Marshall could see that his daughter's friends were missing their hands and feet.

He screamed, a ragged, tortured, piteous wail that pierced the private living quarters of the White House and brought a contingent of Secret Service agents running as Ann shook him awake. The image of the Hale children burned in his memory. He sat upright in bed, shivering in the seventy-degree heat, his wife of twenty-four years gazing at him with alarm. "Jeffery, you were having a dream. My God, are you all right?" Then she was up, talking to the agents who clustered at the door, jotting down a prescription.

Jennifer sat up in the backseat where she had been sleeping and looked out the window. They were in the mountains. To her left an alpine meadow sloped down past the remnants of an old barn, the shingled roof flat against a crumbling foundation of stone. A ridgeline rose above it, catching the first golden light of day. She yawned, still dressed in her gown, and placed a hand on Drake's shoulder. Gerhardt would have killed the boy. But even when their lives were in danger Drake had let the boy go. She thought of the day when Drake had stood in her office, staring at the photograph of Montségur. He had looked at the photograph for a mere instant and had grasped its essence. For Gerhardt it had all been a game, an intellectual exercise, a romantic illusion with which to entertain a child. But for Drake it was real.

As it is for me.
I am falling in love.

Henderson turned into a long gravel driveway that curved up into the woods.

"Where are we?" Jennifer asked.

"Berkshires. My wife and I have friends who own a cabin here. Said we could use it while they're away. We'll be safe here."

Jennifer looked out the window at the modern trilevel home coming into view beyond a grove of Scotch pines. A wide balcony ran along the front of the house, and above she could see a series of tall windows overlooking the pines and the meadow. The exterior of the house was constructed entirely of oak.

They pulled up in front of a two-car garage and climbed out of the Mercedes. The mountain air was redolent of pine. Drake and Jennifer looked up at the house, pleasantly surprised. "When you said cabin, I envisioned a dirt floor and no running water," Drake said. "You build this place?"

"Two summers ago. We literally bolted the foundation to the granite."

"It's charming," Jennifer said.

They entered the house and found coffee and a tin of Mc-Cann's oatmeal in the cupboard. They ate on the deck, then adjourned to the living room to watch the latest on the Ocho Rios bombing and the growing furor in Washington. Jamaican authorities were now confirming that the body of a Mauranian terrorist had been discovered on a nearby beach. The terrorist had apparently drowned. Then there were clips of Senator Rutledge calling for an invasion and an interview with the Mauranian ambassador denying his country's involvement.

They watched in silence until Drake got up and turned it off. Jennifer looked relieved. Henderson stood and pocketed the car keys. "I need some air. I'm heading into town."

"Is that wise?" Jennifer asked.

"They're looking for three people, not one," Jack reasoned. "Besides, if we're going to stay here awhile, we're going to need some food. And I have to stop by the neighbor's anyway, so he doesn't think we're robbing the place. He's expecting me. I was supposed to take my boy fishing here next week."

Jefferson Marshall sat down behind his desk, his brain still fuzzy from the sedative the First Lady had prescribed for him only four hours before. He had a full schedule that day: a meeting at ten with key Senate leaders regarding farm legislation pending in Congress, lunch with the Japanese prime minister at noon, a campaign swing through Detroit at four, and now the growing crisis in Jamaica. To make matters worse, Ellis had squeezed in a press conference at three-fifteen, insisting that the country needed the reassurance of a guiding hand. Already Harold Westerfield had jumped on the issue, denouncing the administration's lack of preparedness on a prominent morning talk show.

Now, as he stared at his National Security Advisor with an anger close to hatred, he wondered how this disaster could have befallen him. After the confrontation in Vaughan's office the night before, they had agreed to meet first thing in the morning to discuss damage control. But for the first time in his life Jefferson Marshall longed to be someone else—a stockbroker, or a doctor like his wife, or a car salesman. He yearned for the anonymity that was the unheralded luxury of the common man. Here he was, the most powerful man in the world, and his life was spinning out of control as one act of violence engendered another.

My God, what have I done?

"How many people know about this, Martin?"

"Besides Burnham, only one. Fox."

"And Gerhardt."

"He's guessing."

"Well, it's a pretty goddamn good guess, wouldn't you say?"

"Sir, I think it's important to remember that we had nothing to do with the bombing at Ocho Rios. It was the cowardly act of a rogue warrior, a man acting entirely on his own without the sanction of the federal government."

"But we paid the man, for Christ sake!"

"To bomb the Jamaican Parliament Building. When it was empty."

"You think that distinction is going to hold up in court?"

"It's never going to get there. Not if we stick to the game plan. Not if you rise to the occasion and lead this country to war."

"It's that simple, huh."

"Basically. Appease the god of vengeance and the bombing incident will go away."

"What about Gerhardt?"

"I'll get his people back."

"In two weeks?"

"Give me Adams's job and your full support and I will have them back in less."

"He will have them killed."

"We don't know that. And we don't want to know that. From our point of view, it's irrelevant."

He was alone. She had disappeared into the bathroom to take a shower. He rose from the kitchen table, opened the refrigerator, grabbed a Coke, and headed out to the deck, picking up a *National Geographic* from an end table along the way. Sunlight filtered down through the pines, and he stretched out on a lawn chair, feeling a drowsiness take hold of his body. It had been twenty-six hours since he had slept. The cabin was a godsend, as luxurious an accommodation as they could have imagined—a miracle, given the circumstances. They would stay here for two or three weeks, then move on. *Where would they go next?* Drake had no idea. Maybe they would head south, to the Keys or to Disneyland, tourist areas where they would blend in. He began leafing through the *National Geographic* with the vague sensation of perusing a travel brochure. Then, turning a page, he came to a color photograph of a tropical city, a forest of trees and skyscrapers set against a cerulean bay. A runway stood in the distance. Drake stared at the photograph, wondering for a moment if he had fallen asleep and was having a nightmare, the voices rising from the past.

Panama.

"Golf Two, this is Golf One, over."

"Go ahead, One."

"We have movement—at least four unknowns inside the COI."

"Copy, One. We have you covered."

The air had been hot that December night. They had climbed out of their rubber rafts and had hustled three-quarters of a mile up the runway, creeping around several light aircraft and going to ground. They were a hundred feet from the mouth of the hangar where Noriega's jet was stored, sandwiched between the open hangar and darkened terminals to their rear. They were exposed, lying on the tarmac, illuminated by the ambient light of Panama City. It was a fucked-up operation, and Drake knew it. They all knew it. In the distance they could see tracer fire pouring down over the city and could hear the muffled explosions and small-arms fire as other American units encountered resistance as they tried to reach their final points of departure. It was five minutes before H-hour, Operation JUST CAUSE, the U.S. invasion of Panama; and the element of surprise was gone. And to make matters worse, the Rules of Engagement had been changed at the last minute. Instead of shooting out the nose gear and the fuel tanks of Noriega's jet, Drake's SEALs were now supposed to enter the hangar and slash the tires. Later Drake would learn that the decision was made because some desk jockey didn't want the United States to have to buy the Panamanians a new jet.

"Golf Two, we have PDF inside the hangar. We are exposed. Our position has been compromised. We are moving to the right. Do you copy—"

From inside the hangar someone shouted a command in Spanish. Sweat poured down his back. Fifty yards to his left a squad from Bravo Platoon was securing another hangar, taking into custody civilian guards watching over planes belonging to the drug cartels. He glanced up over his shoulder at the high-rise apartment buildings overlooking the airfield. Months before, he had recommended that they scrap the full-scale assault and place a sniper team in one of those apartments instead. Armed with a .50-caliber rifle equipped with silencer and nightscope, the SEALs could control the entire airfield, using exploding rounds to disable Noriega's jet should the General appear. A textbook SEAL operation: maximum effect with minimum risk to the few men involved. But his recommendation had been rejected, the planners opting instead to send forty-eight men up the center of a brightly lit runway.

Now, peering through his scope, watching the Panamanians positioning themselves behind steel drums and doors, Drake knew that if he didn't get his men out of there fast they were going to die.

"What's he saying?"

"They're telling us to surrender, sir."

"We move now!"

Suddenly the air exploded. Drake felt something slam into his right shoulder as bullets sparked off the runway. He was bleeding to death as gunfire erupted all around him and tracer fire poured from the hangar. Men were screaming, and he saw immediately that only one other man in his eight-man squad was returning fire, the rest either dead or badly wounded, lying flat under the weight of their packs or writhing in pain. The Panamanians were using fire control, skipping rounds off the tarmac. He was hit again in the wrist. The pain was searing, and he screamed in agony as he shifted his weapon to his left hand and fired into the hangar. In a panic he looked left and saw Jack moving up, firing from the hip, moving his men forward, laying down a protective curtain of fire. Then Jack's voice: *"Heavy wounded. Bravo, get up here!"*

The hostile fire was not diminishing. Out of the corner of his eye he could see sporadic muzzle flashes coming from the darkened terminal. One of Jack's men went down, shot in the head. He slipped a magazine out of his vest and bit through his tongue to kill the pain in his wrist as he pulled back the charging handle and reloaded his weapon. He fired a long burst, aiming at the flashes inside the hangar as the world began to swirl around him. *Please God, not now.* He was losing consciousness. He fought to stay alert, to stay awake, to stay alive. He fought for his men. Then he felt someone beside him.

"Hold on, Phil. We're gettin' you outta here." Jack's voice. Again. *"Get the others."*

His wounded were being dragged to safety. His shoulder hurt. Something hot creased his temple. Tracer fire was burning up the air all around him. He couldn't breathe. There was blood in his mouth. Then lights began to dim and he couldn't hear anything anymore. He reached for his weapon, but it wasn't there. . . .

Twenty-four hours later he awoke. White sheets, white uniforms, soft music instead of gunfire, soothing voices instead of men dying in agony, white bandages instead of blood. Unable to hold a pen, he had asked a nurse to take dictation so that he could write to the families of the dead. He had known those men for three years. He had trained with them, he had partied with them, he had attended some of their weddings, and nothing was going to bring them back. It was a lesson he should have learned as a boy—after all, he had missed him enough, mourned his absence at the head of the dinner table. But nothing could bring his father back, either—not even the shared knowledge of what it was like to die.

The conviction that the tragedy of Vietnam had made men

wiser had proved to be an illusion. Even within the military. But what had he expected? Universal anagnorisis? Not even the Civil War had effected such a transformation, as Henry James, Sr., had expressed ruefully to his sons.

Now, as he set the magazine down over his chest, he recalled the night that she had joined him on the observation deck of the *Avatar.* They had gazed up at the stars just as he had as a boy growing up in Michigan. He would look up at the stars, wondering what the earth was like when the light left those distant planets. Light from an infinity of ages shining down, dappling the earth, throwing all geologic and human history into a relief that was as mysterious as it was incomprehensible. And as he looked up at the pines, he sensed that a critical realignment had taken place within his soul, the fragments of his past reconfigured like planets drawn to a brighter sun.

Then she was there. She had changed out of her gown into a pair of baggy corduroy pants and a white cotton shirt. She looked at the magazine on his chest and said, "Good article?"

"History."

He set the magazine aside and she leaned over him, her chestnut hair spilling around his face, and kissed him on the lips. He drew her in and they kissed again, passionately. Then he had his hand beneath her shirt, cupping her breasts. She leaned her forehead against his as she straddled him, her smile as wide as the ocean, her cheeks flushed with happiness, and he slid his hands down along her hips and unfastened the button of her corduroys, running his hands along the smooth skin of her bottom and then up along the insides of her thighs. He carried her to the bedroom.

And so they made love, undressing each other without haste and without speaking, not wanting it to end, not wanting the intensity of their passion to be diminished by the inflections of language. Nor was there the slightest hint of self-consciousness at their occasional fumblings. They were new to each other, yet they had known each other forever.

"Eddie? Martin Vaughan over at NSC. Listen, the President needs a favor. Yes, that's right. We're trying to track down a couple of people and we're wondering if you might monitor a couple of phone lines. Pardon? I'm sure that can be arranged, but I'll have to check the White House schedule. Philip Drake and Jack Henderson. Now, the first line we'd like you to monitor belongs to a Mary Henderson in Concord, Massachusetts. We need to know everyone she talks to. The second line belongs to Charles Francis Adams. That's right. In Georgetown. Very funny. The third line . . ."

If anyone had told him on his first day of orientation at West Point that he would watch the boy standing next to him bleed to death in the tall elephant grass of Vietnam, or that thirty-two years later he would desperately search for a way to keep that boy's son from dying as well, Walter McKendrick might have marched out of the Old Chapel and never looked back.

He tossed the green duffel onto his desk and glanced dismally about his Pentagon suite. He was there to collect his personal effects. Word had come down: He and Adams had been fired. The President would make the announcement during his address to the nation that afternoon.

He thought about the carnage at Ocho Rios and the cover-up that was taking place that very minute inside the White House. The men Hawking had sent to Jamaica had been unable to stop the bombing. Burnham had turned out to be murderous and un-predictable. According to Fox, the former operative had disap-peared from the face of the earth.

Already a transformation was taking place inside the Penta-gon. The men and women he encountered along the E-ring were restless, their faces lit by the prospect of war. Who could blame them? Seven hundred and fifty Americans had been killed at Ocho Rios. The entire country was spoiling for battle, and there was little he and Adams could do about it until proof of President Marshall's malfeasance was at hand.

So it was up to Adams, the descendant of two American pres-idents and the great-grandnephew of Henry Adams, one of the world's greatest historians. Adams, the last representative of the Eastern Establishment, fighting the last battle of the Cold War.

But they were running out of time. Two weeks, Fox had said, describing Gerhardt's ultimatum. Once Vaughan took over at CIA he would use the Agency's considerable resources to hunt Drake and the others down. And that would happen the minute the President designated Vaughan as Adams's successor.

If it wasn't happening already.

They would close in on Drake and the others the way the North Vietnamese had closed in on that hot November day in '65. And as McKendrick began packing his things he found him-self drifting back to that afternoon—to the most savage one-day battle of the Vietnam War, when three battalions of North Viet-namese tore into the 2nd Battalion, 7th Cavalry strung out in the tall elephant grass of the Ia Drang.

It was the first airmobile campaign of the war, except there was nothing airmobile about the orders they had received that day. They were told to abandon LZ X-Ray and to march to a smaller clearing designated LZ Albany. McKendrick recalled how exhausted they all were, having been on one hundred percent alert for the past two days. He hadn't slept in over sixty hours. They had been choppered into X-Ray at the base of the Chu Pong massif to relieve 1st Battalion, who had beaten back the enemy in a vicious three-day firefight, having been surrounded by more than 2,000 North Vietnamese Regulars. At times the Americans had been nearly overrun, but with the help of artillery and close air support, the 450 men of the 1st had prevailed. McKendrick's men had been shocked by the number of enemy dead. More than 1,000 North Vietnamese lay rotting in the sun. The stench had been unbearable.

Now the B-52s were heading in from Guam to finish up where the 1st had left off. Second Battalion had been ordered to LZ Albany, a four-mile hike through the jungle.

They had been captains then, company commanders, Drake's father, Phil Sr., a tall, good-looking man who had been first in their class at West Point and had often talked about returning there someday to teach American history. It was from Drake's father that McKendrick had developed his love of history, for during the initial months of their plebe year McKendrick had struggled under the heavy course load and probably would have flunked out had it not been for the fortuitous circumstance of having Drake's father as a roommate. While he and his other classmates were following the gridiron exploits of Navy quarterback Jefferson Marshall, Drake's father had immersed himself in literature and philosophy, with preternatural seriousness seeking the universals that have guided men and women since the beginning of history. It was through Drake's father that McKendrick had discovered Arthurian legend, McKendrick bursting into their room one autumn afternoon to find Drake's father reading with the same look of tight-lipped concentration that McKendrick would notice years later in the son.

"Jesus, Phil. What are you reading now—? Hey, Phil? There's a game on."

"*Le Morte d'Arthur.* You should check it out, Walt. It's about the Knights of the Round Table. You'd like it."

Now, as they moved through the jungle, they began to worry about the exhaustion of their men, who were beginning to shed equipment as the march continued on. Suddenly the column came to a halt. Two North Vietnamese had been captured and the battalion commander wanted to assess the situation with his company commanders.

After two hours of marching under the hot sun, the men welcomed the break. Before moving up the line McKendrick had deployed the men in a herringbone formation. The men relaxed as best they could, squatting in the tall grass, eating C rations and talking quietly among themselves.

He had bumped into Phil Sr. as they neared the clearing at the head of the column, and they had talked a bit. The Recon platoon had already moved to the far side of the clearing to the northwest, and 1st and 2nd Platoons of A Company had taken up positions to the northeast and southwest, respectively. There was a copse of trees in the middle of the clearing, and McKendrick and Phil Sr. had just joined the command group when the first mortar rounds started coming in.

For as long as he lived he would remember the look of stark horror on Phil's face as they both realized what was happening. While the troops were resting in the grass along a 550-yard trail, three regiments of North Vietnamese had silently positioned themselves in a deadly U-shaped ambush extending the entire length of the American column.

Without waiting to be dismissed, they had sprinted back toward their companies as small-arms fire began to erupt all around them. They never made it. The North Vietnamese were everywhere: in the trees, on termite hills, in the grass—three regiments firing down upon the column of American soldiers fighting desperately for their lives.

The fire was so intense that bullets were clipping the grass around them as they ran; and above the crescendo of incoming mortar rounds, grenades, and small-arms fire they could hear the terrified screams of men dying all around them.

Suddenly McKendrick was hit. It felt as though someone had whacked him in both legs with a baseball bat and he was down, falling face forward in the dirt, wounded in both thighs, and Phil was crouching beside him in the tall grass, tearing away at a bandage wrapper.

"Hang on, man. We're getting out of here. "

"Phil . . . I think my legs are broken. . . ."

Then Drake's father was quickly up and firing a burst from his M-16, and McKendrick heard the heavy thump of a man falling nearby.

They were cut off. Surrounded. Then he heard the deeper sound of an AK and Phil spun around, tumbling hard on his side where he lay aspirating blood and writhing in pain. In agony McKendrick had crawled over and seen immediately that his friend had taken three rounds in the chest. He had placed a hand over the wounds, trying to stop the bleeding. Then the firing around them slacked off and he could hear men in the grass around them, chattering in Vietnamese. Occasionally the chattering would stop, followed by a short burst from an AK, and McKendrick knew what was happening.

The North Vietnamese were executing American wounded. With a bloody hand he caressed his friend's forehead.

"Be still," he whispered. And as the mortally wounded captain stared at the sky, McKendrick could sense the transformation taking hold of his friend as he quieted down, the body dying as the spirit soared elsewhere.

For Drake's father *had* left the battlefield, borne on the words McKendrick had uttered as the PAVN closed in. He was back in Monterey, standing in his backyard, listening to his young wife repeating the words to their squirming son as he held the baby close with more emotion than he could bear, the day she took their picture, the day he left for Vietnam.

The Blue Oyster Bar and Grill had just opened for lunch when Adams stepped inside and peered down a row of empty booths. The place was bright and cheerful with brass lanterns on the walls and a row of tall windows in the dining room overlooking Cape Cod Bay. Near the entrance to the dining room he could see a chalkboard listing the specials: crab cakes with a wasabi cream sauce; beer-and-molasses barbecued chicken; seared tuna marinated in olive oil, rosemary, and garlic; and wild-rice-stuffed salmon. Adams felt his stomach rumbling. He was hungry. He had flown up to Boston early that morning and had driven down to the Cape, then along Route 28 to Wellfleet and the Blue Oyster.

"Can I help you, pop?" the bartender asked.

"I'm looking for Ricky Martinez." Adams handed the young man a card.

"Just a sec." The bartender flipped up the service end and disappeared down a hallway. A moment later a short, athletic-looking man in his mid-thirties stepped into the bar. Martinez was tan and well dressed: blue blazer, white button-down shirt open at the collar, gray slacks, tassel loafers. He introduced himself, gazing at Adams with a kind of questioning wonder.

"I was just reading about you in the paper. . . ."

"George Ogilvy gave me your address. Is there some place we can talk? In private?"

The carpeted office was spare and businesslike. On a table behind Martinez's desk stood an eight-by-twelve color photograph of an attractive woman of Spanish descent standing behind two boys and a girl. Venetian blinds covered two windows to the left, and on the opposite wall hung photographs of two other restaurants and a picture of the Blue Oyster on the front page of a newspaper. It was obvious that Ricky Martinez had gone on to better things, and Adams was glad to see that the former DEA agent had made a life for himself and had prospered.

"You have a nice place here," Adams remarked.

Martinez beamed with the justifiable pride of a man who has built his business from the ground up. "My wife and I opened this place six years ago. Now we have two others. We open a third next month. In Boston."

Like many naturalized Americans Adams had known, Martinez spoke about his accomplishments with a kind of humble eagerness, as though needing to have his success validated by the approval of others.

"How may I help you, Señor Adams?"

"Panama."

Martinez's face darkened. "Big subject, man."

"Gerhardt."

The restaurant owner was silent, scrutinizing Adams with uncertainty.

"I need to know, Ricky. The bodies are piling up."

"Ghosts."

"Excuse me?"

Martinez shook his head with a trace of sarcasm. "You think a thing is dead and buried, then it comes back to haunt you."

"But for you it was never buried, was it, Ricky?"

Notre Dame was down fourteen points and George Meyer was happy. There was nothing he liked better on a Saturday afternoon than to suck down a few brewskies and watch Division I football. So every Saturday, regardless of season, he selected a videocassette from his substantial collection of football classics and popped it into the VCR. Today's game was one of his favorites. Twice already Lou Holtz had flung his headset to the ground, and it wasn't even the second quarter. This was going to be great! Meyer sipped his Budweiser and hunkered down to watch the snap.

The phone rang. *Shit.*

It was Alice Rhodes.

"I thought you were in Europe, Alice."

"We are. John flew over yesterday."

"Well, I'm glad you called. Your neighbors, the Hendersons, are here. They arrived last night."

There was a troubled pause. "But that's impossible."

"The man was here this morning."

"I just talked to Mary Henderson fifteen minutes ago. Her husband's away on business. That's why I'm calling. I just wanted to let you know that they won't be using the cabin. George? Hang on a sec. . . ."

There was an alarmed conversation taking place at the other end. Then Alice's husband got on the line.

"George? John. You say this guy came over and introduced himself?"

"This morning. He was standing right here in my living room."

"What did he look like?"

"I dunno. Brown hair. Tall. Hooked nose."

"That's Jack."

"Want me to go over there?"

"I don't think so. He probably decided to swing by the cabin on his way home. Besides, anyone about to rob the place would hardly stop by the neighbors' to say hello. And he sure as hell wouldn't be using the name Henderson."

"You got a point there."

"I wouldn't worry about it if I were you."

"You sure?"

"Alice says she's going to call Mary right back, anyway. We'll straighten it out. Hey, what's that I hear in the background? Football?"

Ricky Martinez rose from his desk with a somber look of reflection in which Adams discerned a note of bitterness long suppressed.

"I been working for the DEA for about six years. In 1985, they assign me to Central America. The idea was to go down and help the locals get organized.

"As far as drug trafficking went, Noriega wasn't a whole lot different from many of the other military leaders we dealt with down there. The situation was the same everywhere—Peru, Guatemala, El Salvador—the military people in charge all had a piece of the action. Basically, we became their enforcers. We'd obtain leads and gather evidence and then bust the people they wanted us to bust—lefties, for the most part. We'd arrest them and the security forces would haul them off, and you don't want to know what happened after that. It was the same with Noriega, except with Noriega it was all business. As far as politics went, Noriega didn't give a shit unless he felt threatened. He played both sides—running guns to the Sandinistas and to the rebels in El Salvador, schmoozing with Castro, then running guns to the Contras. But like I said before, when it came to drugs Noriega only cared about making money and turning in his rivals to make himself look good to the *norteamericanos*.

"And it worked for a while, man. The *maricón* had us eating right out of his hand. CIA, too. We should have been hip to what was going on, but we weren't. I mean, how do you explain all those banks and dummy corporations? We knew about meetings he had with the Medellín cartel, but he always explained these away—you know, Manuel Noriega, undercover agent. That kind of shit. And as long as good ol' Manuel kept on producing, nobody wanted to know any different.

"Then one day this kid comes in asking for protection. Early thirties. Clean cut. Looked like a farmboy. Said his name was Lloyd Wheeler and that he had a lot of information to trade. Sounded good to me. I told him that I'd see what I could do, but I'd need some information first just to see what he got. That's when I first started hearing about Gerhardt. Wheeler was a drug pilot. Smuggled guns for Noriega in the beginning, then got a job with the cartels. Things work out fine for a while. Then one day one of his pilots disappears with about ten million dollars' worth of coke. Crashed in the jungle. Problem was, nobody could find the plane. Cartel figured Wheeler made up the story and took off with the stash. So good ol' Lloyd finds himself in trouble. Hit men beating the bushes, just to find out where he is. So he comes to us. Wants to trade his story for asylum. That's when we first learned about the extent of Noriega's corruption. And believe me, man, every pile of shit that Lloyd uncovered for us had Gerhardt's footprints all over it.

"Gerhardt started working with the cartels in '81 when they called him in to help out with a little problem they were having with the M-19, the leftist guerrilla organization backed by Castro that was trying to overthrow the Colombian government. M-19 needed money, so they started kidnapping prominent Colombians. And one of the people they kidnapped was the little sister of Jorge Ochoa. *Muy estupido,* man. Ochoa drew together about two hundred of the biggest traffickers in Colombia and formed the Medellín cartel. That's how the whole cartel business got started. Gerhardt got them weapons and hired the specialists to train the paramilitary force, and about six weeks later Ochoa got his sister back and the M-19 was begging for mercy, and I mean begging, man. And from that point forward Gerhardt was their man.

"Soon Ochoa's balls got so big that he thought he could take on the Colombian government after it shut down one of his processing labs. Decided to off a couple of Colombian officials in retaliation. Cocaine might be Colombia's numero uno cash crop, but in murdering government officials the cartel had stepped over the line and the Colombian government came down hard. Soon the cartel leaders needed a new home. Gerhardt arranged

for them to go to Panama. Turns out that Gerhardt had been doing business with Noriega for years, using him as a source for the
false end-user certificates he needed to ship weapons to countries
that were embargoed for one reason or another. Countries like
Chile and Iran. So Gerhardt spoke to Noriega and the cartel
leaders went to Panama, and resumed business as usual.

"And business was good. Too good. Supply couldn't keep up
with demand. All across America, from gutter to boardroom,
people were packing their noses. By 1984 the demand for the
product had become so great that they needed to find new ways
of smuggling it into the United States, which was getting harder
and harder to do because the U.S. was getting its act together as
far as interdiction was concerned. The Coast Guard stepped up
its patrols, some tough new laws were passed, and we started using AWACS. Then, just as the floodgates were beginning to
close, they opened up again."

"Gerhardt?"

"You bet. After Casey got caught mining Nicaraguan harbors—technically an act of war—Congress passed the Boland II
amendment, which made arming the Contras illegal. The Reagan
administration said fuck Congress, we're going to do it anyway,
and they did."

"I remember. Not only was the resupply effort illegal, but it
violated one of the most fundamental principles of the United
States Constitution: separation of powers."

"Boland II took the CIA out of the resupply game, so Casey
off-loaded the entire operation to the NSC and Oliver North.
Since North couldn't use any of the CIA proprietaries, he hired
local pilots who knew the area. Being in the arms business, Gerhardt picked up on this right away, told the Medellín boys to look
into it. They did. And that's when the dam burst. Suddenly we

had drugs flying up and guns flying down. Coke was being flown in all over the southern United States, and there wasn't a damn thing we could do about it."

"The law of unintended consequences."

"I guess. In Washington the people in charge weren't happy about the situation, but what could they do? Not as though they were going to shut the resupply effort down. Not these guys. So they just looked the other way."

"Is that when you quit?"

"I filed reports. It did no good," Martinez said with disgust. "DEA didn't want to know shit. Like I said before, the Contra resupply effort was a White House operation—hands off. And it wasn't like you could hand the story to the papers. No matter what you thought of North's operation, we had men in the field, people might have been killed."

Adams nodded in sympathy. "You mentioned AWACS. Were any of those airfields in Texas?"

"Two. One was an Air Force base. According to Lloyd, the pilots would dump the coke right there in front of all those flyboys and laugh. The other was an airstrip owned by a company called—let me think . . . Growth Tec. Yeah, that was it. Gerhardt was definitely a part of that. I checked it out. No drugs. They were into something else—shipping industrial products to Chile, to Industrias Cardoen via Panama."

"Industrial products?"

"Zirconium."

Eddie McMahon sat in his cubicle in the sealed communications room deep inside the NSA. A blue light was flashing on one of the computer banks. They were receiving another intercept. He sipped his coffee, turned up the volume slightly, and leaned back in his chair, listening to the two women begin their conversation. Mary Henderson and Alice Rhodes. Then abruptly he put his coffee down and began scribbling on a pad of paper. The conversation ended six minutes later, and he replayed the tape just to make sure. Then he dialed the CIA Director's private line, dreaming of the night in the Lincoln bedroom Vaughan had promised him, wondering which girlfriend to ask.

"Sir? I think I've located the people you're looking for . . . yes, just this minute. They're in the Berkshires . . . in a cabin. No, I don't have the address, but I have the name of the owner. Rhodes. John Rhodes. Yes, thank you, sir. That would be great. Hmmm, let's see . . . how about next Friday night?"

Trailed by his Chief of Staff, David Ellis, and a host of other advisors, Jefferson Marshall strode into the Oval Office and scanned the members of the White House staff who had gathered at his invitation to watch history being made. The electricity in the room was palpable.

The President of the United States took his seat behind the enormous oak desk, unconsciously flexing his shoulders with the kind of aggressive self-confidence he had displayed years before when he and his co-captains had faced their opponents, waiting out the coin toss in the emotionally charged seconds preceding each football game. He had been a national hero once, and he would become a hero again. The nation would soon forgive his failure to implement the tax cut he had promised. He would speak to the people, reminding them of their glorious destiny as Americans. He would galvanize their attention just as he had riveted the attention of his staff. Already, gazing up at their expectant faces, he could sense their vast reservoir of fear and uncertainty evaporating in the light of his commanding presence. Yes, an opportunity of a lifetime had presented itself, just as Vaughan had predicted. A phoenix had risen from the ashes.

Darryl Waters, his press secretary, signaled from the corner. "Ten seconds, Mr. President."

An expression of gravity settled over the President's features.

"Good afternoon, my fellow Americans. Yesterday evening, while our nation was celebrating its independence, nine hundred and thirty-nine men, women, and children were killed when an explosion of uncommon force destroyed the Lion's Head Hotel at Ocho Rios, Jamaica. Immediately upon learning of this tragic event I spoke to the Jamaican ambassador and offered our full assistance in the search for survivors. It saddens me beyond the ability of words to convey that no survivors have yet been found.

"First of all, Ann and I would like to convey our deepest sympathies to all those who have lost friends and family as a result of this awful event. Our prayers are with you. And I want you to know that I will do everything in my power to ensure that your loved ones are brought home as quickly as possible. At this very moment Secretary of State Reeves is meeting with Jamaican authorities to coordinate our mutual effort.

"This morning, at the Jamaican ambassador's request, I dispatched a team of forensic scientists to Ocho Rios. Just a few short minutes ago, they confirmed that the massive explosion that destroyed the Lion's Head was caused by a bomb.

"Let me say to those individuals responsible for this heinous crime, make no mistake about it, I will make it my mission in life to hunt you down. No matter how clever you think you are, no matter how many friends or allies you think you have, I will find you. Accordingly, I have asked National Security Advisor Martin

Vaughan to assume the directorship of the Central Intelligence Agency, effective immediately. The Deputy National Security Advisor, Terrence Fox, will assume Mr. Vaughan's duties at the White House during the interim. Likewise, I have also named Admiral Jason Webster as Chairman, Joint Chiefs of Staff. With no reflection on the honorable service and exceptional abilities of Mr. Charles Francis Adams and General Walter P. McKendrick, I feel our nation must now embark on a new course to stem the tide of international terrorism. And I have authorized Mr. Vaughan to use every means at his disposal to uncover the perpetrators of this despicable crime in which over seven hundred Americans died.

"Here in the United States we look out for our own. We always have, and God willing we always will. Because that is the American way. And when attacked, we fight. That, too, is the American way. Make no mistake about it. Here in America we stand up for what we believe, we stand up for what's right. So those individuals responsible for the bombing at Ocho Rios, I say to you: Your days are numbered. Justice will prevail. Because here in America we are one nation, under God, indivisible, with liberty and *justice* for all."

"I think I'm going to puke," Jack Henderson remarked, turning away from the television set as the President's address to the nation ended. His arm around Jennifer, Drake sat on the couch in silence.

"What are we going to do?" Jennifer asked.

"Nothing, for the time being," Henderson said. But it was clear from his expression that he wasn't happy about the idea.

"But Adams and McKendrick have been fired."

"Won't stop McKendrick," Drake offered by way of reassurance. "Don't worry, Jen. They'll think of something."

But deep inside, Drake was worried, too. No matter how hard Adams and McKendrick tried to overcome the forces arrayed against them, the possibility existed that they might fail. And if they failed, arrangements would have to be made—a deal worked out with Vaughan and Gerhardt. Adams and McKendrick would work out a deal to spare the lives of their operatives. But Drake could not abide the prospect. The very idea nauseated him. Somehow, they would have to find another way.

The sky was limitless and blue. Adams was flying to Dallas. He was taking care of one final detail, though he knew the story now, or at least its essentials. He was flying to see Allen Wexler, chairman of Marshall Oil.

He gazed down at the arid Texas countryside, thinking about the day he had first come to Washington. It had been Donovan who had brought him there. Wild Bill Donovan, the legendary founder of the OSS, grandson of Irish immigrants, recipient of the Congressional Medal of Honor, among his many other awards—Donovan would become the only person in U.S. history to win the nation's top four medals for gallantry and public service—acting Attorney General, founder of the distinguished law firm Donovan, Leisure, Newton & Irvine, winner of a number of landmark cases before the Supreme Court. Yes, for Adams, history was indeed the biography of great men. He had flown to Gravelly Point and taken a cab to Donovan's headquarters on the outskirts of Georgetown and had joined the OSS, and like his mentor had spent the rest of his life alternating between government service and law.

Adams recalled vividly the day they had met. With restless blue eyes Donovan had looked at him and said, half joking, half serious, "Nazis ever get ahold of you, Charlie, they'll turn you into a totem." Few men could match Donovan's exuberance and sense of duty. And Adams had known them all—Lovett, Acheson, Bohlen, Kennan, Harriman, Frankfurter, Bruce, McCloy, and many others. They were the Wise Men, the Natural Aristocracy that John Adams had hoped would prevail in America. They were Republicans and Democrats, some wealthy, some not, some— like Donovan and McCloy—from humble beginnings, but they were men who, like the Founding Fathers, disdained the internecine divisiveness of partisan politics. They were men who took scholarship seriously, who set forth the intellectual ideals to which Adams had aspired—that to arrive at even a semblance of truth you had to examine a problem from both sides, you had to try to see things from other perspectives. You had to be honest in your assessments, you had to try to see things in all their manifold distinctions, because that was the only way that you could judge the quality of your ideas and determine a course of action. In the world of clear thinking, ideology meant death.

Vietnam was proof of that—a war undertaken by men whose ideological convictions prevented them from clearly seeing what was at hand, liberals and conservatives and, alas, even some of the Wise Men he had admired, whose Cold War perceptions had hardened into a rigid framework so that a communist insurgency in the most insignificant of nations loomed as a global threat.

And for the United States the results had been tragic.

When asked for his opinion of the war Adams said it reminded him of the lost army of Aelius Gallus that had set out to conquer Arabia Felix in 24 B.C. only to wander in the wilderness for months, cursed by the stargazers of Sheba. And as the bodies piled up—and for decades afterward—Adams would watch with sorrow as the United States became increasingly polarized, the political debate too often set by people whose ideological convictions were as rigid as any communist Chinese. In the sixties and seventies they had come from the New Left. In the eighties and nineties they were the self-styled revolutionaries of the Right. In either case, they were men and women whose beliefs in healthier times would have been consigned to the margins.

Nevertheless, Adams remained hopeful. Unlike Henry Adams, he did not see history's acceleration as profoundly alienating. To the contrary, the modern world was striking for its beneficence. People were healthier and better educated than ever before. They had more opportunities. And Adams was convinced that one day others would have the privilege, just as he and his forefathers had enjoyed, of being present at the Creation.

Natural Aristocracy—yes. A Republic of Virtue? Who in his right mind would want it? In America you could smoke dope and listen to grunge rock, or loll in front of a TV set, or on Election Day toe the party line, if you cared to vote at all. Or you could raise a family, or try in other ways to improve the world. Or, like the young people whose lives he was trying to save, you could attain the stature of the heroic. That was the beauty of America. You could do a million things. The choice was all yours.

"That'll be three dollars and fifty cents," said the driver over his shoulder.

Adams handed the man a five and climbed out of the cab. He was standing at the base of a forty-five-story tower of glass and steel, the corporate headquarters of Marshall Oil. He entered the lobby and headed for the security booth marked "Visitors."

"Charles Adams to see Mr. Wexler."

"Do you have an appointment?"

Adams handed the security officer a card. With the air of a martinet the officer read the designation and glanced at Adams with impatience "Is this some kind of joke?"

Without saying a word, Adams unfolded the copy of *The New York Times* that he had been carrying under his arm and handed it over. The officer looked at the pictures on the front page.

"I'm the man on the right."

The officer blanched. "I'm sorry, Mr. Adams. Right this way."

Allen Wexler was standing in front of the tall windows that lined the rear wall of his executive suite. Brown eyes, black hair, outwardly trim, wearing a blue pin-striped suit the jacket of which could be seen hanging from the back of the desk chair, silk suspenders emblazoned with oil derricks, and a white shirt of Egyptian cotton, Wexler looked at Adams with the vanquished expression of a man who has spent the last several years of his life trying to overturn the verdict of his conscience.

"It's not the how that interests me," Adams said flatly, removing his glasses. "But the why."

"I didn't know they would kill the girls."

Adams looked at the man across from him with little sympathy. Though the Hale murders were irrelevant to the case that Adams had built against the President of the United States, and, indeed, paled in significance to the universal danger engendered by Gerhardt's nuclear-weapons deal, they were not irrelevant to the moral imperatives that had structured his life or his burgeoning need for justice. As a human being he had been called upon to act, and act he would; he was not about to let it go.

In the intervening years since the murders, Wexler had obviously enjoyed the good life. Upon entering the executive suite Adams had been quick to notice the Monets on the walls, the Hepplewhite and Sheraton furniture, the Bokhara rug, perquisites of a corporate chairmanship that also offered up a salary of five million dollars a year.

So Adams sat down and presented another case, one largely based on conjecture, but accurate enough. Wexler's eyes glazed over with resignation and shame. And then he offered Wexler a deal.

Drake awoke with a start. It was dark. He looked up and saw Jack shaking him awake.

"Quick. Get dressed. We've got company."

"What's going on?" Jennifer whispered with alarm.

"We're leaving. *Now.* Let's go."

They dressed and ran into the living room just as the house was hit by a barrage of spotlights. The sliding glass doors were open, and Drake could see the lawn chair where Jack had been sleeping on the deck. A helicopter jumped over the ridge and zoomed toward them. Then the rotor wash of a second helicopter gusted the pines as it hovered overhead. Drake grabbed Jennifer by the arm and forced her to the floor as the assault team moved in, the doors and windows of the cabin exploding around them. As he went down he saw at least twenty men in black. They were wearing black jumpsuits and balaclava hoods, and from the way they moved through the house Drake could tell that they lacked the coordination of a well-trained unit though armed with CAR-15s and tactical shotguns. "Don't move," he whispered to Jennifer, holding her close. She was shaking. "Philip . . ."

He looked at Jack, and Henderson returned the look, a mixture of fear, rage, and calculation. Then he felt a boot between his shoulder blades, pressing him to the floor, and the cold steel of a twelve-gauge shotgun bearing down against the back of his neck as two men dragged Jennifer across the room. "Hey, look at me," the owner of the shotgun boasted, jabbing the shotgun into Drake's neck for emphasis. "I just bagged me a Navy SEAL."

"Shut the fuck up, Irons," the man beside him coughed in a hoarse whisper. Then another man moved in, sliding his feet to maintain a steady shooting platform, keeping his distance, his CAR-15 held at the high ready position, pointed directly at Drake's head—a man who knew what he was doing.

"You frisk him?"

The man beside Irons shook his head no.

The big man looked at Irons. "Didn't I teach you nothin'? Get cracking, mate."

"How're you holding up, Charlie?" McKendrick asked.

"I feel as though I've circumnavigated the globe." Adams glanced up at the mantelpiece clock. It was half past midnight. "They should be arriving any minute." He was exhausted but alert, at the age of seventy-two running on reserves that he wasn't quite sure he still possessed.

From the living-room window of Adams's town house McKendrick gazed down on the street as two limousines pulled up to the curb. Three men stepped out of the first limousine: Attorney General Everett Smith; Secretary of Defense Richard Elliot; and General Craig Hawking, Chief, Special Operations Command. Four Secret Service agents emerged from the second limousine, followed by the Vice President of the United States.

Adams rose from his chair as McKendrick disappeared downstairs to get the door. A moment later two Secret Service agents entered the room, glancing about as the other men followed. Hawking entered the room with McKendrick, and Adams could see that both men were visibly upset.

"What's wrong?" he asked.

"We got another message from Fox," Hawking answered. "Vaughan had Drake and the others picked up a half hour ago. Gerhardt's people conducted the raid. They're being taken back to the *Avatar.*"

Adams felt sick. He nodded to McKendrick and apologized to the others, inviting them to sit.

The Vice President looked at Adams with an expression of anxiety and concern. "Charles? May I ask what this is about?"

"Operation TORCHLIGHT has been blown, sir."

The group looked at Adams with alarm.

"What about our agents?" the Vice President asked.

"Alive for the moment. They will be tortured and killed if we don't get to them soon, however. That in part is why I've asked you here tonight." Adams glanced at McKendrick and Hawking. "We need your assistance in getting them out."

"Has anyone informed the President?" the Attorney General asked.

Adams looked at the Vice President. Thomas Young had owned a flourishing computer software business in the Silicon Valley before becoming governor of California. He was a bright and conscientious man of forty-six who loved skeet shooting. Adams hardly knew the man at all.

"Unfortunately, that's not an option."

"What? Why on earth not?"

Adams looked at the three men before him and saw that their expressions had shifted from concern to perplexity.

"Walt?"

McKendrick leaned over and pressed the button on the cassette recorder that he had placed on the butler's table in front of the Vice President, and for the next fifteen minutes the men listened in shocked silence to Terry Fox's confession.

"Jesus Christ . . ." muttered the Vice President of the United States after hearing Fox's panicked disavowal following the bombing, one of the subsequent messages that he had left on Hawking's answering machine.

The tape ended and Richard Elliot looked up at Adams in disbelief. "Are you certain that Fox is telling the truth?"

"I am," Adams replied. "First of all, the confession was taped the day before the bombing occurred. Second, the body of the Mauranian terrorist confirms that the bombing at Ocho Rios was not just a ghastly coincidence, but that Burnham was responsible. And third, I'm certain if we pry open the records of the bank they used to pay Burnham, we would find proof of that as well. But there's more."

Adams lifted a small pocket tape recorder from the mantelpiece. "The voice you're about to hear is that of Ricky Martinez, a former DEA agent assigned to Panama City in the mid-eighties. The next voice you'll hear belongs to Allen Wexler, chairman of Marshall Oil, who agreed to make a statement earlier this evening in the presence of his attorney when I visited him in Dallas."

Adams clicked the button, and the men listened. When the second tape was over, Richard Elliot held his head in his hands. "This is going to be worse than Watergate," he moaned.

"What about the tactical nuclear weapons?" the Vice President asked.

"Thankfully, that part of the operation has been contained, thanks to the agents Marshall and Vaughan betrayed. The nukes were being offered by a former member of the Politburo. Alexi Konalov. The KGB picked him up yesterday.

"Gentlemen, the tapes you've just heard are what the CIA commonly refers to as raw intelligence. Let me try to put this in perspective. About three years ago Gerhardt's adopted daughter discovered that Gerhardt was responsible for the Hale murders. Exactly how she made that discovery, we don't know. Irrelevant, really. Nevertheless, it provided her with sufficient motivation to turn Gerhardt in. At that point she began sending the CIA information concerning Gerhardt's activities, including, most recently, information concerning the nuclear deal Gerhardt was brokering between Konalov and the Iraqis. Then, shortly after Operation TORCHLIGHT's inception, Marshall got nervous."

"Regarding his past relationship with Gerhardt."

"That and the Hale murders—yes. He couldn't risk our taking Gerhardt into custody. So in desperation he turned to Vaughan. Vaughan offered Gerhardt a deal of some kind that Gerhardt apparently rejected. At that point Vaughan came up with the idea of bombing the Jamaican Parliament, hoping to create the illusion that the Mauranians were exporting their brand of communism—a scheme that would allow the President a way of canceling TORCHLIGHT without creating a firestorm within the administration. After the bombing was tied to the Mauranians, the President could claim that General McKendrick and I had been negligent and should be fired. And anyone else who chose to complain could be fired, too, with few repercussions, given the enormous popularity Marshall would enjoy having successfully invaded Maurania. And once that had occurred, TORCHLIGHT would be history. Then, apparently for reasons at which we can only guess, Burnham went off and did his own thing."

"Killing nine hundred people," Everett Smith murmured with sadness and disgust.

"Yes. Marshall and Vaughan covered it up and went on with the Mauranian ploy as planned."

"Martinez mentioned zirconium," the Vice President said.

"An essential compound in the manufacture of cluster bombs. Evidently Gerhardt and Marshall were shipping zirconium to Chile by way of Panama. Industrias Cardoen was Saddam Hussein's principal supplier of such weapons. With the ability to shred everything within ten football fields down to coleslaw, cluster bombs were just what Saddam needed to decimate the human waves that the Iranians were sending against his forces during the Iraq–Iran War. With Marshall's help, Gerhardt obtained the export licenses to have the stuff shipped to Panama, where it would be diverted to Chile."

"And no one found out about this?"

"There were officials who knew, but after the Gulf War everyone went into denial. Nobody wanted to discuss export licenses or anything else. Not after American boys had died in the Gulf War. Prior to Saddam's invading Kuwait, you see, the United States had been, in certain limited ways, assisting Iraq in their war with Iran. For good reason. Without Western assistance Iraq would have lost the war. And nobody in his right mind wanted that. In addition to controlling Iraq's abundant oil reserves, the Iranians would have turned Iraq into a breeding ground for Islamic terrorism. What later occurred in Afghanistan is a case in point. The Soviets kept the fundamentalists under

control. The Soviets gone, thanks in part to the Stingers we supplied to the Mujaheddin, Afghanistan became Terrorist Central.
The World Trade Center bombing was a direct result of that—an
example of what we in the intelligence community call blowback.
So, faced with the prospect of an Iranian victory in the Persian
Gulf, the United States began to tilt toward Iraq, despite our considerable reservations about Saddam Hussein. And as I said before, as we later learned from the situation in Afghanistan, we
were justified in doing so.

"There were, however, two repercussions. One, it embold-
ened Saddam to invade Kuwait. Two, it bolstered Saddam Hussein's nearly insatiable desire to obtain classified technology from
the West. And once the Iraqis began waving all those petrodollars
around, a number of corporations in western Europe and the
United States jockeyed for position. Gerhardt set up the procurement networks. Very complex and very difficult to trace, even
though the United States tried on numerous occasions to curtail
technology transfer when it pertained to weapons of mass destruction, and pressured other countries to do the same. Still,
thanks in large part to Gerhardt, Saddam was able to construct a
number of chemical- and biological-warfare facilities and came
very close to building an atomic bomb.

"Gerhardt's business relationship with Marshall was a part of
that network. Why Marshall got involved is something we don't
know. What we do know is that exportation of zirconium to Chile
was illegal. And when Hale became a government witness, agreeing to testify, this business relationship was suddenly about to be
exposed. Gerhardt started putting pressure on Marshall, who was
a senator at the time, urging him to use whatever contacts he had
developed to ferret out Hale's location. It was at this point that

Marshall got in touch with Wexler. Wexler was working for Justice at the time. He had just gone through a divorce, needed the money, hated his job, and figured that Hale was a scumbag anyway. So, having access to the Witness Protection Program files, Wexler turned over Hale's address to Marshall, who then handed it over to Gerhardt. Neither Wexler nor, apparently, Marshall expected Gerhardt to butcher the entire family."

"And a year later Wexler found himself on the fast track to the chairmanship of Marshall Oil," Thomas Young commented, shaking his head.

"Yes."

Anguished silence. The men, Adams could see, were dwelling on the implications of what they had heard, one of which was the unspoken certainty that once the scandal became public their party would lose the election.

Then Walter McKendrick spoke. "Gentlemen. The longer we delay, the greater the likelihood that we will be unable to prevent our people from being tortured and killed. I helped send them into harm's way, and I can get a group of men together and get them off that ship. It will be an unauthorized operation for which I will take full responsibility."

General Craig Hawking walked over and stood by McKendrick's side. "That goes for me, too."

Thomas Young stood and faced the two men standing before him. "Thank you very much, gentlemen, but that responsibility is not yours to take." He gazed at Adams. "It is mine."

And in one breathless second every man in the room knew that the transfer of power had begun, that they were looking at the man who would become, even for a brief few months until the election, the next President of the United States.

"Charles. You must be exhausted. Please sit," the Vice President said. Then he looked at the group assembled before him. "From what I can see, we've got a hell of a lot to accomplish in a very short amount of time. Walt? Craig? What's it going to take to assault that ship?"

She had betrayed him.

In the days following her disappearance Gerhardt could think of nothing else. He was obsessed by her betrayal, and the obsession was wearing him down. That afternoon he had napped until four o'clock. Sleep was his only refuge. He would swallow two Percodans with a glass of wine and knock himself out, awaking hours later, his mind blank with happiness an instant before the fires of memory consumed his soul.

From the night of her disappearance and his subsequent conversations with Vaughan he had been forced to confront the enormity of her deception. She had been feeding information to Adams for three years. For three years she had been planning his destruction. She had taken his love for her and had twisted it to her own designs.

He knew the lingering memory of the Hale murders, like blood on Lady Macbeth's hands, had threatened to stain the smooth marble surface of their life together. So he had been assiduous in his mourning. He told her that it had been the work of the cartels. But somehow she had learned the truth.

And now the tactical-nuclear-weapons deal had disintegrated along with everything else; overnight his greatest accomplishment had become his greatest humiliation. The KGB had rolled up Konalov and his men. He had gotten the word that morning when the Iraqi Minister of Defense had berated him over the phone, unconcerned about who might be listening in. It didn't matter. He was finished in this business. The Hizbollah affair had nearly destroyed his credibility; once his clients got wind of his latest debacle, no one would ever trust him again.

Now, as he sat in her office aboard the *Avatar*, he felt like a man without a country. He had thrown open the windows, but the magnificence of the ocean on this bright summer day seemed to mock him and he had drawn the shades. Even the ocean had become a hostile territory.

There was a knock on the door.

"What is it?" he demanded.

It was one of the security men Rexer had brought on board. "They're on the way, sir. They should be landing in fifteen minutes."

"Have Rexer bring them into the main salon."

He gazed at her things one last time. Then, on the wall above the bookcase, he noticed the gilded frame. The photograph was missing. And he knew exactly which photograph it was. Every time they had spoken in her office he had glanced at it with the proud satisfaction of a father whose exploits have taken on mythic proportions by their children. He had told her of the time he had spent there, and she had cherished the memory; it had been one of the things they had shared. But now as he stared at the empty frame he began to see the missing photograph from a different perspective. A woman's name formed on his lips, and he realized that for Jennifer there had been a deeper significance to the fortress at Montségur. He leapt at the frame, clawing it from the wall, tears of rage coursing down his cheeks. Instead of symbolizing her love for him, the empty frame mirrored his fate. The worship and love that had once been his now belonged to another. To the chatelaine of the mountain fortress.

Esclarmonde.

And as he stood over the broken frame, thinking that his life was over, he suddenly had an idea. Then he gathered himself, knowing what punishment to inflict on the woman who had betrayed him.

"Sir, I'm picking up an inbound chopper."

"Range?"

"Forty-six miles and closing fast. She's headed for the *Avatar.*"

In the Combat Information Center of the *Wasp,* Captain Bobby Hopf looked at the grim faces of the men surrounding him. A naval amphibious assault carrier, the *Wasp* had been part of a Marine Expeditionary Unit set to deploy to Maurania until it had been diverted, courtesy of Secretary of Defense Richard Elliot and Admiral Jack Tanner, Chief of Naval Operations, who were now present. Also filling the spacious quarters of the command center were General Walt McKendrick; General Craig Hawking, Chief of Special Operations Command; Lieutenant Commander John Kelly, the assault force commander; the two SEAL lieutenants who would lead the assault; the Aviation Combat Element commander; and the colonel in charge of the Marine Maritime Special Purpose Force that would act as a follow-on force once the SEALs had secured the *Avatar*'s main deck and bridge.

McKendrick looked at Hawking with a tension that was hard to conceal. "What do you want to do, Craig?"

Secretary of Defense Richard Elliot glanced up, incredulous. "We intercept them. That's what we do, goddamn it."

"Not a good idea," Hawking replied. "If there were only bad guys aboard it would be different—we could threaten to shoot them down. But with Drake, Henderson, and Jennifer aboard, they'll call our bluff. And we don't want to lose the element of surprise when we board that ship. Unfortunately, we have no choice but to stand down 'til we're ready."

"But what about our people?"

"If Gerhardt wanted them dead, they'd be dead already," Hawking observed. "My guess is that Gerhardt will hold them hostage until he's safe."

"Or play with them for a while," Elliot grumbled in frustration.

McKendrick shifted in his chair. "What's our ETA?"

"Captain?" Hawking asked.

Captain Hopf glanced at a console. "Forty minutes, sir."

"Can you get us there in thirty?" Kelly asked.

"Can't make any promises, son. Got the pedal to the metal as it is."

McKendrick shook his head. "We have to launch early, Craig."

"Can't take that chance. The Sea Knights don't have that kind of range. Send 'em early, and by the end of the operation those birds will be in the water—a lot of men with them. I'm sorry, gentlemen. We wait."

"Well, well," Gerhardt exclaimed. "What cozy little gathering do we have here?" He glanced at Rexer and at the three security men who stood over the prisoners. The security men were armed with Heckler and Koch MP-5s. One man handed off his weapon and removed the hoods as Jennifer, Drake, and Henderson lay propped against the sofa, bound and gagged.

The prisoners squinted in the bright sunset. Gerhardt examined them closely for a moment. Then he stepped in front of Jennifer. "Schätzelein," he cooed in mock solicitude. "Whatever on earth are you doing here?" He looked over at Rexer again, and the muscular security chief stepped forward and ripped the adhesive tape from her mouth. She screamed in agony. In anger and desperation, Drake lunged at Rexer but was knocked down by Irons. Laughing, Irons pressed his submachine gun against Henderson's head as Rexer casually walked over and kicked Drake hard in the stomach. Drake groaned, curling in pain.

"Easy, Dennis. We want Mr. Drake to dive later this afternoon," Gerhardt said, turning his attention once more to Jennifer. "Well? I'm waiting. What? Something wrong? No explanation for dear old Dad?"

She stared up at him in defiance, and deep in his soul Gerhardt could feel the crazy coursing of blood as the very quality he had most loved in her, the very thing in her that had reminded him of himself, the quality from which their kinship had sprung, was turned against him.

"No? I didn't think so," Gerhardt seethed. "Then perhaps you won't mind if I acquaint you with some of what *I've* been going through." He walked over to an intercom and pressed a button. A moment later the galley door opened and Clarence appeared. Clarence looked at the three men with guns, his eyes suddenly wide with fright, and Jennifer's face twisted in horror as Rexer raised his MP-5 and pumped three rounds into the elderly Jamaican's chest. The old man crumpled to the ground. She was crying hysterically now. "Shut up," Gerhardt commanded. He walked over and backhanded her twice across the face. Then to Irons he said, "Lock her in her room. Get the bitch out of my sight."

Drake lay on his side, staring up at Gerhardt with hatred.

"I know what you're thinking," the arms dealer said with vindictive glee. "You're thinking that if I let Strickland and Rexer touch her, you're going to kill me. Actually, the thought did cross my mind, since they did such a nice job with the Hale children."

"That's right, mate," Rexer added, placing a boot on the side of Drake's head as he squatted down to within a few feet of Drake's face. Drake could smell the big South African's rancid breath. "After I worked on the brats, I gave Hale the knife and told him to do his kids a favor. The fucker slit the throats of his own children. Couldn't take their screaming anymore. Then he begged me to do the same to him. I put the fucker out of his misery then."

They were kneeling on the afterdeck, hands on top of their heads. Behind them, two men were dragging Clarence by the arms. They dropped the elderly chef on the deck, and Clarence groaned. Strickland looked at Henderson and Drake and laughed as the two men snapped a sixty-pound weight belt around the Jamaican's thin frame and tossed him overboard.

"Sharks be eatin' good tonight," Billy Ray Irons joked.

"What about these two?" asked the other.

"The boss wants them kept alive," Strickland said, licking the perspiration off his mustache. "In the meantime, they can earn their keep. Whadaya say, boys? Feel like diving?"

They were in the water. It was eight-thirty in the evening and the sun looked huge on the horizon, flaring red where it touched the sea. There were no support divers this time, no oxygen lines dangling in the water, just the inflatable, tethered to the *Avatar* by a line. Maki and his team of divers were gone, replaced by a security element of at least twenty men. Drake could see a guard on the observation deck, armed with a CAR-15. Another man stood beside him unpacking something from a long plastic case that sat atop the Formica bar next to the pool. Then Drake saw that it was a Stinger. Gerhardt's men were armed with shoulder-fired guided missiles.

They descended to fifty feet, where Henderson scribbled a message on an underwater slate and passed it to Drake. The message said: "You OK?"

Drake nodded. He was thinking of Jennifer, and the desperation was tearing him apart.

Henderson wrote another message. "Have to disarm guard when we climb aboard."

Drake rubbed the slate clean and wrote: "Any ideas?"

Shaking his head, Henderson took back the slate, and a few seconds later handed Drake the reply: "Think of something. Maybe we could use gold as distraction, weight belts as weapons. Work out details on the way up."

"We got 'em in the water, sir," Strickland said. "Jennifer's locked up tight. We'll be under way in an hour, as soon as the explosives are rigged."

"Did you cut the buoy line?"

"Not yet. I want to give the assholes time to swim inside the wreck first. Wouldn't want to ruin the surprise." Strickland chuckled.

"Send two men out in the inflatable. When Drake and Henderson surface, kill them. Make it hurt. Give whoever volunteers for the job a little incentive to do it right. Let me know when they get back. I want to see the bodies." Gerhardt swiveled in his office chair, his cheeks flushed. "And tell Dennis that we're leaving in an hour and a half. I want those charges set to go off immediately after. I'll tell Spector. If anyone finds out about the explosives, you know what to do. I want everything to appear as normal as possible."

Black water surrounded them. In the penumbra of his dive light Drake could see plankton sweeping past, and as he descended he could feel the current becoming stronger. Jack halted, unsure if he should continue; they were consuming too much air pulling themselves down the buoy line. Drake dropped down beside him and took over the lead. The rushing water felt cold against their faces.

They pulled themselves down, hand over hand. Then, just as Drake thought they would have to give up and return to the surface, the current subsided. Drake shined his light on his dive computer: 185 feet. Darkness surrounded them. They had dropped into a pocket of still water created by the *Norfolk*'s superstructure. Swinging his light toward the port rail, he could see the current rushing past, tapering toward the bow with increasing velocity. They dropped down through the open hatch.

The gun deck stretched before them, illuminated by their lights. Drake handed the end of his penetration line to Jack and drifted down through the hole to the berth deck, trying to come up with an idea that would not get them killed. He swam beneath the rotting overhead, sweeping his light in front of him, then up along the framework of rusted steel. Large sections of the overhead were missing. He turned and saw the beam of Jack's light shining down in the darkness. The side of his head throbbed where Rexer had pressed his boot. His ribs ached. He kept on, thinking of Jennifer and the way her hair smelled of jasmine. Then he could see the paymaster's issuing room, standing before him like the darkened hangar where Noriega's jet had been stored. He looked back at his penetration line trailing in the distance. Jack's light was invisible somewhere in the darkness beyond, the man who had saved his life watching his back. Jack had been right, of course. They would have to fight. McKendrick and Adams would never make it in time.

But as he swam toward the paymaster's issuing room, Drake knew that it wasn't going to be easy. The moment they approached the *Avatar*, the thermal-imaging cameras would pick up their movement. And as a precaution Rexer had confiscated the knives as well as the flares they always carried in case they were swept away by the current.

The weight belt idea wasn't bad, but they were going to need a bigger diversion than the gold. He thought about the field of eight-inch shells lying two decks below. Some of those munitions were probably live, but getting one to the surface would require too much air. Besides, what would they do once they got it on board—if they got it on board? Initiate a Mexican standoff? No. That wasn't going to work. The flares might have come in handy, but Rexer had confiscated them—or had he?

Flares.

Instinctively Drake looked up, as though gazing at the surface. Rexer might have taken their supply of flares, but Drake knew where he could find more. And a nice five-gallon plastic tank of gasoline to go along with them. All within arm's reach.

The inflatable.

Forget the gold; if they started for the surface now they could cut their decompression in half, allowing plenty of time to quietly surface when they were not expected. They could silently rise up behind the inflatable beyond the range of the cameras and grab what they needed. And chances were fairly good that they would get away with it. The trickiest part would be getting close enough to the *Avatar* to toss the open gas tank onto the afterdeck and then a lighted flare. Maybe they could send up a lift bag alongside the yacht. That would create a diversion, especially if the assholes thought there was a quarter of a million dollars' worth of gold dangling beneath it. Drake was getting excited. Goddamn. This was going to work! Once the deck was burning they would climb aboard and subdue one of the guards. Once armed, they would quickly hunt Gerhardt down. And with a gun to the arms dealer's head, they would control the ship. Chances were good that Jennifer was still alive. Gerhardt would want her to suffer. Which in the scheme of things meant that he and Jack would be the first to die. And they sure as shit weren't dead yet.

He swam back to the gun deck, signaled to Jack that he was okay, and penciled: "I have a plan." Then he wrote the plan down in detail and handed it to Jack. He could tell that Jack was excited, too.

They ascended toward the main-deck hatch, and Drake directed his light up into the open water. The current had shifted. Looking up through the open hatch, Drake felt as though he were standing inside a storm cellar, gazing up at a hurricane. He stared at the moving water, then, holding his mask in place, slipped his head above the hatch, peeking in the direction of the buoy line.

The line was gone.

Drake dropped down beside Henderson and wrote on the slate: "They cut the line."

Jack shook his head and wrote beneath it: "Knew those assholes would do something."

Okay, so that idea's out. Think of another, Drake thought. But as he racked his brain he knew that whatever they decided, his resolve would go unchecked. For he had learned something in the past ten days, since the night McKendrick had stood before him on the beach in what seemed a lifetime ago, evoking the memory of his father. He had learned that what was good in life was good because men and women made it so, often at great personal cost, sometimes even at the cost of their lives. That was the sacred trust that bound men and women to the past and what tied the past to the future. That is what transformed men and women into Mankind—the idea that no matter what happened, you had an obligation to go on. Not to fulfill your destiny, but to act in passionate defiance of it. Like Hector of Troy. Or Arthur of Camelot. Or the thirteenth-century heroine of Montségur, Esclarmonde de Perelha. You went on to protect the people you love. You went on to prevent men like Gerhardt from destroying the world.

Shining his light up, Drake extended his right hand through the main-deck hatch. The current buffeted his hand as though he had slipped it outside the window of a speeding car. They couldn't stay inside the *Norfolk* much longer without using air that they would need for decompression. They would have to bail out and work the problem from there. But what if there was a surface current? They would be swept away. *Don't think about that. Think about the problem at hand.*

He took his penetration line and rubbed it along the edge of a rusted band of steel, cutting the line into an eight-foot section. Then he had another idea. He handed the line to Henderson and swam along the gun deck, scanning the framework until he found a bar of rusted steel. Hovering a foot above the gun deck, he began bending it back and forth, expecting the rotted deck to collapse at any minute. Henderson swam over and immediately caught on to what Drake was up to and began hunting for a weapon himself. Soon he found one, having dropped down through a large opening in the gun deck to the infirmary. He returned to Drake's side wielding an L-shaped section of steel, part of a bed frame. A minute later, Drake had detached the steel bar. They were ready.

Beneath the open main-deck hatch Drake made two small loops at either end of the eight-foot line, then clipped one end to Jack's harness and the other end to his own so that they would not become separated during their ascent and decompression. Then, holding their masks in place, they vaulted into the current.

They bumped once along the foredeck and up over the turret as they inflated their vests, Drake's fins brushing the barrel of an eight-inch gun. They were speeding toward the starboard rail, their lights flashing along pieces of wreckage and then out into the dark. Ten feet above the foredeck Drake began purging air from his vest to slow his ascent. His light, dangling from the lanyard on his wrist, swung around and he could see Henderson doing the same. Suddenly they jerked to a stop.

Monofilament.

The current rushed past them with such force that the second stages were nearly ripped from their mouths. Their masks flooded. If they hadn't worn their mask straps beneath their hoods they would have lost them completely. Drake felt cold water in his nostrils, his body automatically curbing his reflex to breathe. He forced himself to breathe anyway. He could see the beam of Jack's light fluttering behind him eight feet away. They were bucking against the current that surged all around them. A long strand of monofilament had snagged his tank valves. Straining against the current, Drake reached up, located the line, and tried to free it. No dice. Then with both hands he pushed the bar of steel over his head and began working it back and forth against the line. An instant later, the line snapped.

They were free. Sweat trickling down his arms and chest, Drake cleared his mask and checked his depth as Jack pulled himself close. They were drifting in the current at 150 feet. Drake signaled that he was okay and together they began their ascent. The current began to subside. The silence echoed around them, the water no longer rushing past their ears. They began their decompression at fifty feet, switching off their lights to save power. Then, in the darkness, they heard the sound of an approaching outboard.

From his seventh-floor Director's suite at Langley, Martin Vaughan congratulated himself on a job well done. The situation had nearly spun out of control, but Drake, Henderson, and the girl had been safely contained. It was unlikely that Burnham would ever show his face again—not if he knew what was good for him. And Adams and McKendrick? They were out in the cold. They didn't know anything about Wexler. And even if they suspected that Marshall had once been Gerhardt's business partner, what could they prove? If they went before the press, their accusations would sound delusional. Bobby Ray Inman stuff. Besides, the press wasn't about to rehash something that had skirted the edges of the Iran-Contra affair, even if it did involve the President of the United States. They were on the prowl for fresh meat. And Vaughan had dangled before them the juiciest tenderloin of all. Maurania. Already within the halls of Congress he could hear the tom-toms pounding.

Vaughan shuffled his papers together. He had just put the finishing touches on the President's address to the nation scheduled for the following night—the second that week. At eight o'clock next evening the President of the United States would demand that the government of Maurania extradite the individuals responsible for the bombing at Ocho Rios, a necessary prelude to the invasion soon to follow. The President's previous address had been terrific, but Vaughan had really pulled out the stops for this one. He would review it with the President first thing tomorrow morning.

A president who would be a shoo-in for reelection.

Five decks below in the *Avatar*'s hold, Dennis Rexer was wiring the last of the charges. He had placed the high explosive amidships, then strung the incendiary charges along the *Avatar*'s four watertight compartments. The high-explosive charge would detonate first at their convenience, once they were aboard the chopper and hovering nearby. The charge had been rigged against the starboard hull in such a way that the *Avatar* would remain afloat for no longer than an hour. The incendiary charges would begin exploding fifteen minutes later, the initial explosions bracketing Jennifer's room so that she would roast alive as she lay tied to the bedposts. Rexer chuckled to himself as he crimped the final blasting cap. For an old guy, the boss really had a sense of humor.

• • •

The sun had slipped below the horizon and darkness was falling fast. The mercenary manning the helm of the inflatable throttled back the engine so that his partner could glass the water once more, searching for Drake and Henderson's bubble trail. They were a quarter of a mile astern of the *Avatar*, drifting along with the mild current. Drake and Henderson had been in the water for an hour. The ocean was glossy and flat, and within seconds the two mercenaries had spotted the twin convex eruptions knuckling the surface of the water two hundred feet away. Together with Strickland they had worked out a plan. They would wait until Drake and Henderson were out of air and had surfaced. Then the fun would begin. They had even brought along a pair of night-vision goggles to carry the game into the night. They would toss a couple of fragmentation grenades into the water as Drake and Henderson bobbed helplessly on the surface, not close enough to kill, but close enough to cause internal bleeding. Then they would take turns with the speargun, aiming for the extremities. A couple of hours later, when Drake and Henderson resembled pincushions, they would handcuff the two divers together and tow them back to the *Avatar* to collect the prize money.

But the mercenary named Sam was getting bored. When they were fifty feet behind Drake and Henderson's position, he slipped on a tank.

"Hey? Where do you think you're going?" his partner asked.

"Need some action. I'm gonna pop these guys in the ass and jump-start the night."

"But Strickland said to keep our distance—"

"Fuck him. I'm the one with the speargun. What's he think these guys are gonna do?"

He picked up a Russian pneumatic speargun equipped with a laser sight and slipped quietly into the dark water, zeroing in on the two light beams faintly visible below him in the distance. Alone in the inflatable, George switched on a spotlight and concentrated it on the bubbles rising to the surface in front of him fifty feet away.

Moving silently underwater, Sammy brought the speargun up to the ready position. He had spent his youth spearfishing in the Florida Keys, but he had never speared a man before and was looking forward to the experience. Ahead, the light beams were clearer now, though in the darkness he still couldn't see the divers. Didn't matter. He would wait until the last minute to switch on the laser. As he moved closer, he could see a vague bundle from which the lights extended. Then, as he crept closer still, he realized that something was wrong. Instinctively he halted. Taking aim, he flicked on the laser and the thin red line struck the bundle, but as he directed the laser down, expecting to see torso and legs, the beam extended again into the darkness. An icicle of fear expanded in his chest and he listened, not daring to breathe, to the exhaust bubbles coming from the bundle ahead of him, realizing that they were continuous, not the rhythmic sound of two divers decompressing. Unwilling to admit his mistake, he bolted forward and for a horrified instant gazed upon the empty scuba rig hovering in the water. Two lights had been tied to the tank valves, their beams flaring out into the black water. Two second stages had been turned mouthpiece up, slowing leaking air.

Panicked, he kicked toward the surface, ascending three feet before he was grasped from behind, two powerful arms ripping the mask from his face and the second stage from his mouth as another set of hands wrestled away the speargun. He reached behind, clawing at the diver who was propelling him down into the depths. A steel bar pressed against his throat, and he struggled violently as his lungs burned for air. Then, at a depth of seventy-five feet, the pressure around his neck subsided and he reflexively inhaled, choking on a lungful of water as the light vanished from his eyes.

Drake ascended, his lungs aching for air. Even with the speargun he knew that he would have no chance of eliminating the other mercenary unless he surfaced behind the inflatable. When he could swim no farther he silently broke to the surface, fully expecting his head to explode from a well-placed shot. He was fifteen feet astern of the inflatable, and in the dark he could see the back of the other mercenary as the man stood at the helm directing the spotlight down on the bubbles rising in the water in front of him. A sound-suppressed MP-5 was slung over the mercenary's right shoulder. Quietly Drake lifted the speargun from the water and moved in until he was six feet from the inflatable, feeling a twinge of guilt about shooting the man in the back. Then he thought about Jennifer. He squeezed the trigger.

The spear entered the small of the man's back, plunging upward through the heart and breaking a rib as it exited through his chest. In shocked disbelief the man looked down at the barbed point protruding from his chest, then turned and looked at Drake and let loose an agonized scream. Drake jerked the line back as hard as he could and the mercenary screamed again, spinning around as he tumbled backward over the gunwale and into the water, floundering a minute before going limp. Drake tossed the MP-5 into the inflatable and climbed aboard as Jack surfaced twenty feet away. The *Avatar*'s running lights sparkled in the distance.

. . .

On the observation deck of the *Avatar* Billy Ray Irons tipped the flask against his lips and took another pull. He was sucking down some Tennessee small-batch corn whiskey and feeling good about it, though not quite good enough. He glanced down at the deck chair to his right where he had laid the thirty-five-pound Stinger and removed a small glass vial from his pocket, inserting it into each nostril and tapping twice. He sniffed deeply and sighed to no one in particular: "Oh yeah, baby. . . ." He held the vial of cocaine up to Locotelli. "Want any?"

"You're fucking crazy, Irons."

He hadn't fired a Stinger since his army days in Bosnia. Didn't matter. Not with the kind of money he was making. His mother had told him about the ad. Security work. High pay. Military background required. The fucker was right up his alley. They had given him a pager and told him to be on call—the South African and the bald-headed fuck. Then came the Hale job. Rexer had carved those people up pretty bad, but they had paid him twenty grand just for making Hale watch. Twenty grand just for holding some guy's head.

His stomach grumbled. He turned toward Locotelli and flicked his cigar overboard. "Hey, dickhead. Cover me while I grab a sandwich."

"Wait a minute. . . ."

"What?"

"I thought I heard something. A scream . . . out there . . ."

Irons cocked an ear to the wind and shot a skeptical glance at his counterpart. The fucker had been jumpy all afternoon, ever since Rexer had shot the nigger.

"There it is again."

"You dumbfuck," Irons said with derision. "Sammy and

George are carving up the two assholes we brought back with the girl. They're out in the inflatable. Lighten up, Locotelli, will ya?"

Through the large rectangular windshield of the *Avatar*'s bridge Captain Alberto Alvarez looked out upon the darkened sea, his own mood darkening as he watched the trail of red sparks drifting down from the observation deck as one of the guards flicked his cigar into the sea. He did not care for the security team that Strickland and Rexer had brought aboard the *Avatar.* These people had no ties to any of the people on board and they showed no compunction about killing in cold blood—not that Strickland and Rexer were any different. Still, in the past, Gerhardt had kept these people under control. Now things were falling apart fast. After Jennifer's disappearance Gerhardt's behavior had turned erratic. And the shooting of Clarence had shocked the entire crew. It was time to make a move. No two ways about it. Perhaps he should fly to Mexico. Over the years he had stashed away enough money to live in comfort should the need arise. Now it was time. Once they reached Lyford Cay he would make arrangements. He smiled to himself—one of the advantages to commanding your own ship was that you could get away with things like this. Too bad about the girl. What a luxury it would be to take her along. But that could never happen now. Such a shame. He would have enjoyed having a piece of that.

He looked out the window, smiling to himself, dreaming of naked women tanning themselves on tropical isles. Then the Chief Engineer's voice came over the radio: "Engine room to bridge."

"Alvarez."

"Captain, there's something funny going on down here. I think you better take a look."

They were out of their dry suits, cruising back toward the *Avatar* at half-speed, Henderson manning the helm while Drake gathered the equipment they would need. The inflatable had proved to be a mini-arsenal, thanks to the two mercenaries who were now drifting facedown in the Gulf Stream. In addition to the MP-5, Drake found two sets of handcuffs, a pair of night-vision goggles, four fragmentation grenades, and two spare magazines. In a cabinet beneath the helm lay a box containing a Very pistol and seven multistar flares as well as several smoke flares and a knife. He handed the knife to Jack along with the Very pistol and a couple of grenades and smoke flares. Then he stuffed the rest of the gear into his pockets, thinking that if the mercenaries had dropped the grenades into the water it would be he and Jack floating facedown in the Gulf Stream, and not the two assholes they had killed fifteen minutes earlier.

Once they reached the *Avatar* they would have to move quickly and quietly. Since the people monitoring the thermal-imaging cameras were expecting the mercenaries' return, they would have no problem cruising up to the swim platform undetected. The key lay in eliminating the guard on the afterdeck before they were recognized and without alerting the two guards on the observation deck. If they were able to accomplish those two vital tasks, they stood a good chance of reaching Jennifer. But if they were spotted on the afterdeck and got bogged down in a firefight, they would have no chance at all.

Their plan was simple: They would eliminate the guard on the afterdeck, then take a staircase down to the corridor to Jennifer's stateroom, where Rexer's men had dragged her two hours before. Once they had rescued Jennifer, they would return to the inflatable, where Henderson would prepare to cast off while Drake eliminated the two guards on the observation deck, grabbed a Stinger, and soaked the rest in gasoline. A well-placed flare, shot from the inflatable, would take care of the rest. Then they would head for the nearest ship, using the inflatable's radar system and radio. There were several ships in the area; maybe they were rescue craft.

Drake lifted the binoculars to his eyes. They were an eighth of a mile out, approaching the *Avatar* from the port side so that they could take out the guard on the afterdeck without worrying about a stray round smashing into the sliding glass doors that separated the lounge from the main salon. On the observation deck a guard peered nervously into the darkness while the other guard raised a flask to his lips and teetered as he gripped the rail. Drake recognized the mercenary with the flask. It was Irons. Irons put the flask to his lips again and gave his partner the finger.

"See anything?" Henderson asked.

"Yeah. Irons. He's up on the observation deck getting smashed, and his buddy's having a tough time handling it."

"What about the guy on the afterdeck?"

"Smoking a cigarette. Taking it easy."

They were moving quickly now, skimming the water, the *Avatar*'s lighted decks expanding as they angled in toward the swim platform. On the observation deck Locotelli, alerted by the whining of the inflatable's engine, looked out into the dim light surrounding the *Avatar.* The guard on the afterdeck tossed his cigarette overboard and looked in their direction, too. Drake felt a nervous flutter in the pit of his stomach. He slung the MP-5 over his shoulder, barrel down, and turned himself sideways so that his features would be partially obscured as he stood in the bow, coiling line. They came abreast of the yacht, and with an oily baseball cap snugged down on his head, Jack throttled back the engine as Drake gave the thumbs-up sign to the guard above, who waved and moved off. There was no sign of Irons.

They were thirty feet from the port side of the swim platform, and the afterdeck guard leaned over the rail, his weapon slung over his shoulder, barrel up, waiting to catch the line. "Come on, come on, I haven't got all day," he grumbled, and Drake tossed him the line so sloppily that it bounced off the stern rail and onto the swim platform. Cursing, the guard climbed down to the swim platform, and Drake leveled his weapon and fired, killing the man instantly with a single round to the head. The mercenary slumped to his knees and fell facedown on the swim platform.

Quickly Henderson nosed the inflatable up against the *Avatar* and Drake hopped out, tied off the line, handed the guard's MP-5 to Jack, and slid the body into the water, allowing the current to do the rest. Henderson aimed his weapon up toward the observation deck, where they could hear belching followed by the raucous sound of Billy Ray Irons's laughter. Otherwise the *Avatar* was quiet, the afterdeck deliberately darkened to enhance the guard's night vision. They moved up onto the deck, when suddenly they heard voices on the helicopter platform coming toward them. Gerhardt and someone else. The tail of the Sikorsky projected out over the top of the lounge. Jack kept his weapon pointed up in that direction as Drake hit the button on the lift and covered the afterdeck. They descended into the equipment room, out of sight. Through the heavy screened enclosure they could see a mercenary watching TV and munching a sandwich. Drake opened the enclosure and the mercenary looked at Drake and scrambled for his weapon. Drake shot the man twice in the chest, then hopped off the lift and switched out the lights. Despite the detour, Drake was feeling optimistic. They were almost there.

She was lying on her back, her hands and feet tied to the bedposts, and through the open windows of her stateroom she could hear the sound of the approaching inflatable. They had gone out to ambush Philip and Jack, and now they were returning. She knew about the plan because the three men guarding her had joked about it, sensing her growing panic. But she had calmed herself, evoking the image of a woman deep in prayer, leading a procession down the mountainside. Like Esclarmonde she would ignore the men charged with overseeing her death. And she would continue to believe that Drake and Henderson were alive until proven otherwise. She knew that Gerhardt would want her to view the bodies to increase her suffering. But even then she would not submit. She closed her eyes. There was nothing they could do to her now.

Gerhardt had been standing in the corridor opposite Jennifer's office on the bridge deck, watching Spector carry the last of the luggage out to the glass-enclosed reception area. He had informed Alvarez that he would be leaving for a couple of days, and the Colombian had accepted the explanation as routine. Now, as he made final arrangements to leave the *Avatar* for good, Gerhardt wondered if perhaps he should order Spector to load the Stingers on board as well. Imported from Saudi Arabia following the Gulf War, they had cost him plenty, including a summer cruise to Dubrovnik, where they had been loaded aboard. Jennifer had spent the week in Venice. He had sailed back up the Adriatic and had met her at the Hôtel des Bains. She had taken him to see Giovanni Bellini's *Pietà* at the Correr. He shivered at the memory. No. He would have to leave the Stingers behind. There could be nothing left in his life that would remind him of the whore who had once been his daughter. He would destroy the *Avatar*, and sell the houses. He would expunge her from memory. Only then would he be free of the pain that lashed his soul.

Spector mounted the staircase with a large valise in hand, and together they stepped out onto the helicopter platform.

"There're two open suitcases in my stateroom," Gerhardt commanded. "I haven't quite finished packing, but everything's laid out on the bed. Take care of that for me, will you. I have a few more papers in my office to collect."

Spector nodded in compliance, and Gerhardt looked down past the afterdeck, noticing for the first time the inflatable bobbing in the darkness as the sound of drunken laughter filtered down from the observation deck. Gerhardt flushed with anger. "Where's Gerald?"

"In his stateroom, I think. Taking a shower."

"Get him. Go to the bridge and get a master key. I want to talk to him. Now."

Gerald Strickland was leisurely soaping his dick when Spector barged into the bathroom. He dropped the soap and glared at the breathless chopper pilot in a fit of rage. "WHAT THE FUCK DO YOU THINK YOU'RE DOING!"

Spector couldn't keep a straight face. "The boss is going apeshit. The guys you sent out in the inflatable are back, and nobody bothered to tell him. He wants you topside. Guess you and your date better pack it in."

Without bothering to rinse, Strickland stepped out of the shower, dressed, collected his radio and MP-5, and headed for the afterdeck, thinking that his ass was in a sling, sure as God grew little green apples. He reached the main salon, looked out the sliding glass doors, and saw that the afterdeck was empty. *What the hell?* He stepped onto the afterdeck and peered down at the inflatable, looking for bodies. Nothing. *If those cocksuckers fucked up . . . And where in Christ's sake is the guard?*

He walked over to the lift and pressed the button with the idea of checking out the equipment room, then the crew's recreation room beyond. He wanted to get the problem solved before getting his ass chewed by Gerhardt. Damage control. He descended on the platform and, looking through the screened enclosure inside the equipment room, saw that the lights were out. A television cast a flickering cobalt shadow across the opposite wall. A trail of shiny liquid too thick to be water led out across the black linoleum floor. *Oil?* He stepped off the lift and crouched beside the puddle. The scent of copper filled his nostrils. *Jesus. Did they drag bodies in here?* He got up and reached for the light switch. From inside his pocket the radio beeped twice—his private line. Gerhardt. *Fuck.*

"What's happened to the men you sent out in the inflatable? Where are the bodies of Henderson and Drake? Well? I'm waiting for an answer!"

"I don't have one, sir."

"You goddamn get one! You hear me? Where's Dennis?"

"Still rigging the explosives."

"When he's done I want him guarding the chopper. I can't depend on any of the morons you hired as a security team. And there's a man on the observation deck. Drunk."

Cursing, Strickland slipped the radio back into his pocket. He paused, sensing movement nearby to his right. He tightened his grip on the MP-5 and began to bring the barrel on line. Too late. A heavy steel bar slammed into his mouth, pulverizing his lips and shattering his teeth back to the molars.

"What time are the explosives set to go off? Jack, give him something to write with."

Henderson tossed a small notepad and a pen onto the floor where Strickland sat slumped against the compressor. The door to the soundproofed compressor room was closed.

Strickland squinted at the notepad and coughed up more teeth and blood through his mashed lips. He picked up the pen, wrote something on the paper, and shoved the notepad aside. Drake picked it up. The message said, "Fuck you."

"Tough guy, huh?" Drake observed lightly. "Jack, I think it's time we handcuff this sorry sack of whale shit to the compressor. Right hand only—that's the one he writes with; presumably that's the one he wipes his ass with, too."

"I thought he used Rexer's tongue."

"What're you gonna do?" Strickland tensed for another blow.

"I'm going to tell you a little story, that's what I'm going to do. You see, Gerald, in about thirty seconds we'll be saying goodbye and the lights are going to go out and you're going to be sitting here all alone, except for your buddy over there," Drake said, indicating the dead man, "and he's not going to be much help. And shortly after the explosions occur this room is going to fill up with water. It's going to start trickling in around your feet and then it's going to rise up icy cold around your chest and then it's going to climb up your neck and then you're gonna be sticking that ugly schnozzola of yours straight up in the air while straining with both hands to lift that compressor off the floor. At that point you'll be sucking down your last breath. Now, people say that drowning is painless. Maybe so. But I got to tell you, Gerald, the last guy I pulled out of the *Andrea Doria* had thrashed around so violently that he had lacerations all over his face. So, being a considerate man, I'm going to offer you a deal."

"What kind of deal?" Strickland asked skeptically.

"Tell us when those charges are set to explode, and I'll guarantee you a way out of here. Not that you'll be able to free yourself right away, of course. But you'll be able to save your sorry ass."

"Promise?"

"Gerald? Would I lie to you?"

Strickland thought about this for a moment. Then, figuring he had no choice in the matter, he confessed, "Rexer will detonate the high-explosive charge when we're in the air. It's set to go off against the hull somewhere amidships and slowly scuttle the ship. The incendiary charges go off fifteen minutes after that, in ten-minute intervals. Starting just forward of Jennifer's room."

"What time does the chopper leave?"

"Ten minutes."

Without speaking, Drake opened the door. There was no way they could sabotage the helicopter. The instant Spector got behind the controls and realized something was wrong, he would inform Gerhardt and the alarm would go off. Gerhardt would kill Jennifer and have them hunted down. They had to rescue Jennifer first, maintaining the element of surprise.

They stepped outside the compressor room.

"Hey! What about me!" Strickland demanded. "You fucking promised me a way out of here, you lying cocksucker!"

Drake reached inside his pocket and removed the serrated diving knife and tossed it into Strickland's lap.

"Won't work on the handcuffs, Gerald. Think of it as a gift from Katie and Monica Hale."

With an anticipation he had not known since the Hale murders, Dennis Rexer was now hurrying forward through the watertight compartments, activating the timers on the incendiary charges. He was in the engine room bending over a device when Alvarez tapped him on the shoulder. Because of the noise of the turbines he had not heard the Captain or the Chief Engineer approach.

"Hey! What do you think you're doing?" Alvarez shouted with indignation, peering over Rexer's shoulder. "What's that you've got there?"

"None of your fuckin' business, mate."

"Explosives?"

"Now you've ruined it for yourself." He drew a silenced Beretta and shot the Chief Engineer in the chest. The man tumbled backward against a turbine and slumped to the deck.

"You maniac," Alvarez shouted. "What do think you're doing!"

"This." The big South African grinned, pointing the nine-millimeter at the Colombian's bearded face and pulling the trigger. *"Vaya con Díos, maricón."*

• • •

"Hey, Locotelli, look at this! I'm watering the fish!"

With belly outthrust and his pants around his ankles, Billy Ray Irons cradled his hands behind his head and directed a stream of urine into a large rectangular hole. The access panel to the aquarium lay upended three feet away.

"Oh, my God—" In a panic Locotelli peered down over the forward rail, then rushed to the stern rail of the observation deck, expecting to see either Strickland or Rexer charging up the staircase, preparing to kick ass. What he saw instead was the shadowy figure of a man crossing the afterdeck while another emerged from the lift, then a muzzle flash an instant before his head exploded. And like the headless horseman, Locotelli soared through the night air, slamming straight into Billy Ray Irons's backside.

Drake raced up the stairs. Henderson hopped off the lift and crouched at the foot of the staircase to provide cover. Their luck had run out, and Drake had to get to Irons before Irons could alert the whole ship. What he feared most was now happening. They were getting bogged down in a firefight. And they were running out of time.

He was falling.

His MP-5 submachine gun clattering against the fiberglass, his heart revving like a turbocharged engine, Billy Ray Irons plunged into the aquarium. He thrashed to the surface, pants around his ankles, kicking like a mermaid and coughing up water.

He moaned and gazed frantically about the lighted space,

praying that he was somehow mistaken, that he had fallen into the swimming pool instead. But he saw Gerhardt gaping at him from the other side of the glass. Then, to his horror, he became aware of a long torpedo-shaped object hovering in the blue water only five feet away. *My gun? Where the fuck is my gun?* His shaking sent fine tremors lapping against the glass. *It's slung over your shoulders, you idiot!*

But the barracuda had thoughts of its own. He was eyeing the baby eel that had suddenly begun to dance in the shimmering water. It was a good deal shorter than the eels he was accustomed to eating lately, almost too short to bother. But what was that behind it? An egg sac? He hadn't tasted one of those yummy morsels in ever so long. Not since he was a young stud cruising the coral walls of the Caymans. Looked like the eel man was serving up a two-course dinner tonight. He parted his hungry jaws in anticipation, and lunged.

Gerhardt had been in his office, collecting the last of his papers, when he heard the splash. He hurried into the main salon, papers still in hand, and gaped in disbelief at the man thrashing about inside the aquarium. The man was naked from the waist down, his pants around his ankles. Gerhardt reached for his radio but couldn't speak, too stupefied to do anything but stare. The man looked at him in supplication before they both became aware of another set of eyes, glowing gold inside the tank. The man turned and gazed down through the clear water, and his eyes suddenly went wide with fear. The barracuda lunged, and Gerhardt could hear Billy Ray Irons's strangled screams echoing inside the tank as the powerful fish tore at the mercenary's crotch, Irons thrashing wildly as he desperately pulled at the slippery fish, the water turning bright red around his midsection. Then Irons had the submachine gun up and was firing, the glass aquarium shattering and crashing to the floor as the entire room resounded with gunfire and Irons's terrified screaming as barracuda and man, still joined, sailed out of the enormous tank in a cascade of fish, flesh, water, glass, and coral. The barracuda was flopping on the floor no less violently than Irons clutching his shredded groin. "Medic!" he wailed. "I need a medic!" Shocked into reality by the cascading glass, Gerhardt did some bellowing of his own, backing out of the flooded salon with soaking feet. Then, looking up in the dim light toward the sliding glass doors at the far end of the salon, he caught a glimpse of two men on the afterdeck and his heart nearly exploded out of his chest. He raised the Motorola to his lips. "Dennis! They're here! Drake and Henderson are on board and heading for the girl! You've got to head them off. Now!"

Lieutenant Commander Jack Kelly glanced at his watch and picked up a microphone: "Get the Blackhawks up in the air. I want to know everything that's going on aboard that ship before we go in."

Richard Elliot looked up with a hopeful expression. "You can do that?"

Kelly nodded. "The Blackhawks are equipped with stealth technology. We use them as sniper platforms. Inside is a chair designed to keep the shooter motionless. We take the .50-caliber Barrett M-82A1 sniper rifle, mount it to a tripod on the chair, and plug the scope into the Blackhawk's thermal imager and intensifier. Not only will the shooter be able to pinpoint possible targets on the weather decks, but he'll be able to locate people inside the

Avatar as well. From five miles out. Once we get a read on where everyone is, they'll move into position two miles from the *Avatar*, port and starboard, and provide cover while the assault force lands. Bad guy pops up, the assault force confirms the target and calls in the shot. We call them Guardian Angels."

"Amazing."

"How much longer before we're in position to launch the Sea Knights?" Hawking asked.

"Fifteen minutes," Kelly replied.

McKendrick looked at Hawking. "Mind if I go for a ride?"

Admiral Tanner looked up in surprise. "Now, I don't think that's a good idea, Walt. An officer of your position and responsibilities—"

"I've been relieved, remember? By order of the President of the United States."

Hawking gazed at the SEAL commander. "What do you say, Jack?"

Kelly replied without hesitation. "He got us here. Walt, you want in, the privilege is all yours."

Even from a corridor two decks below, Dennis Rexer could hear the sound of shattering glass and gunfire. He was working his way forward from the stern, setting the timers. He tried raising Strickland, but there was no answer. Then he heard Gerhardt's summons. He thought about the conversation that he had over-heard earlier between Gerhardt and Strickland. The inflatable was back, but Sammy and George were missing. He removed the small detonator from his pocket, pressed the button, and felt the *whump* of the high-explosive charge. The *Avatar* shuddered, dust floating down from the gratings above. The charge had been rigged so that the *Avatar* would remain afloat for less than an hour; Gerhardt had wanted the yacht to burn for a while first. Then he headed forward to where Drake and Henderson would come. Toward the girl.

The observation deck was empty. Drake swept his MP-5 from left to right, then heard Irons screaming. The sound was coming from the hole ten feet away. Drake moved past the Stingers and looked down into the blue light just in time to see Irons wrestling with the barracuda. He didn't need to see more. He hustled down the staircase and grabbed Jack. "We gotta move."

"What about Irons?"

"He joined the castrati."

Gunfire erupted in the main salon, followed by the shattering of glass. Drake and Henderson raced across the afterdeck and along the starboard rail, ducking inside a door as two crewmen rounded the corner from the bow.

"This way," Henderson said.

They moved toward a stairwell. Then, from deep below, came the *whump* of a powerful explosion and the *Avatar* shook beneath their feet. They looked at each other for a moment. There was no way they were going to escape in the inflatable now, not with everyone aboard abandoning ship. They had ten minutes to reach Jennifer's room before the first of the incendiary charges went off. And they would have to get there no matter what obstacles they encountered along the way.

Inside Jennifer's stateroom three mercenaries huddled together, talking among themselves, deciding what to do. They had heard gunfire emanating from the main salon and wanted to head top-side, but were reluctant to abandon their posts. Then they felt the explosion.

"What the fuck was that?"

A vase slid off a table and crashed to the floor.

"Jesus Christ!"

The third mercenary glanced at the locked bedroom door.

"Forget about her, Chuck. We didn't sign up for this shit. Don't you get it? This ship is going down!"

Seated on the concrete floor of the compressor room, Gerald Strickland felt the explosion too. He had spent the last five minutes trying to pick his handcuffs, but had quit in frustration. Now he began jabbing at the lock with a renewed sense of urgency, unsure whether the deep vibration shaking his intestines was coming through the floor or from the creeping sense of panic that was bubbling up inside his soul like a stinking tar pit. He brought the tip of the knife down toward the miniature hole, but his hands were shaking and in the darkness the knife deflected off the tempered steel, penetrating his forearm. He shrieked, then lost control entirely, flailing about the floor and crying like a baby until he was spent.

Drake and Henderson entered the stairwell on the starboard side and moved down the stairs, their MP-5s in the high ready position, Henderson taking point. An armed mercenary rounded the corner, and Jack pumped a round into his chest and the man tumbled back down the stairs. They moved in tandem, reaching the berth deck, and halted before the open corridor.

Jack shifted his weapon to the opposite shoulder and peeked around the corner so that only the barrel of his weapon and his left eye would be visible to anyone looking in his direction. A mercenary was running in the opposite direction, weapon in hand. Jack popped off another round, and Drake heard the man tumble to the floor. Drake recalled his training: The man who controls the corners wins.

The corridor was clear. Again they moved in tandem, Drake taking point, Jack covering the rear. The door to Jennifer's stateroom was locked. Drake pressed his ear against the wall. He could hear a radio playing rock. There were no other sounds.

He relayed the information to Henderson by hand signal and scanned the corridor one last time. One dead mercenary at the foot of the stairs, one dead mercenary near Gerhardt's stateroom, a set of abandoned luggage. Drake blew away the lock, shoving Jennifer's door open with the barrel of his MP-5. Then Drake and Henderson were inside, moving quickly through the open door of Jennifer's bedroom, zeroing in on the mercenary near the bed. The man had his shirt off and his weapon up. But Drake was there first, firing a six-round burst that stitched the mercenary's heart and sent him sprawling against a dresser and down to the floor.

"Clear," they shouted to each other, scanning their fields of fire. They checked the body, their weapons ready. The man was dead.

Drake lowered his weapon and bent down, removing the tape from Jennifer's mouth.

She was crying. "I thought—"

"Come on. Let's get you out of here."

• • •

Standing in the corridor outside Jennifer's office, Gerhardt felt the deep vibration as the high-explosive charge detonated against the *Avatar*'s hull. *Where in the world is Spector?* If he didn't show up soon they were finished. They had to make their move now before the incendiaries went off. It was their only shot, and with Spector at the controls of the Sikorsky, they would make it. Strickland and Rexer would just have to fend for themselves. But time was running out. He pressed the radio to his lips and spoke with an increasing sense of urgency. "Freddie? Come in, Freddie. Come in, I say. Goddamn it, Spector, where the fuck are you?"

Freddie Spector was in Gerhardt's stateroom, hiding beneath the bed. He had been lying there for ten minutes, ruing his decision not to bolt when he first felt the explosion. Gerhardt had ordered him to finish packing the last of his bags and he had complied, knowing about the explosives and what Gerhardt had planned. Now he was staring out into the corridor at a dead man. Something bad was going on, and if he didn't get out of there soon it was going to happen to him. He had been walking down the corridor with Gerhardt's bags when the dead mercenary had come tumbling down the stairs. He had dropped the bags and hauled ass back to the bedroom. Then the second mercenary got shot. Now he could hear gunfire coming from Jennifer's room, as well. It was time to move. Now. He crawled out from under the bed and with trembling heart peeked into the corridor. The coast was clear. He bolted.

•   •   •

She stumbled as she got off the bed.

"Can you walk?"

"My hands and feet are numb." Gripping his MP-5 in his right hand, Drake put his other arm around Jennifer as Henderson headed back to the outer door. They checked the corridor. It was clear.

Keeping his eyes on the corridor, Henderson said, "She okay?"

"She's doing fine, Jack. Let's get the fuck out of here."

Spector raced up the stairs to the bridge and down the corridor toward the glass reception room where Gerhardt was waiting.

"Where were you?"

"Trapped."

Noticing his fright, Gerhardt grabbed Spector by the shirt collar and made the young pilot the deal of a lifetime. "You fly us out of here and I'll deposit ten million dollars in any Cayman account of your choice. In fact, I've got a better idea—why don't we fly straight to the bank right now." He was serious.

Ten million dollars! Spector thought. A world of possibility danced before his eyes. He thought about the house he would build, a bachelor's pad filled with the latest techno-toys. A Spanish villa right on the Florida coast, with a pool and a white sandy beach stretching for miles on either side. He could do it, he knew he could; when it came to flying helicopters he was the best there was. He looked at Gerhardt with the proprietary air of a businessman protecting his investment. "Don't you worry about a thing, boss," he said with growing assurance. "You just let ol' Freddie do the flying."

Henderson moved out into the corridor and suddenly he was down, a gunshot reverberating in his ears. Drake threw Jennifer to the floor and dashed into the corridor, his MP-5 blazing on full automatic, catching sight of Rexer as the South African drew back behind the base of the stairwell. He continued firing as he grabbed Jack by the harness and dragged him to safety inside Jennifer's stateroom. He reloaded, popped a smoke flare, and tossed it in Rexer's direction, followed by a fragmentation grenade. He slammed the door shut as the grenade exploded.

Henderson was lying on his back, groaning. Drake examined him and saw immediately that a round had entered the right armpit and exited through the collarbone. The wound was serious.

"Jack, can you hear me?"

"Yeah . . ." The voice seemed to be coming from a million miles away. Jack gritted his teeth.

Drake looked at Jennifer, who was in shock. He took her by the arm. "You're going to have to cover the door. How're your hands and feet?"

"Okay."

"Come on." He got her into position to the side of the door. He could smell smoke seeping through the blasted lock. He handed her Jack's MP-5. "Ever fire one of these before?"

She shook her head.

"It's easy. The selector's set on automatic. Hold the weapon level like this, aim target center. The door moves, shoot it."

"Philip?"

"I love you, Jen. Watch the door."

He grabbed a couple of clean towels from the bathroom, knelt down beside Jack, and quickly dressed the wound.

The gunfire came again, spraying the corridor beyond the closed door. Rexer was still alive. *Fuck.* He knew the corridor was swirling with smoke, and he also knew that Rexer's fire had been a probe. The smoke flare and grenade had bought them some time, but now time was running out. Rexer was setting up to make his move. And somewhere below, incendiary charges were ticking away, ready to explode. He looked up at the skylight, then dragged Henderson to the side of the room.

"What are you doing?"

"Stand back."

Jennifer moved to a corner as Drake pointed his weapon at the skylight and shot out the thick Plexiglas, shards of clear plastic dropping like snow. Then he disappeared inside the bedroom and quickly emerged, pulling the dresser to the center of the room beneath the open skylight. He slid a chair beside it. He lifted Henderson to his shoulder and climbed to the top of the dresser, straining as he lifted him up through the skylight and onto the foredeck. He glanced up the observation deck, praying that no one was there. Then he looked down again as the door exploded in a hail of splinters, rounds chiseling the dresser beneath his feet.

Rexer was standing in the doorway, his eyes narrowed and smarting from the smoke as he raised his CAR-15 toward Drake the instant he realized that Jennifer was standing only six feet away and firing into the pit of his stomach. The South African tumbled back and collapsed to the floor, clawing for his weapon. Drake hopped down from the dresser and kicked it away. Then the world suddenly burst into flames as the first of the incendiary charges exploded, knocking him to the ground.

• • •

Five miles out, the SEAL sniper designated Angel One peered through his scope, trying to make sense of the nightmare unfolding before him. Flames were billowing out of the *Avatar*'s bow, and even from this distance he could see people in the water. The *Avatar* was listing to starboard so heavily that he could see the port deck. And to make matters worse, he was reading three prone bodies inside the *Avatar* with low heat signatures.

From his position in the copilot's seat General Walter McKendrick could also see the flames illuminating the night sky. "How bad is it?"

The SEAL sniper informed him, and McKendrick got on the line with Kelly aboard the *Wasp:* "Jack, we got trouble. The *Avatar* is listing at least twenty degrees to starboard and there are flames shooting out of the bow. There appears to have been an explosion of some kind. We also have three possible dead or wounded inside, as well as a number of survivors in the water. Request permission to approach, over."

Inside the *Wasp*, Secretary of Defense Richard Elliot slammed his fist on the table and said in frantic desperation, "Goddamn it. We've got to get in there! Jack?" Captain Bobby Hopf picked up the microphone. "Launch the rescue choppers and be prepared to pick up survivors in the water. And for God's sake make sure they stay *behind* the *Avatar* unless otherwise instructed by Angel One. Angel One, this is the *Wasp*. Rescue choppers are inbound to target. . . ."

Kelly got on line. "Walt, permission granted. But be careful out there. Angel Two, this is Sierra Charlie. Proceed to starboard position and provide cover for Angel One. Angel Two, do you copy?"

Admiral Tanner looked up at Kelly with a somber expression. "If they're still alive and we don't find them soon . . ."

Smoke filled the room. To the left, the forward wall of Jennifer's stateroom was missing, replaced by a shimmering curtain of fire. The flames were brick orange, curling into the sky and jetting black smoke. Drake got to his feet and saw Jennifer lying on the floor fifteen feet away. He ran to her side. She was breathing. He slid his arms beneath her, shoved the dresser and chair back into position, and climbed up, pushing Jennifer through the open skylight and onto the foredeck as black smoke billowed toward the sky. Then he pulled himself up and located Jack beneath a crumpled sheet of galvanized steel. He was still alive. He looked out at the ocean. There were people in the water; otherwise the ocean was empty and black. Then he thought could he hear the sound of a helicopter approaching somewhere in the distance.

Directly below, in Jennifer's stateroom, Dennis Rexer had yet to die. He lay on the floor with a ceiling of heavy black smoke swirling inches above his head, unable to move from the waist down, his spinal cord severed. He had pleaded to the god he prayed to, begging him to end the terrible pain gnawing inside his chest, and his god had answered him. And now as he lay on the deck, he watched in abject horror as the serpent rose up through the burning floor and began flailing back and forth, snaking toward him, blistering his face with its tongue of white-hot flame. It was one of the propane lines that led to the galley, to the grill that Clarence had ordered installed the year before. It whipped toward his face again, and he grabbed its glowing neck to turn it away and saw his hands melt, then shrieked in agony as the serpent leapt through his cauterized hands, burrowing into his face and down through the very core of his body.

From the copilot's seat inside Angel One, Walt McKendrick stared at the red flames billowing out of the enormous hole in the *Avatar*'s foredeck. He felt sick. He swept his gaze along the decks, searching for Drake, Henderson, and the girl, but all he could see were men scrambling about or diving into the water. Along the yacht the lights flickered. Suddenly the *Avatar* was engulfed in darkness.

"Angel One, this is Sierra Charlie." Kelly's voice. "Any sign of the hostages?"

"Negative."

McKendrick leaned toward the pilot. "Bring us down. Fifty feet off the bow."

"Sir?"

"Do it now, son."

Gerhardt and Spector hurried through the glass-enclosed reception area and out to the platform. The *Avatar* was listing to starboard. They could hear a helicopter nearby and another farther off, but moving in fast.

Taking the arms dealer by the arm, Spector crossed the sloping platform, opened the Sikorsky's door, and strapped Gerhardt in. Then, as he was freeing up the chocks, he noticed a CAR-15 lying a few feet away. *Better take that along just in case.* Spector tossed it into the chopper beside Gerhardt and climbed into the cockpit.

Water was pouring into the compressor room. First it started as a trickling sound in the darkness, then it touched his leg with icy fingers. Strickland recoiled in shock. He lay slumped against the compressor, gripping the knife, lost in a nightmare defined by two unimaginable alternatives. He wanted to toss the knife away but couldn't, as much as he tried to muster the courage. And yet even as the water rose to his waist and moved up his spine he couldn't save his life either, unable to confront the grisly task that lay before him. And so he waited until he was on his feet and straining against the compressor that held him down, just as Drake had predicted. And when he could wait no longer, he pressed the dull blade to his flesh and began to saw, vomiting from the pain, his eardrums bursting from the shrill violence of his screams, his mouth tasting saltwater and blood. Then, as he squeezed the stump of his freed hand, he placed his shoulder against the unlocked door and pushed with what little remaining strength he had. But he had waited too long. On the opposite side of the door lay three feet of water, sealing the compressor room like a tomb. The water rose above him, and he thrashed about like a hooked fish. A minute later he was dead.

Kneeling on the splintered foredeck of the *Avatar*, Drake looked up at the Blackhawk hovering above the observation deck and reached for a flare. With the next incendiary device set to explode beneath them any minute, he couldn't stay where he was. He popped the flare and waved it back and forth three times, then threw it as hard as he could up onto the observation deck. He lifted Jack to his left shoulder and curled his right arm around Jennifer and struggled to his feet. Then he ran.

Freddie Spector switched on the ignition and listened as the engines hummed. The gauges glowed with green light. The Blackhawk hovering above the observation deck was creating a terrible downdraft, but he could handle it, even though owing to the *Avatar's* heavy list they wouldn't have much clearance once they eased off the platform and were pushed down toward the sea. But what the fuck. He had been in tight situations before. . . .

From the cockpit of Angel One, McKendrick gazed with a joy he had not known in years through the windshield at the man waving the flare. The flare arced through the air toward them, landing on the observation deck beside the pool. "There they are," the pilot shouted.

"Sierra Charlie, this is Angel One. We have visual. Drake plus two wounded—Henderson and the girl. He is moving them to our position now."

"Copy, Angel One." McKendrick could hear cheering in the background. But it wasn't over yet. From the looks of things the whole ship was wired with explosives, and in the next ten seconds they would be hovering forty feet above a site where the next incendiary charge could explode. McKendrick looked at his crew with pride, watching them prepare for the extraction, thinking that these were the best men he had ever known. The side door was open and the crew chief was readying the hoist.

"Okay," McKendrick sang. "Let's go get 'em!"

The staircase listed at a forty-five-degree angle. With Jack over his left shoulder and Jennifer cradled beneath his right, he mounted the stairs, struggling to maintain his balance. Each time he glanced to his left he could see ocean looming directly below. He wasn't thinking anymore, he was bruised and exhausted, propelling himself forward by sheer force of will. He held them tight and kept on moving. Then, just as he reached the last set of stairs, the aft section of the bow exploded.

He crouched, shielding Jennifer and Jack from the blast, feeling the intense heat against his back. When he looked down he saw that the entire staircase below them was missing. He gained the observation deck, moving past the carnage that was once Locotelli. The Blackhawk hovered forty feet above, and he quickly slipped Jennifer and Jack into the harness, feeling the stiff rotor wash buffeting his back. Then, as he prepared to snap himself in, the Sikorsky slid off the platform, dipped, and rose up beside them.

Inside the glowing cockpit, Freddie Spector had waited long enough. Adjusting the collective and cyclic sticks, he gently allowed the Sikorsky to slide off the steep platform and away from the Blackhawk hovering above the observation deck.

They dipped low over the water and then rose up, and gazing out the side window as the yacht listed in their direction, Gerhardt could see a man preparing to extract, kneeling over a woman lying beside him and another man, their figures illuminated by the dull-orange flames that rose out of the bow. He began to shake. It was as though he were in Salzburg sitting in his private box at the opera, watching transfixed as the horror of her betrayal was reenacted on stage. She would leave him forever and would remain beyond his reach this time, and he would spend the last years of his life tormented by the knowledge that somewhere in the world she was alive. But this was not opera. And he was not the helpless supplicant who had beseeched her from the balcony window three days before. He had a weapon now; there was an assault rifle in his lap. He would kill the thing that tormented him; he would kill them all.

He slid open the window and fired a long burst, the smell of cordite filling his nostrils, his ears deafened to the sound of Spector's frantic warning. He saw the man lifting something to his shoulder and then a white plume streaking toward him, and in the last moment of his life he recognized the irony of his fate as his final wish was granted: He had indeed killed the thing that tormented him.

He had annihilated his soul.

Muzzle flashes came from a side window, and the rounds were clattering all around him. Drake dove for the Stinger that Irons had left on the chair and switched it on. Instantly the missile locked onto the Sikorsky. Through the sight he could see Spector staring in horror. The Sikorsky began to wheel away, and then as he pulled the trigger he caught sight of the shooter, the cherubic face grimacing against the arrow aimed at his heart, and an instant later the Sikorsky exploded, pieces of flaming wreckage bursting into the sky before dropping into the sea.

Then he was being lifted off the observation deck, Jennifer beside him, Henderson above. They were swinging out to sea.

The rushing air was cool against his face, and he felt Jennifer holding him. "Where are we?" she asked.

"We're going home, Jen."

"My father?"

"Didn't make it."

"Then we really are safe, aren't we. . . ."

Red flames shot out of the bow, curling toward the sky, and as they held each other, the Blackhawk crew pulling Henderson aboard, Drake gazed at the *Avatar* with the feeling of having been transported through time. The entire length of the *Avatar*'s hull lay exposed as the great yacht listed to starboard. Then the *Avatar* shuddered violently as the remaining incendiary charges detonated along her hull. And as the flames mushroomed toward the sky, he thought he saw the *Norfolk* ghosting through the dark waters of 1917, illuminating the ocean with her haunting intensity.

From his suite at the Hay-Adams, Charles Francis Adams looked out past Lafayette Park to the White House. He had selected this suite because of the view and because it evoked the spirit of the man whose ideas had pervaded his intellect since the time he could read. The building had once belonged to his family, at least in part; a home turned into a hotel. And gazing out the window, he reflected that if Henry Adams were present by his side he would doubtless remark that the same might be said of that magnificent structure across the street. But Adams would have taken issue with the remark, claiming that the events that were about to occur proved otherwise.

There was a knock on his door, and the delegation entered: McKendrick, Lieutenant Commander Jack Kelly, Thomas Young, Hawking, Everett Smith, Richard Elliot, two U.S. marshals, and a man and woman whom Adams recognized immediately, though never having met them before.

The man was tall and handsome, dressed casually in jeans and a blue blazer, and the woman was casually elegant as well, dressed in a long silk dress of teal. Despite the numerous small cuts and bruises that marred her features, Adams thought that the dark-haired girl was one of the most beautiful women he had ever seen.

Walter McKendrick smiled. "Jennifer, Phil, I'd like you to meet Charles Adams."

Jennifer looked up at Adams and extended her hand. "Thank you," she said.

"No, my dear. It is we who should be thanking you." Adams turned to Drake. "How's Jack?"

"Doing fine, sir." Drake grinned. "He's in Walter Reed recovering from surgery. His wife and son are there. They'll be going home in a few days."

"And you?"

Drake glanced warmly at Jennifer. "Vacation."

Adams nodded with approval. Then he said, "You did a hell of a job out there—you and Jack both."

Drake looked at Adams, then at the man who had sought him out in what seemed a lifetime ago. He looked at Walt McKendrick and said, "We're a team."

Terry Fox met them at the North Entrance to the White House and the delegation moved through the West Wing toward the Oval Office. David Ellis was striding past the Roosevelt Room when he saw the crowd heading in his direction. He looked at Adams and McKendrick and assumed that they had enlisted the aid of the Vice President, the Attorney General, and the Secretary of Defense to plead their case. But the young man and the woman confused him. He had never seen them before. Then there were the three other high-ranking military officers besides McKendrick. And, even more disturbing, the two U.S. marshals.

"We're here to see the President," Thomas Young announced.

Ellis was nonplussed. He looked at the Vice President and

said, "He's in conference with Director Vaughan. You don't have an appointment."

Attorney General Everett Smith looked at Ellis and said in a stentorian tone, "It might be best if you cancel the President's appointments today."

The two U.S. marshals spoke briefly to the Secret Service agents standing outside the Oval Office, and a moment later the agents opened the door and stepped aside.

Seated at his desk, reviewing the speech that Vaughan had written the night before, Jefferson Marshall looked up in shock at the group gathered before him.

"What is the meaning of this outrage!" Vaughan demanded. "Ellis!"

The Chief of Staff looked on helplessly.

Then Vaughan's eyes fell on Fox. The Deputy National Security Advisor sidled behind the group, trying his best to make himself small. And suddenly Vaughan wasn't looking at people anymore; he was staring at prison bars. "Why, you spineless cocksucker!" he growled as Fox shrank back even farther.

"May I remind you that there's a lady present," Adams said evenly. "Martin, meet Jennifer Lane and Philip Drake. I asked them to join us because I thought you'd like to have an opportunity to meet two of the people you betrayed. Unfortunately, the other person you betrayed, Jack Henderson, can't be here today; he's in the hospital recovering from a gunshot wound."

Vaughan stared at Adams with a loathing so intense that it seemed to ignite the room. Then, as the two U.S. marshals stepped forward to place the former National Security Advisor under arrest, Vaughan lunged. But Drake was filled with loathing of his own, thinking of the way Clarence had been shot and drowned, of the fiery death that had awaited Jennifer. He stepped in front of Adams, caught Vaughan by the throat, and brought the overweight advisor down hard, pressing him to the floor as the two U.S. marshals bent down to snap on the handcuffs. The Oval Office was filled with the sound of Martin Vaughan's sobbing. Then the two U.S. marshals led the former National Security Advisor away.

For a moment there was silence.

Adams laid a piece of paper on Jefferson Marshall's desk. "Regarding the people *you* betrayed, Mr. President, I only wish that they could be here today. But unfortunately they can't. Because they're in their graves."

Jefferson Marshall sat slumped in his chair, not daring to look at the men who stood in judgment before him. Without looking at the paper that Adams had placed on his desk, he asked, "Resignation or confession?"

"A little of both, I should think," Adams advised him. "It's your address to the nation."

EPILOGUE

One month later

The party was in full swing. From the bow of the *Lady Ann*, Drake, Jennifer, McKendrick, Adams, Jack and Mary Henderson, and the Hendersons' son Andrew gazed out at the lovely gray houses and cobbled street of Nantucket harbor, sipping cocktails and Cokes, listening to the Duke Ellington CD that Jennifer had slipped on the stereo. They had spent the day sailing from Boston, enjoying themselves, Adams and McKendrick having broken away from official duties in Washington to spend the weekend with the people they would come to know quite well in the upcoming years. Jack's shoulder was almost completely healed. That afternoon, having anchored off the Nantucket shoals, he and Drake had climbed into the dinghy and taken Andrew fishing, the sandy-haired boy brimming with excitement as he proudly showed his mother the fine bluefish that he had landed with his father's help.

The nation, indeed the world, had been shocked by the revelations contained in Jefferson Marshall's final address. But the American people had also been deeply reassured: Once again the rule of law had prevailed. Thomas Young, his wife and children standing by his side, had taken the oath of office minutes after the President's speech, and in the succeeding weeks the new President had become enormously popular, most Americans, now aware of the facts surrounding TORCHLIGHT, harkening to the leadership and moral courage of the man who would run for office and, against all odds, win the election in November.

Following his resignation, Marshall had been granted immunity from prosecution in return for his testimony in the upcoming trial of Martin Vaughan. Regarding the information that he had passed to Gerhardt, the former President would receive a suspended sentence. He would move to Switzerland, a divorced man, and spend the rest of his days living in disgrace.

Allen Wexler would never accept the deal that Adams had offered him. The day following Adams's departure the corporate chairman helped himself to a hearty breakfast of Seconals and champagne. A maid found him in his bedroom six hours later. A month later the papers reported that Wexler's seventeen-million-dollar estate had been left to a private foundation specializing in the needs of indigent children.

As for Martin Vaughan, odds were, among the habitués of Washington's more fashionable watering holes, that the former National Security Advisor was going to spend a very long time in a place called Marion, Illinois. His deputy, Terry Fox, also took up a new residence, having left government to open up a liquor store in Tucson, Arizona.

Leading a team of Navy divers, Drake would return to the *Norfolk*, but no matter how many times he entered the paymaster's issuing room, he never got accustomed to its mortuary stillness. Then, a week after Hurricane Stephanie had forced them back to Newport, Drake returned to the *Norfolk* again. But this time the paymaster's issuing room was gone, the interior of the armored cruiser reconfigured by the turbulence of the sea, the gold scattered like autumn leaves among the wreckage.

And Drake would stay with Jennifer. When you find someone you love that much, you never let go.

And as for Chickie Burnham? The former CIA paramilitary would spend a number of days relishing hot tubs, martinis, and naked women from his villa high in the Argentine mountains. But for all his success, Chickie Burnham had failed to learn one elementary lesson that Martin Vaughan would have an occasion to confront on a daily basis as he faced the stark walls of his cell: that no matter how carefully you plan your life, you can never predict the future. And for Chickie Burnham, the dark clouds were already forming beyond the horizon.